SINA GRACE · SIOBHAN KEENAN · CATHY LE

Ghosted in L.A.

™

VOL. 2

BOOM! BOX™

BOOM! BOX™

GHOSTED IN L.A. Volume Two, August 2020. Published by BOOM! Box, a division of Boom Entertainment, Inc. Ghosted in L.A. is ™ & © 2020 Sina Grace. Originally published in single magazine form as GHOSTED IN L.A. No. 5-8. ™ & © 2019, 2020 Sina Grace. All rights reserved. BOOM! Box™ and the BOOM! Box logo are trademarks of Boom Entertainment, Inc., registered in various countries and categories. All characters, events, and institutions depicted herein are fictional. Any similarity between any of the names, characters, persons, events, and/or institutions in this publication to actual names, characters, and persons, whether living or dead, events, and/or institutions is unintended and purely coincidental. BOOM! Box does not read or accept unsolicited submissions of ideas, stories, or artwork.

BOOM! Studios, 5670 Wilshire Boulevard, Suite 400, Los Angeles, CA 90036-5679. Printed in China. First Printing.

ISBN: 978-1-68415-541-5, eISBN: 978-1-64144-707-2

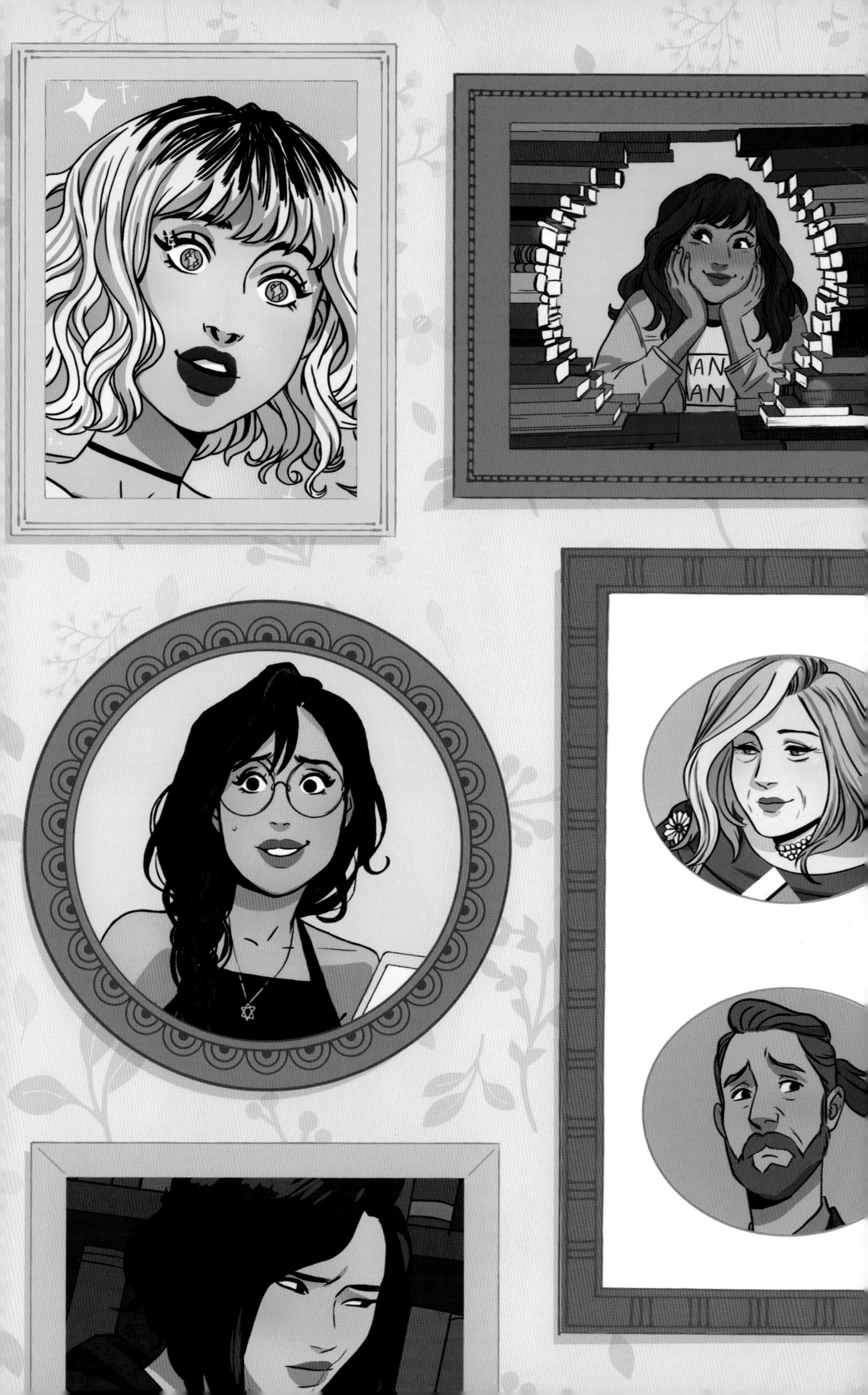

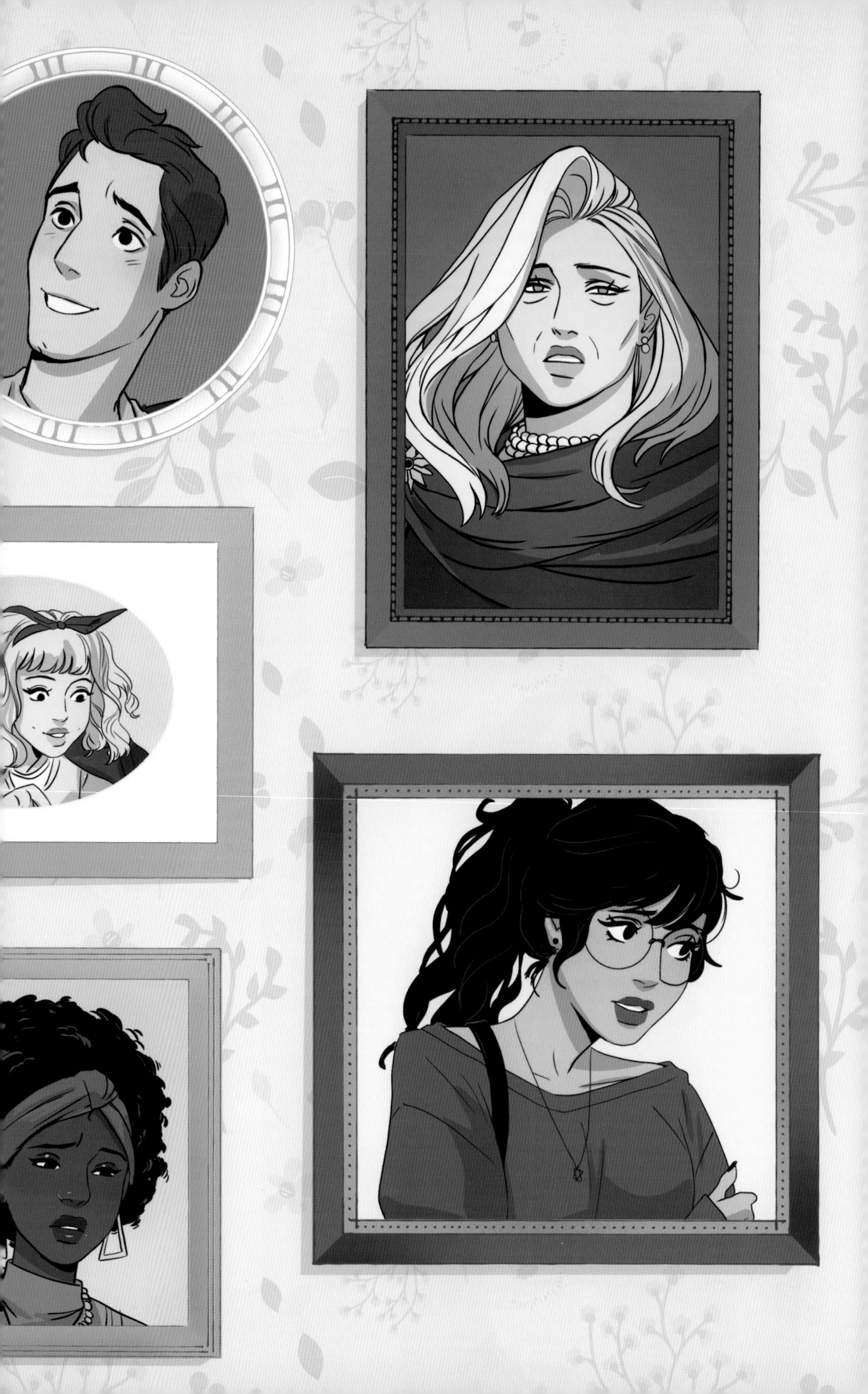

Created & Written by......................**Sina Grace**

Illustrated by................**Siobhan Keenan**
With ....Sina Grace

Colors by.......................................**Cathy Le**

Letters by.................................**DC Hopkins**

Cover by ....**Siobhan Keenan**

Series and Collection Designer..............**Michelle Ankley**
Assistant Editor..**Allyson Gronowitz**
Editor...**Shannon Watters**

The Bechdel Cast is a Production of iHeartRadio. All rights reserved. Used with permission.

Chapter Five

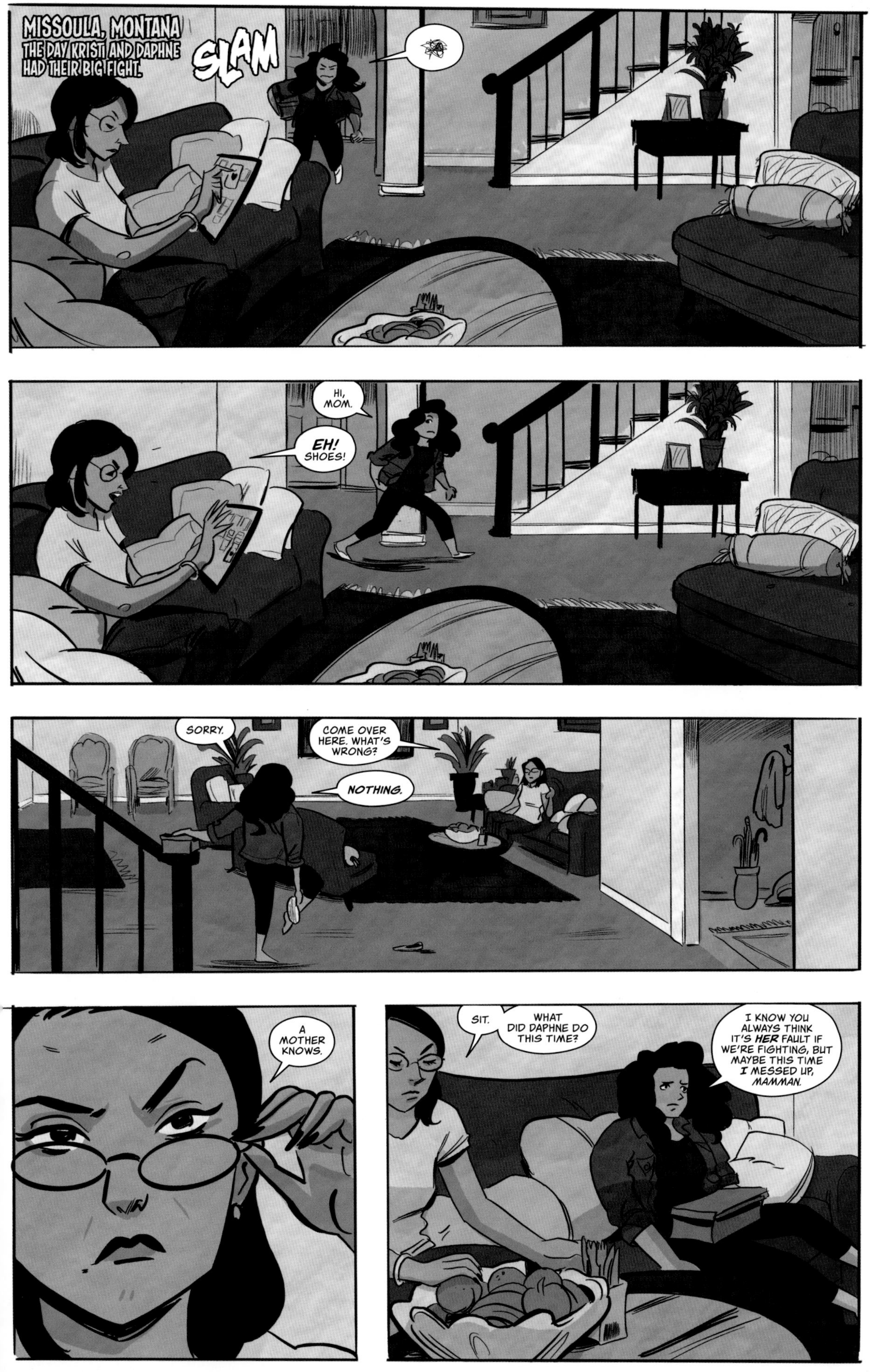
MISSOULA, MONTANA
THE DAY KRISTI AND DAPHNE HAD THEIR BIG FIGHT.
SLAM
HI, MOM.
EH! SHOES!
SORRY.
COME OVER HERE. WHAT'S WRONG?
NOTHING.
A MOTHER KNOWS.
SIT.
WHAT DID DAPHNE DO THIS TIME?
I KNOW YOU ALWAYS THINK IT'S HER FAULT IF WE'RE FIGHTING, BUT MAYBE THIS TIME I MESSED UP, MAMMAN.

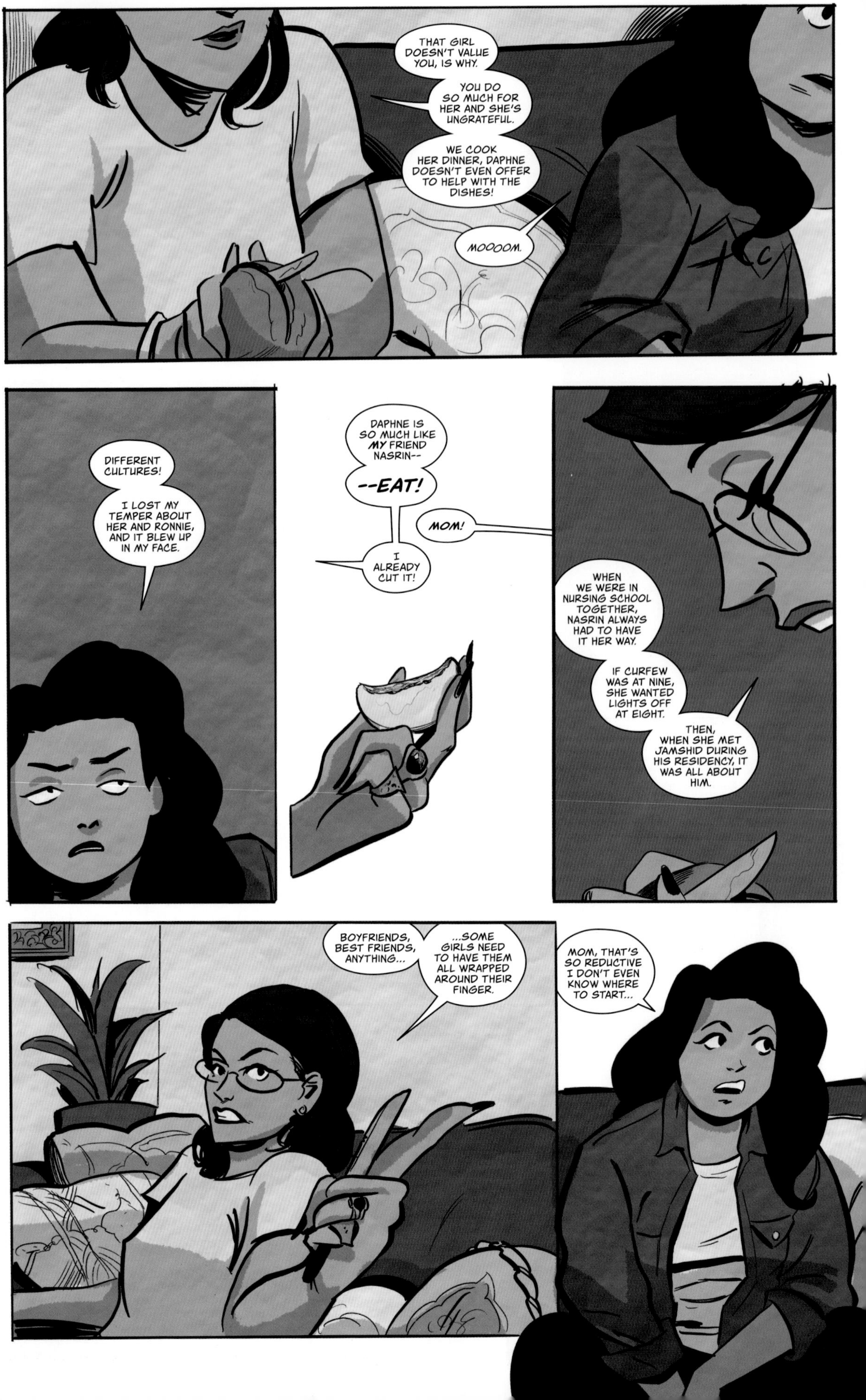
THAT GIRL DOESN'T VALUE YOU, IS WHY.
YOU DO SO MUCH FOR HER AND SHE'S UNGRATEFUL.
WE COOK HER DINNER, DAPHNE DOESN'T EVEN OFFER TO HELP WITH THE DISHES!
MOOOOM.
DIFFERENT CULTURES!
I LOST MY TEMPER ABOUT HER AND RONNIE, AND IT BLEW UP IN MY FACE.
DAPHNE IS SO MUCH LIKE MY FRIEND NASRIN--
--EAT!
I ALREADY CUT IT!
MOM!
WHEN WE WERE IN NURSING SCHOOL TOGETHER, NASRIN ALWAYS HAD TO HAVE IT HER WAY.
IF CURFEW WAS AT NINE, SHE WANTED LIGHTS OFF AT EIGHT.
THEN, WHEN SHE MET JAMSHID DURING HIS RESIDENCY, IT WAS ALL ABOUT HIM.
BOYFRIENDS, BEST FRIENDS, ANYTHING...
...SOME GIRLS NEED TO HAVE THEM ALL WRAPPED AROUND THEIR FINGER.
MOM, THAT'S SO REDUCTIVE I DON'T EVEN KNOW WHERE TO START...

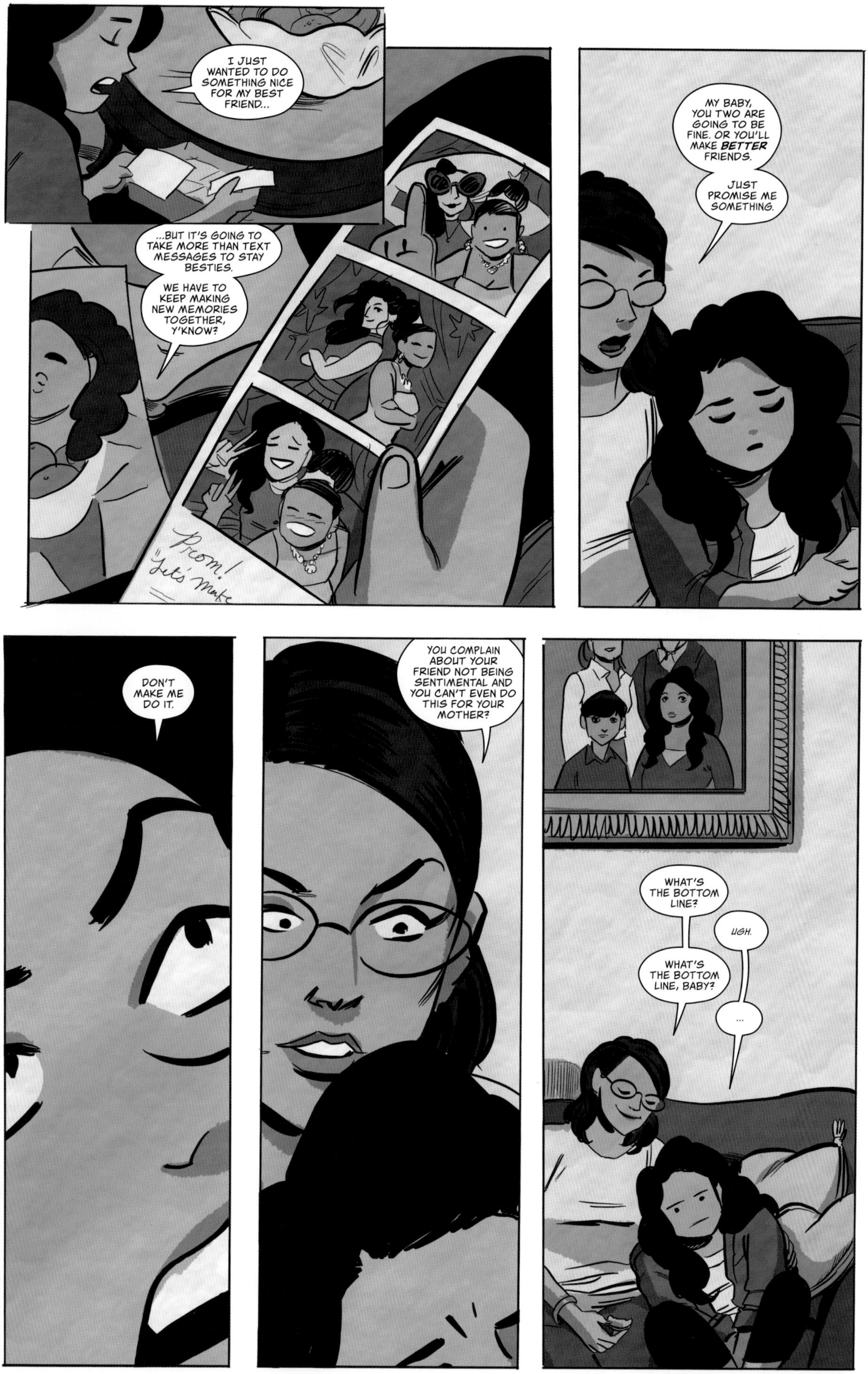
I JUST WANTED TO DO SOMETHING NICE FOR MY BEST FRIEND...
...BUT IT'S GOING TO TAKE MORE THAN TEXT MESSAGES TO STAY BESTIES.
WE HAVE TO KEEP MAKING NEW MEMORIES TOGETHER, Y'KNOW?
Prom!
"Let's Make
MY BABY, YOU TWO ARE GOING TO BE FINE. OR YOU'LL MAKE **BETTER** FRIENDS.
JUST PROMISE ME SOMETHING.
DON'T MAKE ME DO IT.
YOU COMPLAIN ABOUT YOUR FRIEND NOT BEING SENTIMENTAL AND YOU CAN'T EVEN DO THIS FOR YOUR MOTHER?
WHAT'S THE BOTTOM LINE?
UGH.
WHAT'S THE BOTTOM LINE, BABY?
...

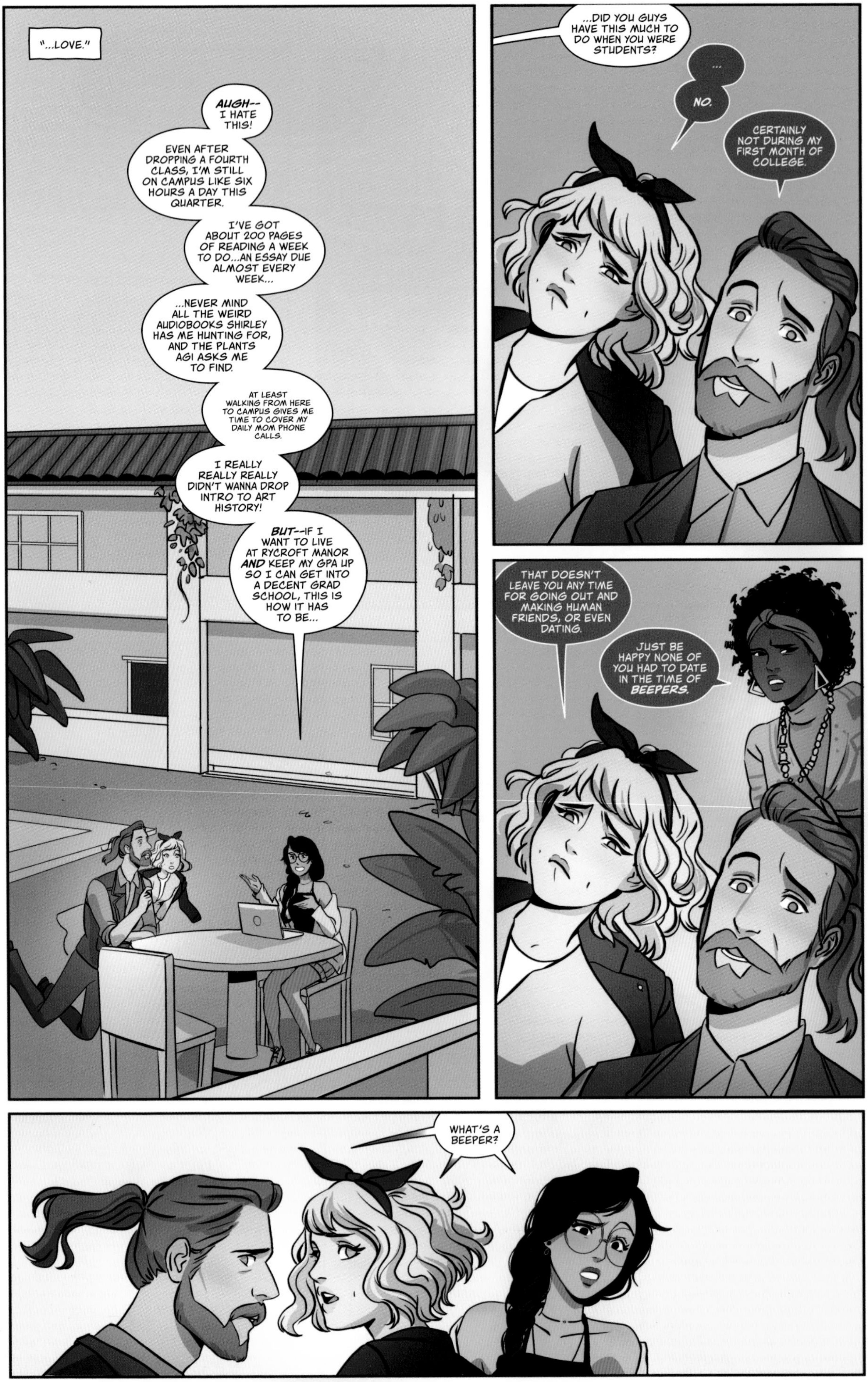
"...LOVE."
AUGH--I HATE THIS!
EVEN AFTER DROPPING A FOURTH CLASS, I'M STILL ON CAMPUS LIKE SIX HOURS A DAY THIS QUARTER.
I'VE GOT ABOUT 200 PAGES OF READING A WEEK TO DO...AN ESSAY DUE ALMOST EVERY WEEK...
...NEVER MIND ALL THE WEIRD AUDIOBOOKS SHIRLEY HAS ME HUNTING FOR, AND THE PLANTS AGI ASKS ME TO FIND.
AT LEAST WALKING FROM HERE TO CAMPUS GIVES ME TIME TO COVER MY DAILY MOM PHONE CALLS.
I REALLY REALLY REALLY DIDN'T WANNA DROP INTRO TO ART HISTORY!
BUT--IF I WANT TO LIVE AT RYCROFT MANOR AND KEEP MY GPA UP SO I CAN GET INTO A DECENT GRAD SCHOOL, THIS IS HOW IT HAS TO BE...
...DID YOU GUYS HAVE THIS MUCH TO DO WHEN YOU WERE STUDENTS?
...
NO.
CERTAINLY NOT DURING MY FIRST MONTH OF COLLEGE.
THAT DOESN'T LEAVE YOU ANY TIME FOR GOING OUT AND MAKING HUMAN FRIENDS, OR EVEN DATING.
JUST BE HAPPY NONE OF YOU HAD TO DATE IN THE TIME OF BEEPERS.
WHAT'S A BEEPER?

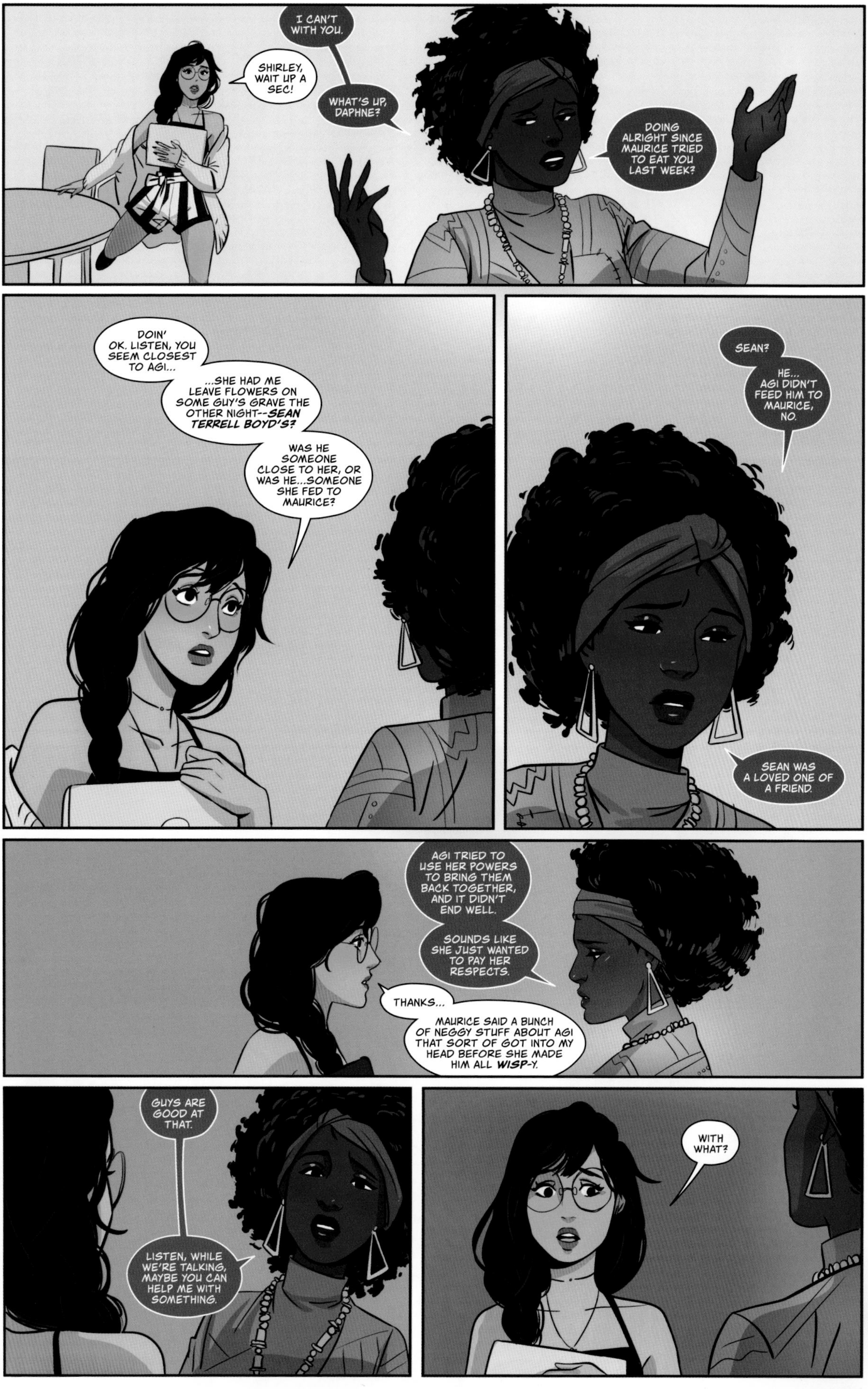
SHIRLEY, WAIT UP A SEC!
I CAN'T WITH YOU.
WHAT'S UP, DAPHNE?
DOING ALRIGHT SINCE MAURICE TRIED TO EAT YOU LAST WEEK?
DOIN' OK. LISTEN, YOU SEEM CLOSEST TO AGI...
...SHE HAD ME LEAVE FLOWERS ON SOME GUY'S GRAVE THE OTHER NIGHT--SEAN TERRELL BOYD'S?
WAS HE SOMEONE CLOSE TO HER, OR WAS HE...SOMEONE SHE FED TO MAURICE?
SEAN?
HE... AGI DIDN'T FEED HIM TO MAURICE, NO.
SEAN WAS A LOVED ONE OF A FRIEND.
AGI TRIED TO USE HER POWERS TO BRING THEM BACK TOGETHER, AND IT DIDN'T END WELL.
SOUNDS LIKE SHE JUST WANTED TO PAY HER RESPECTS.
THANKS...
MAURICE SAID A BUNCH OF NEGGY STUFF ABOUT AGI THAT SORT OF GOT INTO MY HEAD BEFORE SHE MADE HIM ALL WISP-Y.
GUYS ARE GOOD AT THAT.
LISTEN, WHILE WE'RE TALKING, MAYBE YOU CAN HELP ME WITH SOMETHING.
WITH WHAT?

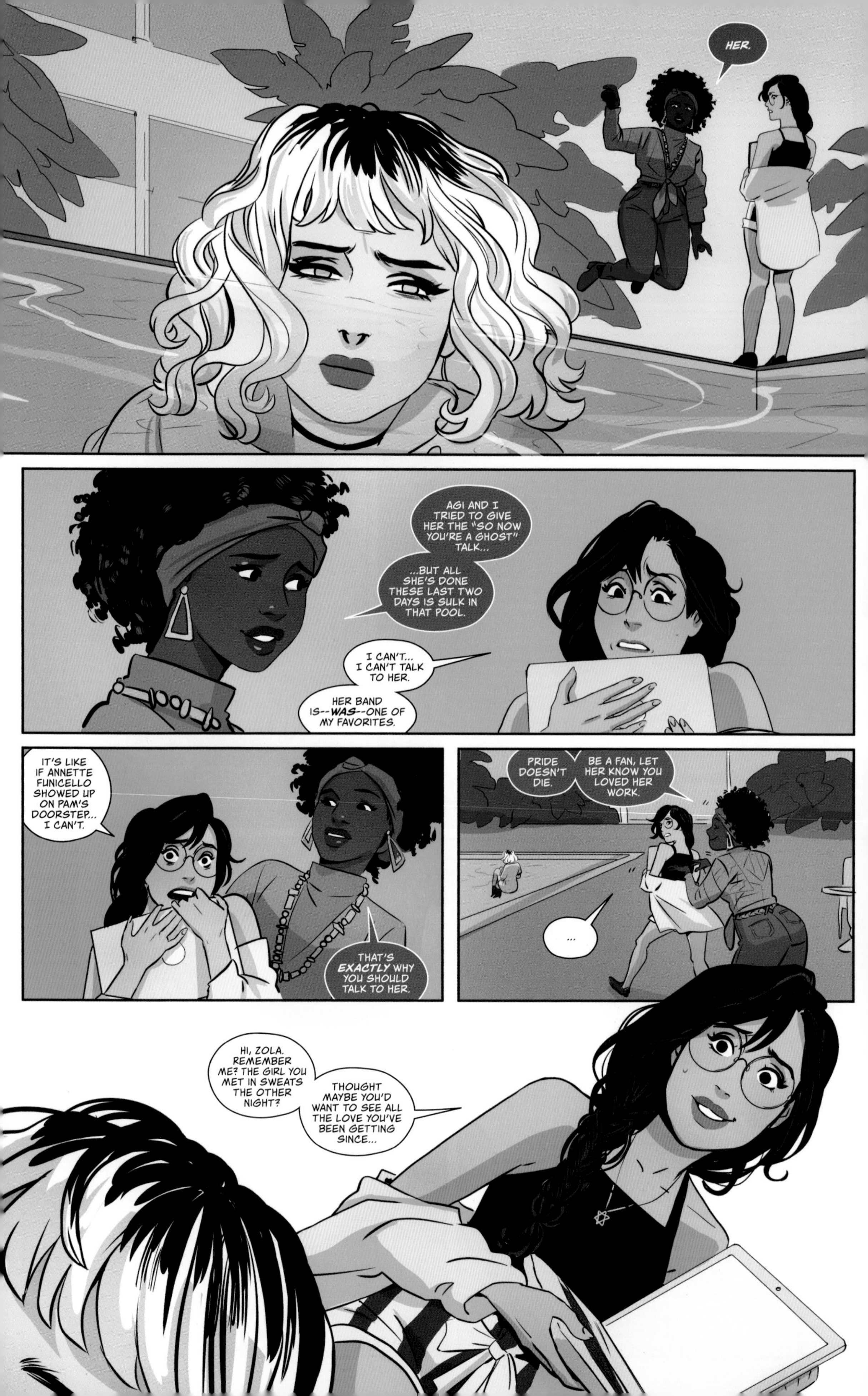
HER.
AGI AND I TRIED TO GIVE HER THE "SO NOW YOU'RE A GHOST" TALK...
...BUT ALL SHE'S DONE THESE LAST TWO DAYS IS SULK IN THAT POOL.
I CAN'T... I CAN'T TALK TO HER.
HER BAND IS--WAS--ONE OF MY FAVORITES.
IT'S LIKE IF ANNETTE FUNICELLO SHOWED UP ON PAM'S DOORSTEP... I CAN'T.
THAT'S EXACTLY WHY YOU SHOULD TALK TO HER.
PRIDE DOESN'T DIE.
BE A FAN, LET HER KNOW YOU LOVED HER WORK.
...
HI, ZOLA. REMEMBER ME? THE GIRL YOU MET IN SWEATS THE OTHER NIGHT?
THOUGHT MAYBE YOU'D WANT TO SEE ALL THE LOVE YOU'VE BEEN GETTING SINCE...

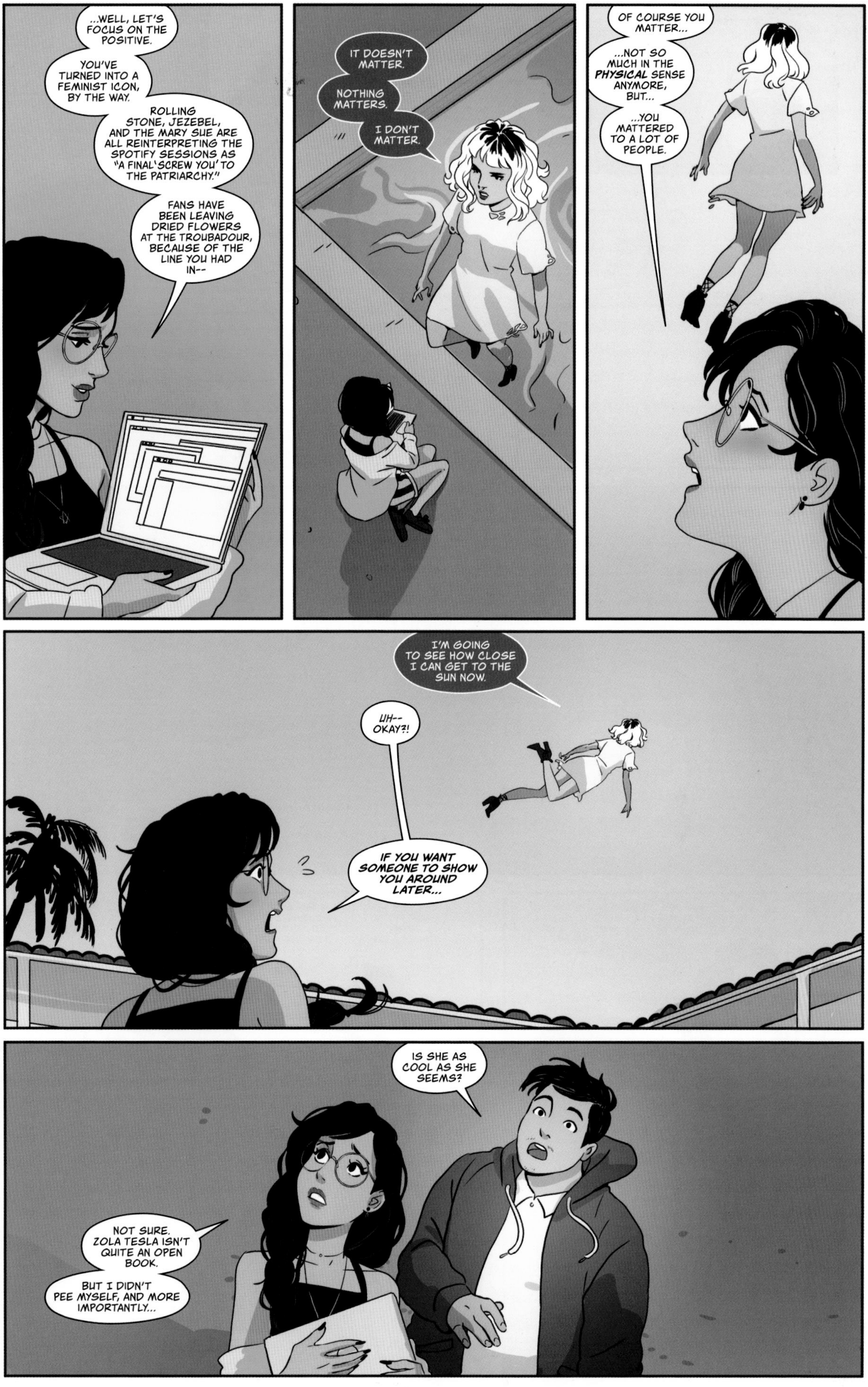
...WELL, LET'S FOCUS ON THE POSITIVE.
YOU'VE TURNED INTO A FEMINIST ICON, BY THE WAY.
ROLLING STONE, JEZEBEL, AND THE MARY SUE ARE ALL REINTERPRETING THE SPOTIFY SESSIONS AS "A FINAL 'SCREW YOU' TO THE PATRIARCHY."
FANS HAVE BEEN LEAVING DRIED FLOWERS AT THE TROUBADOUR, BECAUSE OF THE LINE YOU HAD IN--
IT DOESN'T MATTER.
NOTHING MATTERS.
I DON'T MATTER.
OF COURSE YOU MATTER...
...NOT SO MUCH IN THE PHYSICAL SENSE ANYMORE, BUT...
...YOU MATTERED TO A LOT OF PEOPLE.
I'M GOING TO SEE HOW CLOSE I CAN GET TO THE SUN NOW.
UH-- OKAY?!
IF YOU WANT SOMEONE TO SHOW YOU AROUND LATER...
IS SHE AS COOL AS SHE SEEMS?
NOT SURE. ZOLA TESLA ISN'T QUITE AN OPEN BOOK.
BUT I DIDN'T PEE MYSELF, AND MORE IMPORTANTLY...

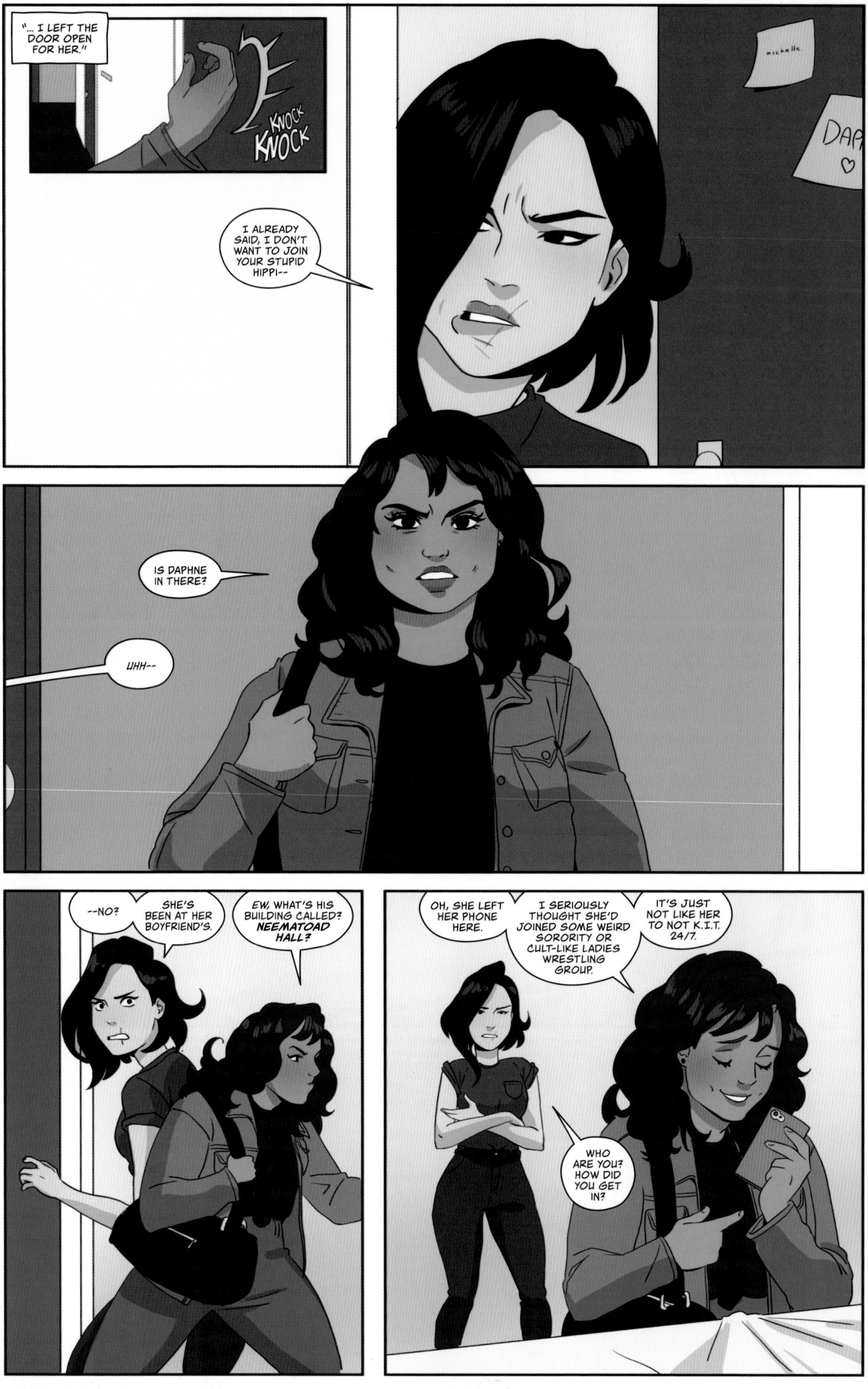
"... I LEFT THE DOOR OPEN FOR HER."
KNOCK KNOCK
michelle
DAPH ♡
I ALREADY SAID, I DON'T WANT TO JOIN YOUR STUPID HIPPI--
IS DAPHNE IN THERE?
UHH--
--NO?
SHE'S BEEN AT HER BOYFRIEND'S.
EW, WHAT'S HIS BUILDING CALLED? NEEMATOAD HALL?
OH, SHE LEFT HER PHONE HERE.
I SERIOUSLY THOUGHT SHE'D JOINED SOME WEIRD SORORITY OR CULT-LIKE LADIES WRESTLING GROUP.
IT'S JUST NOT LIKE HER TO NOT K.I.T. 24/7.
WHO ARE YOU? HOW DID YOU GET IN?

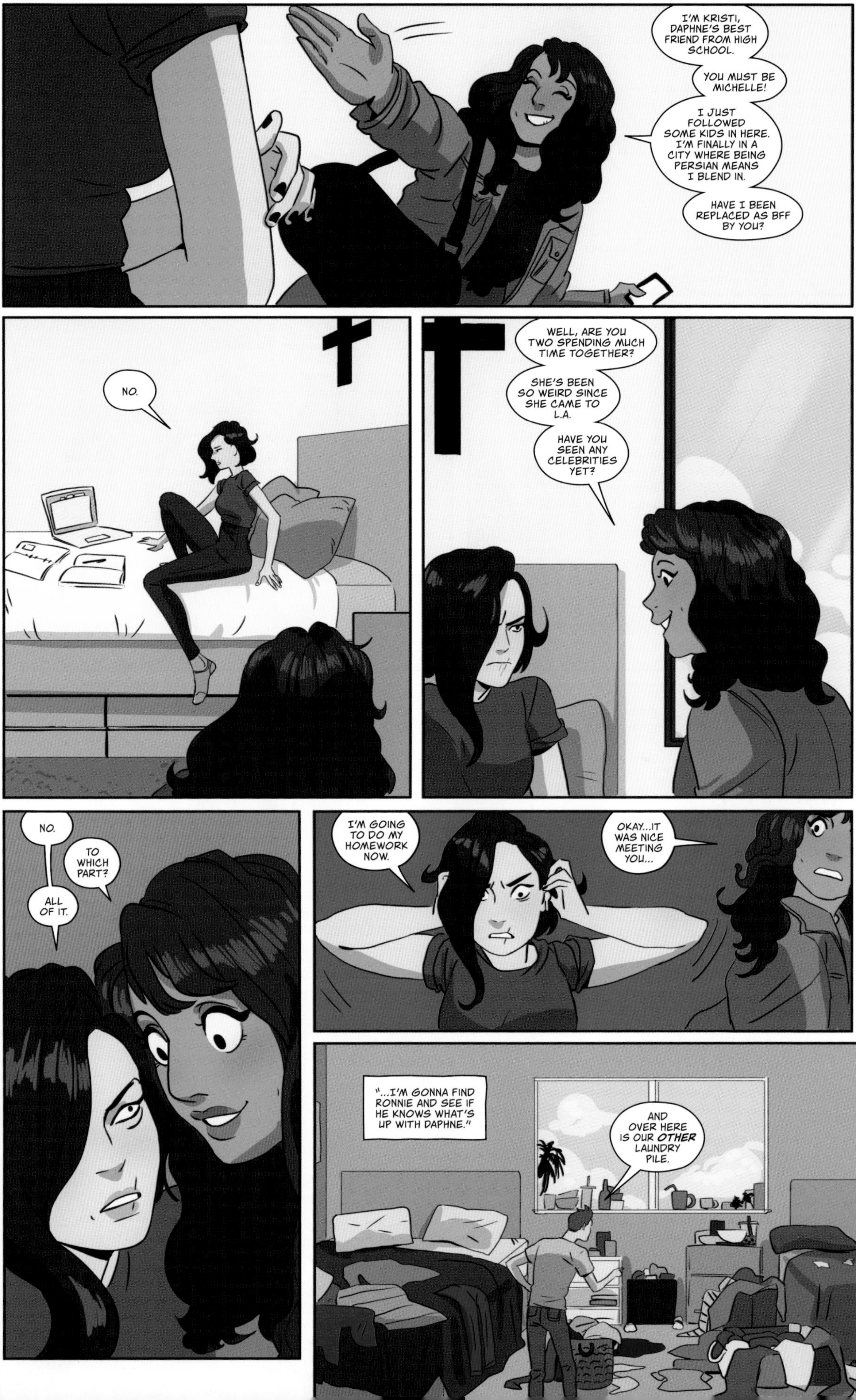
I'M KRISTI, DAPHNE'S BEST FRIEND FROM HIGH SCHOOL.
YOU MUST BE MICHELLE!
I JUST FOLLOWED SOME KIDS IN HERE. I'M FINALLY IN A CITY WHERE BEING PERSIAN MEANS I BLEND IN.
HAVE I BEEN REPLACED AS BFF BY YOU?
NO.
WELL, ARE YOU TWO SPENDING MUCH TIME TOGETHER?
SHE'S BEEN SO WEIRD SINCE SHE CAME TO L.A.
HAVE YOU SEEN ANY CELEBRITIES YET?
NO.
TO WHICH PART?
ALL OF IT.
I'M GOING TO DO MY HOMEWORK NOW.
OKAY...IT WAS NICE MEETING YOU...
"...I'M GONNA FIND RONNIE AND SEE IF HE KNOWS WHAT'S UP WITH DAPHNE."
AND OVER HERE IS OUR ***OTHER*** LAUNDRY PILE.

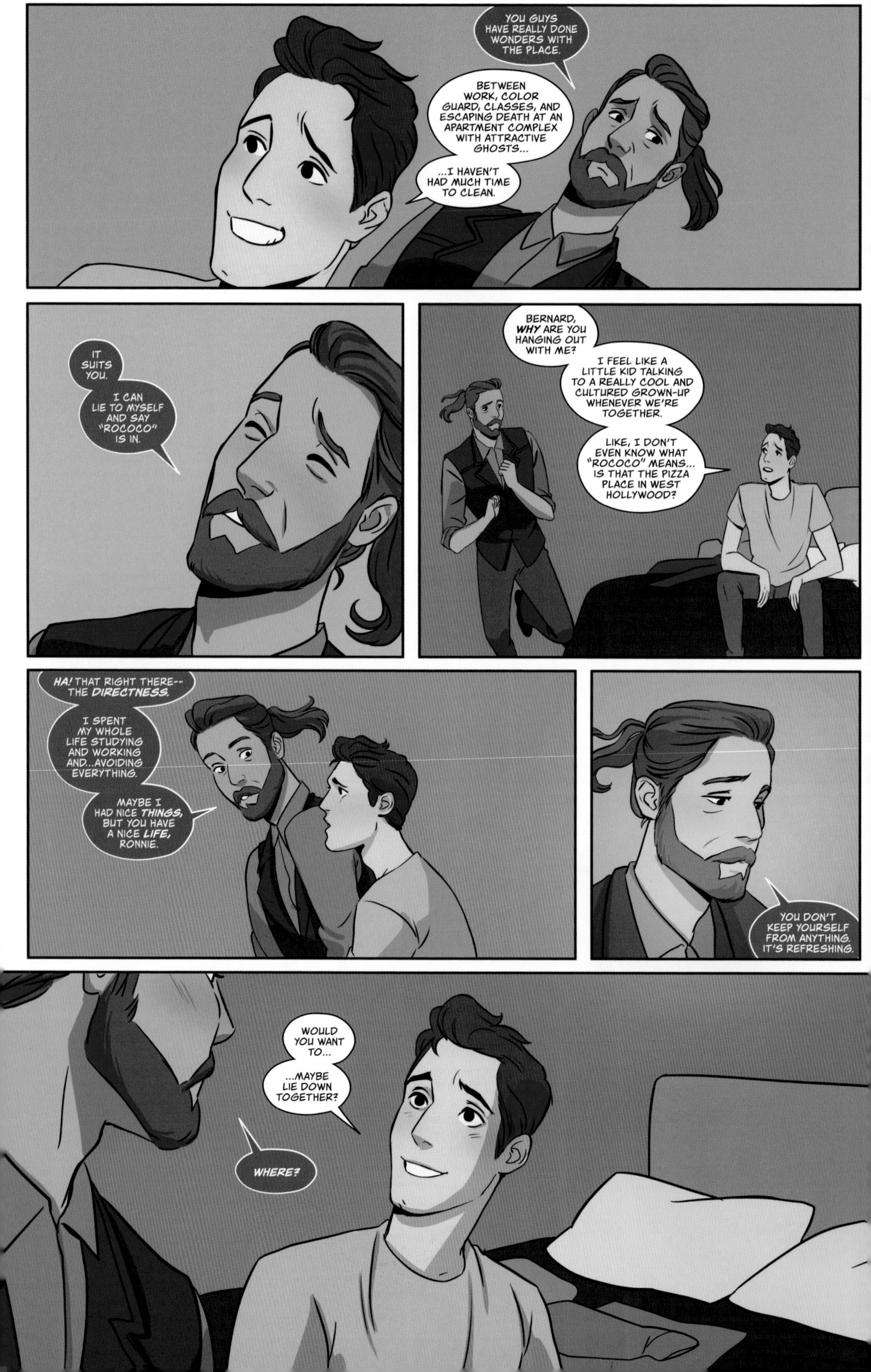
YOU GUYS HAVE REALLY DONE WONDERS WITH THE PLACE.
BETWEEN WORK, COLOR GUARD, CLASSES, AND ESCAPING DEATH AT AN APARTMENT COMPLEX WITH ATTRACTIVE GHOSTS...
...I HAVEN'T HAD MUCH TIME TO CLEAN.
IT SUITS YOU.
I CAN LIE TO MYSELF AND SAY "ROCOCO" IS IN.
BERNARD, WHY ARE YOU HANGING OUT WITH ME?
I FEEL LIKE A LITTLE KID TALKING TO A REALLY COOL AND CULTURED GROWN-UP WHENEVER WE'RE TOGETHER.
LIKE, I DON'T EVEN KNOW WHAT "ROCOCO" MEANS... IS THAT THE PIZZA PLACE IN WEST HOLLYWOOD?
HA! THAT RIGHT THERE-- THE DIRECTNESS.
I SPENT MY WHOLE LIFE STUDYING AND WORKING AND...AVOIDING EVERYTHING.
MAYBE I HAD NICE THINGS, BUT YOU HAVE A NICE LIFE, RONNIE.
YOU DON'T KEEP YOURSELF FROM ANYTHING. IT'S REFRESHING.
WOULD YOU WANT TO...
...MAYBE LIE DOWN TOGETHER?
WHERE?

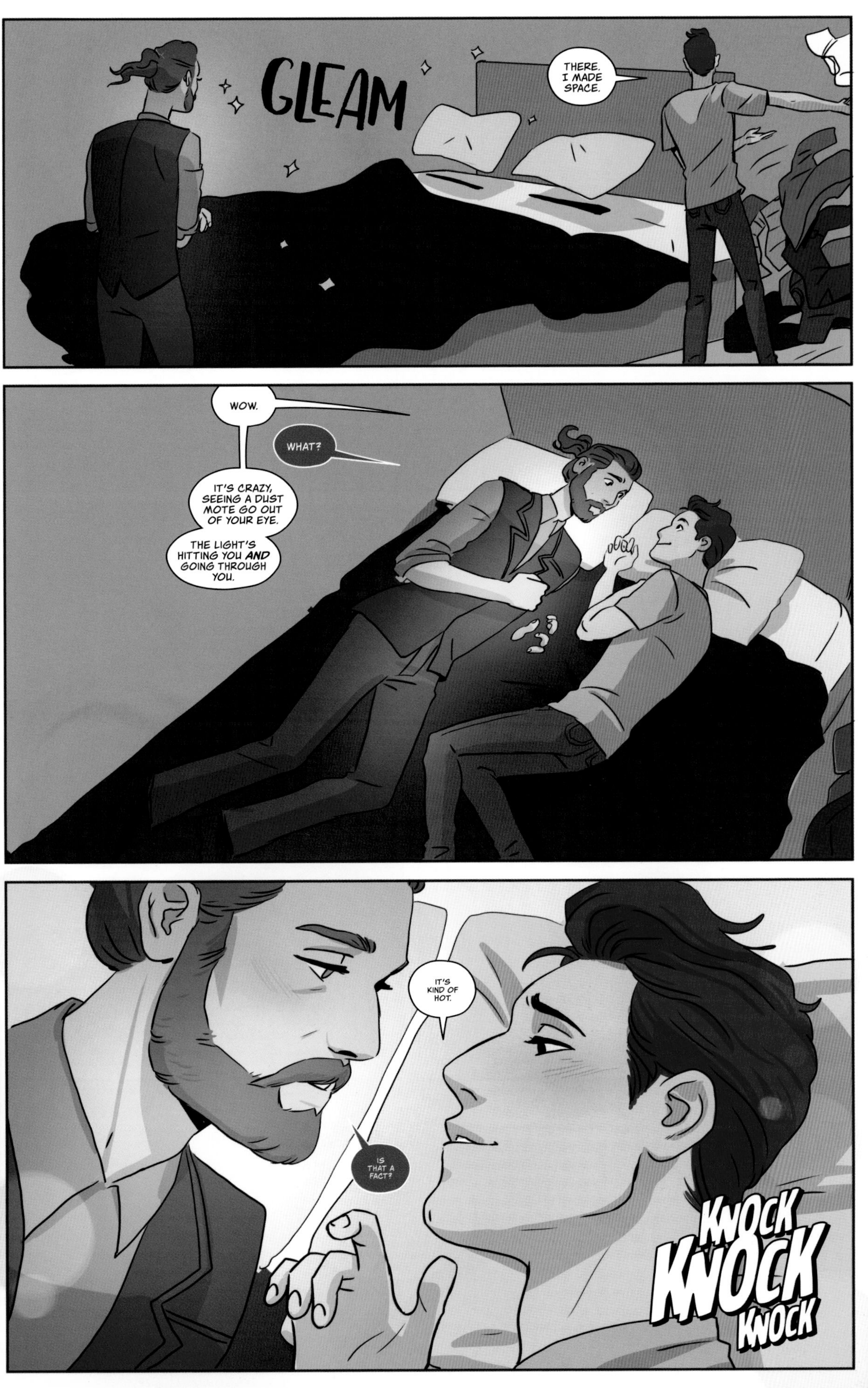
GLEAM
THERE. I MADE SPACE.
WOW.
WHAT?
IT'S CRAZY, SEEING A DUST MOTE GO OUT OF YOUR EYE.
THE LIGHT'S HITTING YOU AND GOING THROUGH YOU.
IT'S KIND OF HOT.
IS THAT A FACT?
KNOCK
KNOCK
KNOCK

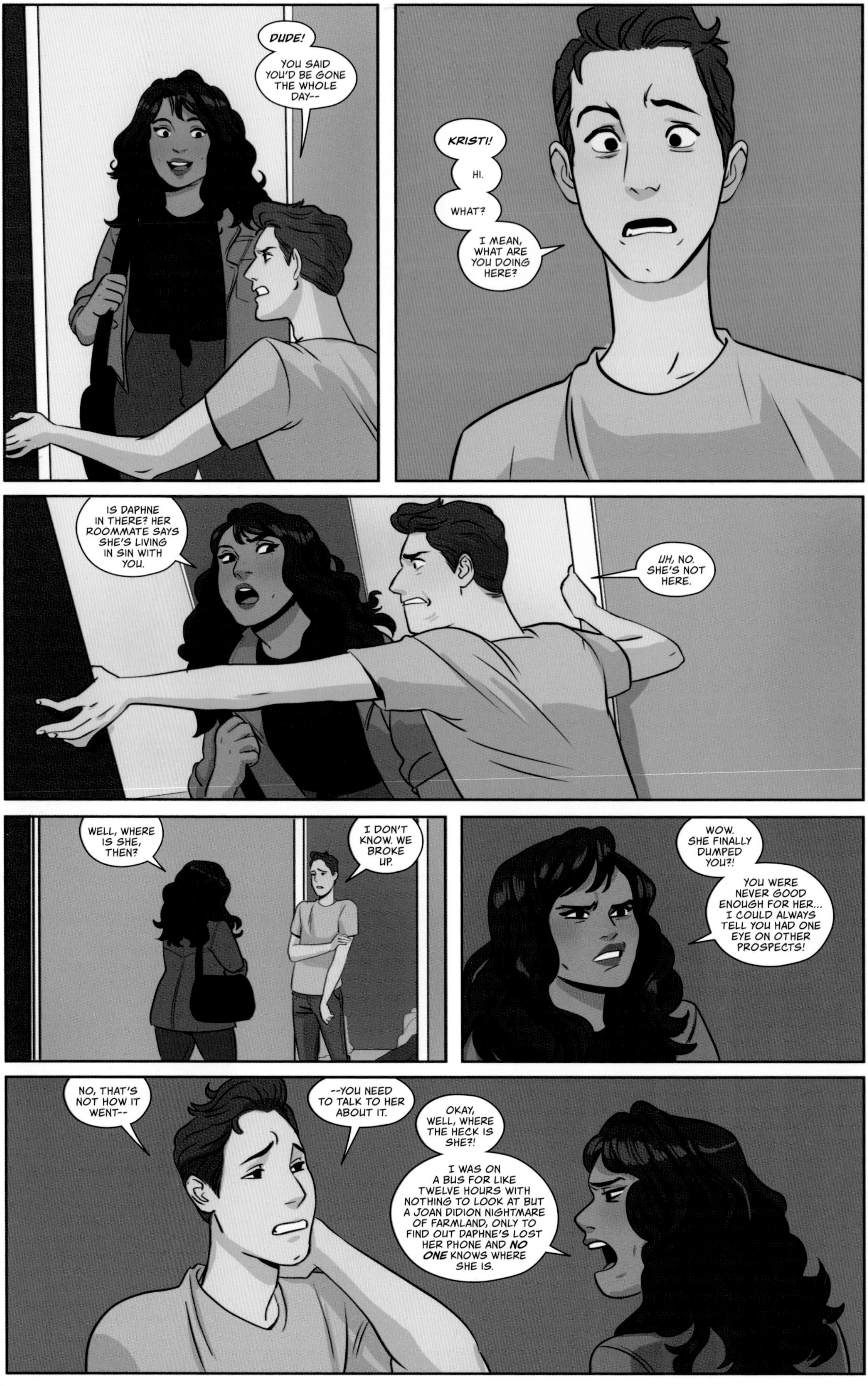
DUDE!
YOU SAID YOU'D BE GONE THE WHOLE DAY--
KRISTI!
HI.
WHAT?
I MEAN, WHAT ARE YOU DOING HERE?
IS DAPHNE IN THERE? HER ROOMMATE SAYS SHE'S LIVING IN SIN WITH YOU.
UH, NO. SHE'S NOT HERE.
WELL, WHERE IS SHE, THEN?
I DON'T KNOW. WE BROKE UP.
WOW. SHE FINALLY DUMPED YOU?!
YOU WERE NEVER GOOD ENOUGH FOR HER... I COULD ALWAYS TELL YOU HAD ONE EYE ON OTHER PROSPECTS!
NO, THAT'S NOT HOW IT WENT--
--YOU NEED TO TALK TO HER ABOUT IT.
OKAY, WELL, WHERE THE HECK IS SHE?!
I WAS ON A BUS FOR LIKE TWELVE HOURS WITH NOTHING TO LOOK AT BUT A JOAN DIDION NIGHTMARE OF FARMLAND, ONLY TO FIND OUT DAPHNE'S LOST HER PHONE AND NO ONE KNOWS WHERE SHE IS.

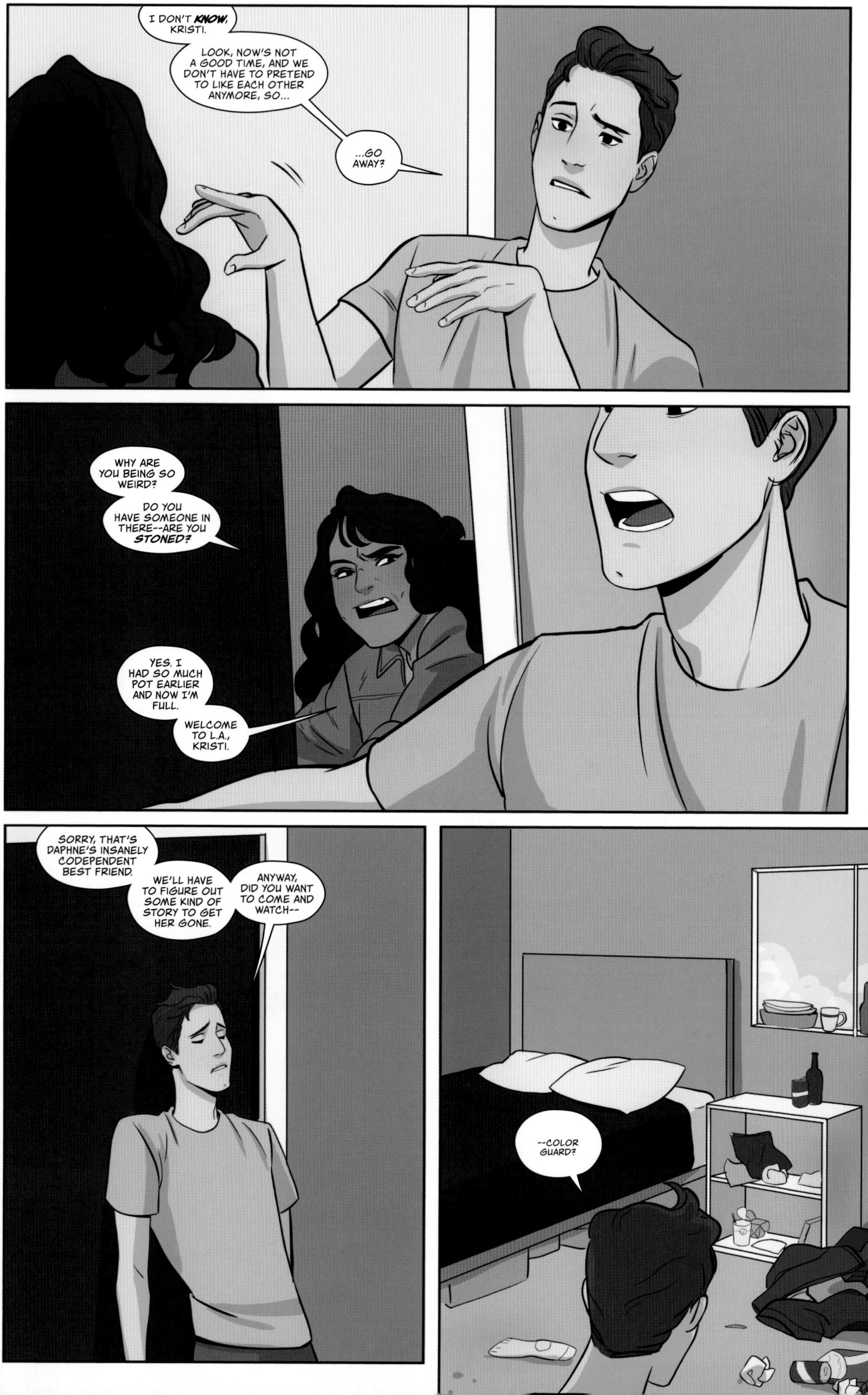
I DON'T KNOW, KRISTI.
LOOK, NOW'S NOT A GOOD TIME, AND WE DON'T HAVE TO PRETEND TO LIKE EACH OTHER ANYMORE, SO...
...GO AWAY?
WHY ARE YOU BEING SO WEIRD?
DO YOU HAVE SOMEONE IN THERE--ARE YOU STONED?
YES. I HAD SO MUCH POT EARLIER AND NOW I'M FULL.
WELCOME TO L.A., KRISTI.
SORRY, THAT'S DAPHNE'S INSANELY CODEPENDENT BEST FRIEND.
WE'LL HAVE TO FIGURE OUT SOME KIND OF STORY TO GET HER GONE.
ANYWAY, DID YOU WANT TO COME AND WATCH--
--COLOR GUARD?

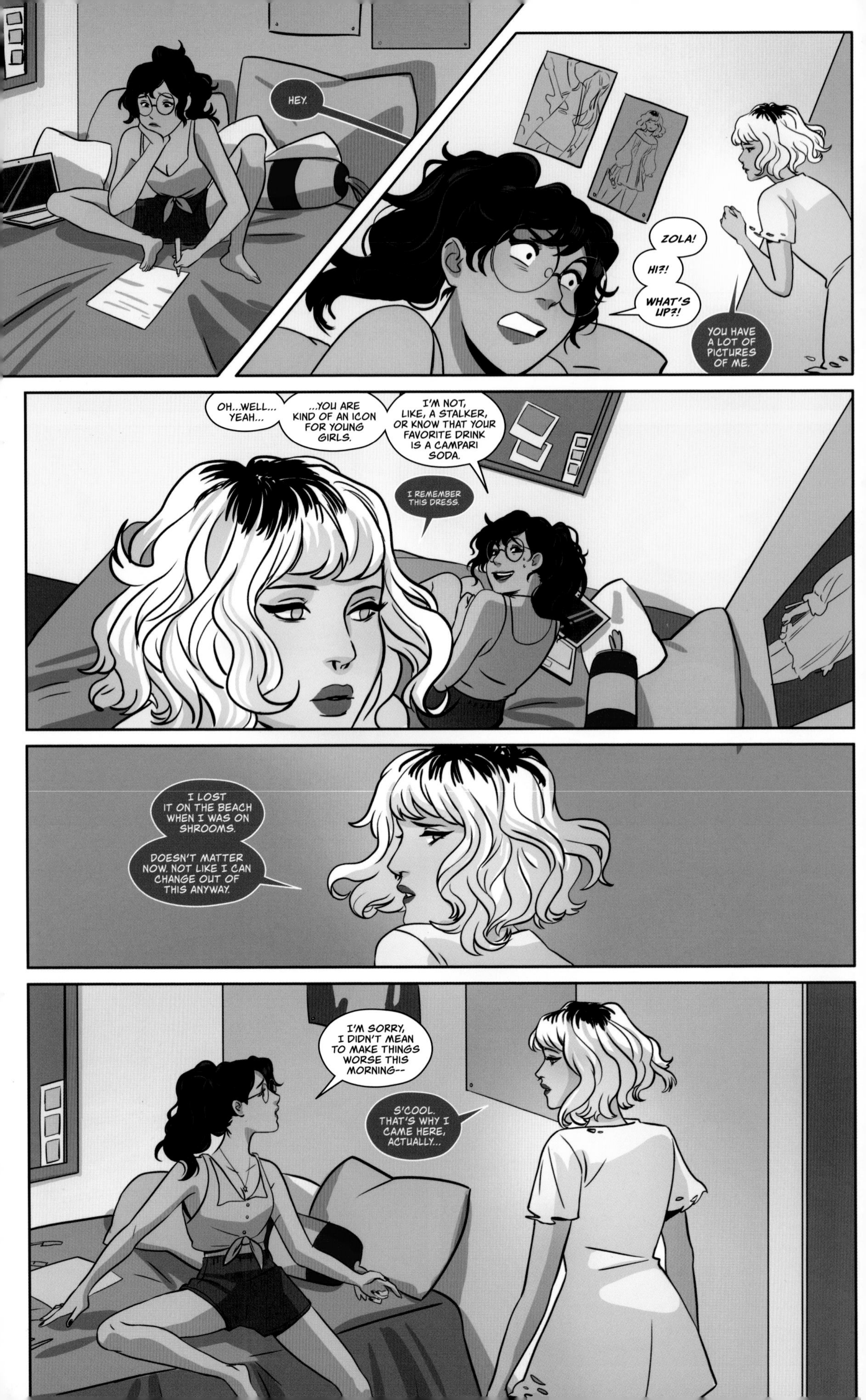
HEY.
ZOLA!
HI?!
WHAT'S UP?!
YOU HAVE A LOT OF PICTURES OF ME.
OH...WELL... YEAH...
...YOU ARE KIND OF AN ICON FOR YOUNG GIRLS.
I'M NOT, LIKE, A STALKER, OR KNOW THAT YOUR FAVORITE DRINK IS A CAMPARI SODA.
I REMEMBER THIS DRESS.
I LOST IT ON THE BEACH WHEN I WAS ON SHROOMS.
DOESN'T MATTER NOW. NOT LIKE I CAN CHANGE OUT OF THIS ANYWAY.
I'M SORRY, I DIDN'T MEAN TO MAKE THINGS WORSE THIS MORNING--
S'COOL. THAT'S WHY I CAME HERE, ACTUALLY...

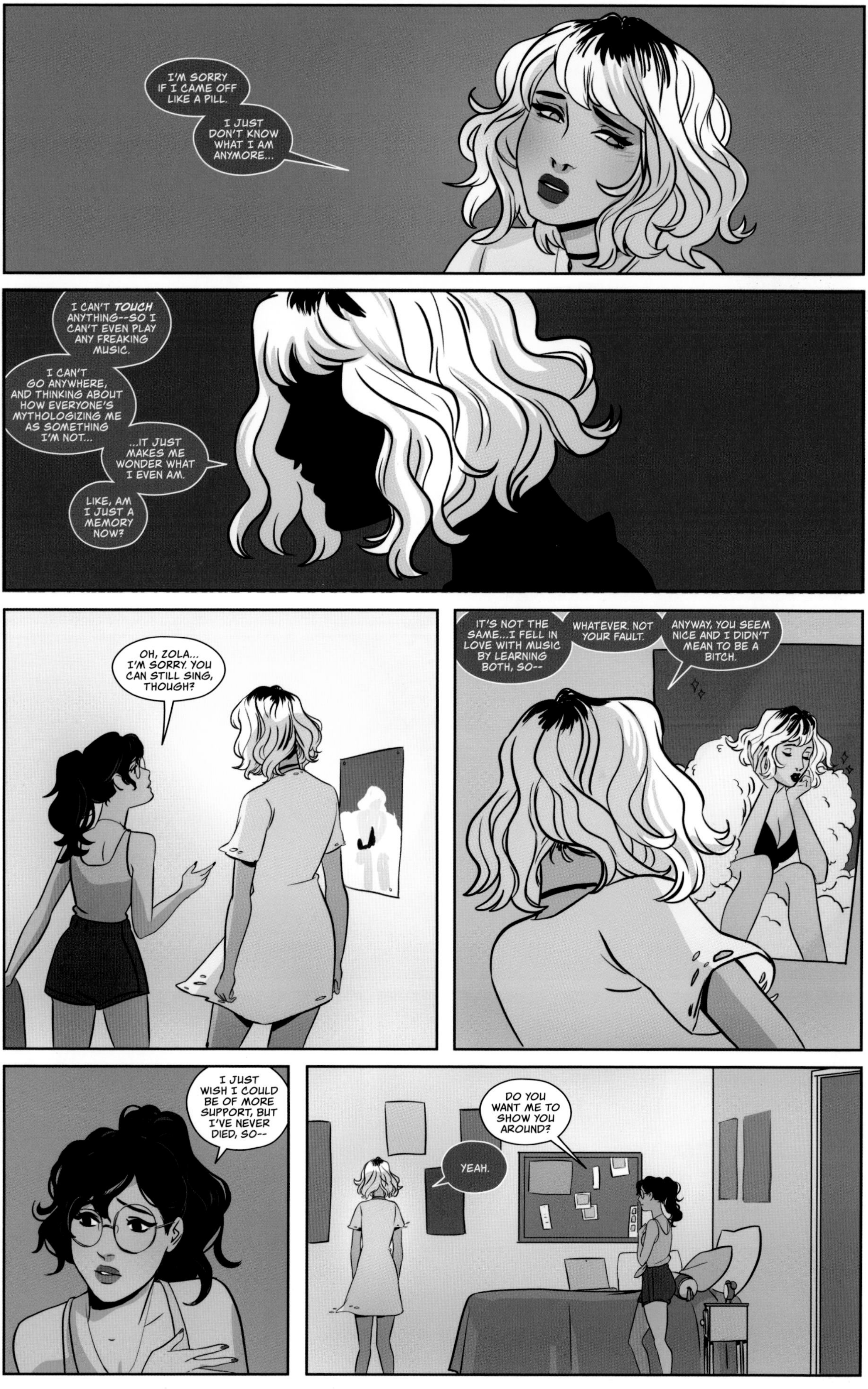
I'M SORRY IF I CAME OFF LIKE A PILL.
I JUST DON'T KNOW WHAT I AM ANYMORE...
I CAN'T *TOUCH* ANYTHING--SO I CAN'T EVEN PLAY ANY FREAKING MUSIC.
I CAN'T GO ANYWHERE, AND THINKING ABOUT HOW EVERYONE'S MYTHOLOGIZING ME AS SOMETHING I'M NOT...
...IT JUST MAKES ME WONDER WHAT I EVEN AM.
LIKE, AM I JUST A MEMORY NOW?
OH, ZOLA... I'M SORRY. YOU CAN STILL SING, THOUGH?
IT'S NOT THE SAME...I FELL IN LOVE WITH MUSIC BY LEARNING BOTH, SO--
WHATEVER. NOT YOUR FAULT.
ANYWAY, YOU SEEM NICE AND I DIDN'T MEAN TO BE A BITCH.
I JUST WISH I COULD BE OF MORE SUPPORT, BUT I'VE NEVER DIED, SO--
DO YOU WANT ME TO SHOW YOU AROUND?
YEAH.

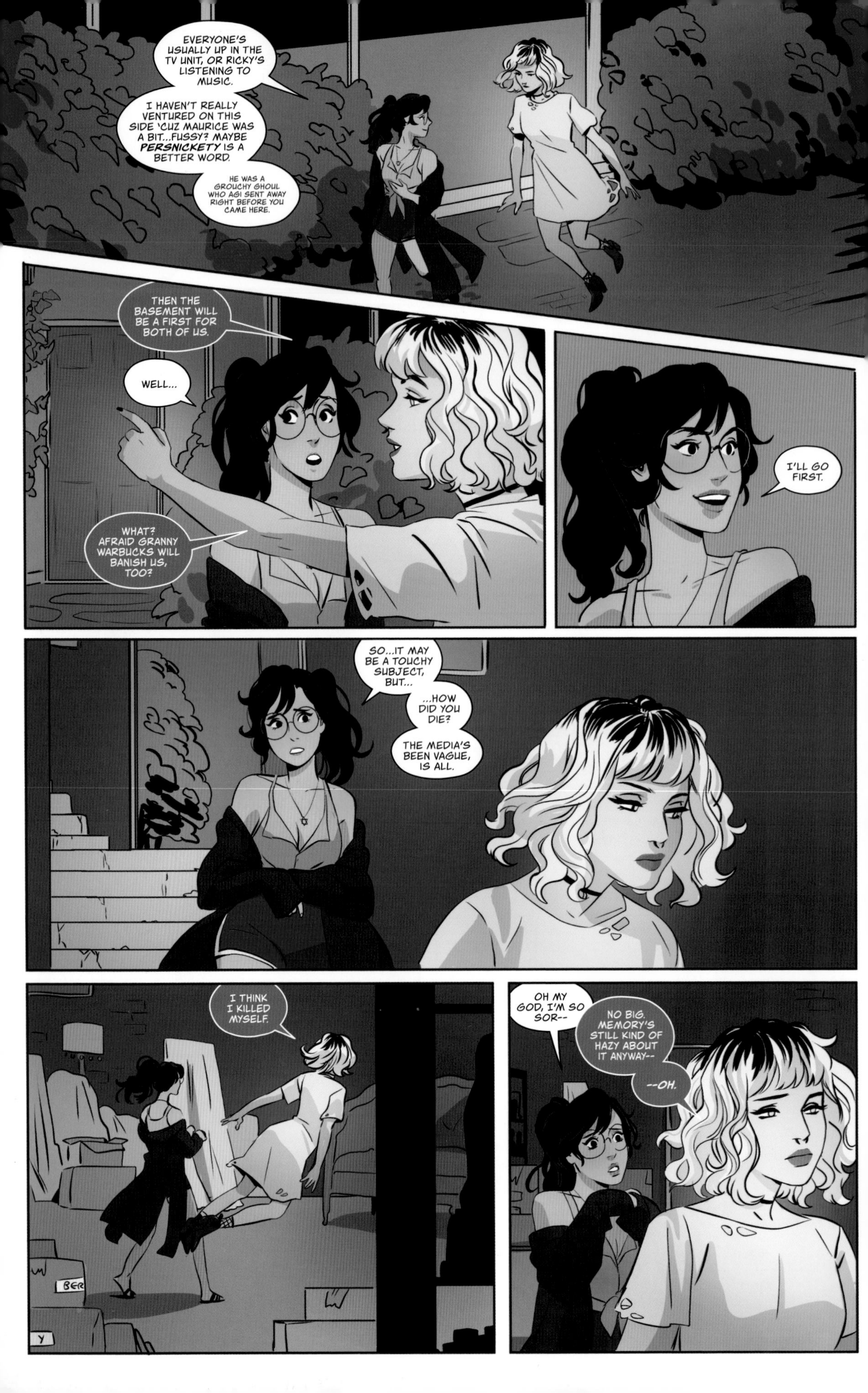
EVERYONE'S USUALLY UP IN THE TV UNIT, OR RICKY'S LISTENING TO MUSIC.
I HAVEN'T REALLY VENTURED ON THIS SIDE 'CUZ MAURICE WAS A BIT...FUSSY? MAYBE PERSNICKETY IS A BETTER WORD.
HE WAS A GROUCHY GHOUL WHO AGI SENT AWAY RIGHT BEFORE YOU CAME HERE.
THEN THE BASEMENT WILL BE A FIRST FOR BOTH OF US.
WELL...
WHAT? AFRAID GRANNY WARBUCKS WILL BANISH US, TOO?
I'LL GO FIRST.
SO...IT MAY BE A TOUCHY SUBJECT, BUT...
...HOW DID YOU DIE?
THE MEDIA'S BEEN VAGUE, IS ALL.
I THINK I KILLED MYSELF.
OH MY GOD, I'M SO SOR--
NO BIG. MEMORY'S STILL KIND OF HAZY ABOUT IT ANYWAY--
--OH.

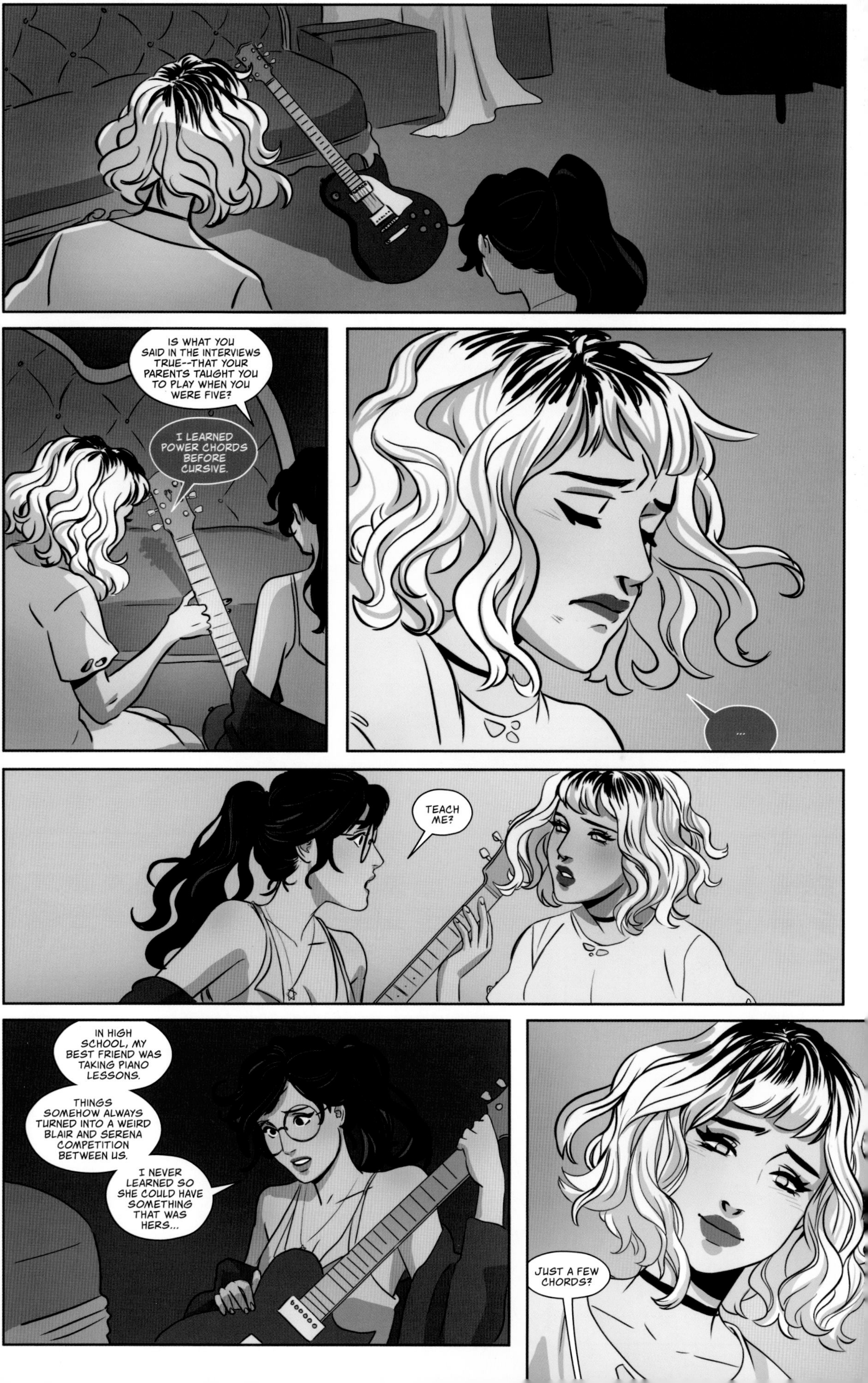
IS WHAT YOU SAID IN THE INTERVIEWS TRUE--THAT YOUR PARENTS TAUGHT YOU TO PLAY WHEN YOU WERE FIVE?
I LEARNED POWER CHORDS BEFORE CURSIVE.
...
TEACH ME?
IN HIGH SCHOOL, MY BEST FRIEND WAS TAKING PIANO LESSONS.
THINGS SOMEHOW ALWAYS TURNED INTO A WEIRD BLAIR AND SERENA COMPETITION BETWEEN US.
I NEVER LEARNED SO SHE COULD HAVE SOMETHING THAT WAS HERS...
JUST A FEW CHORDS?

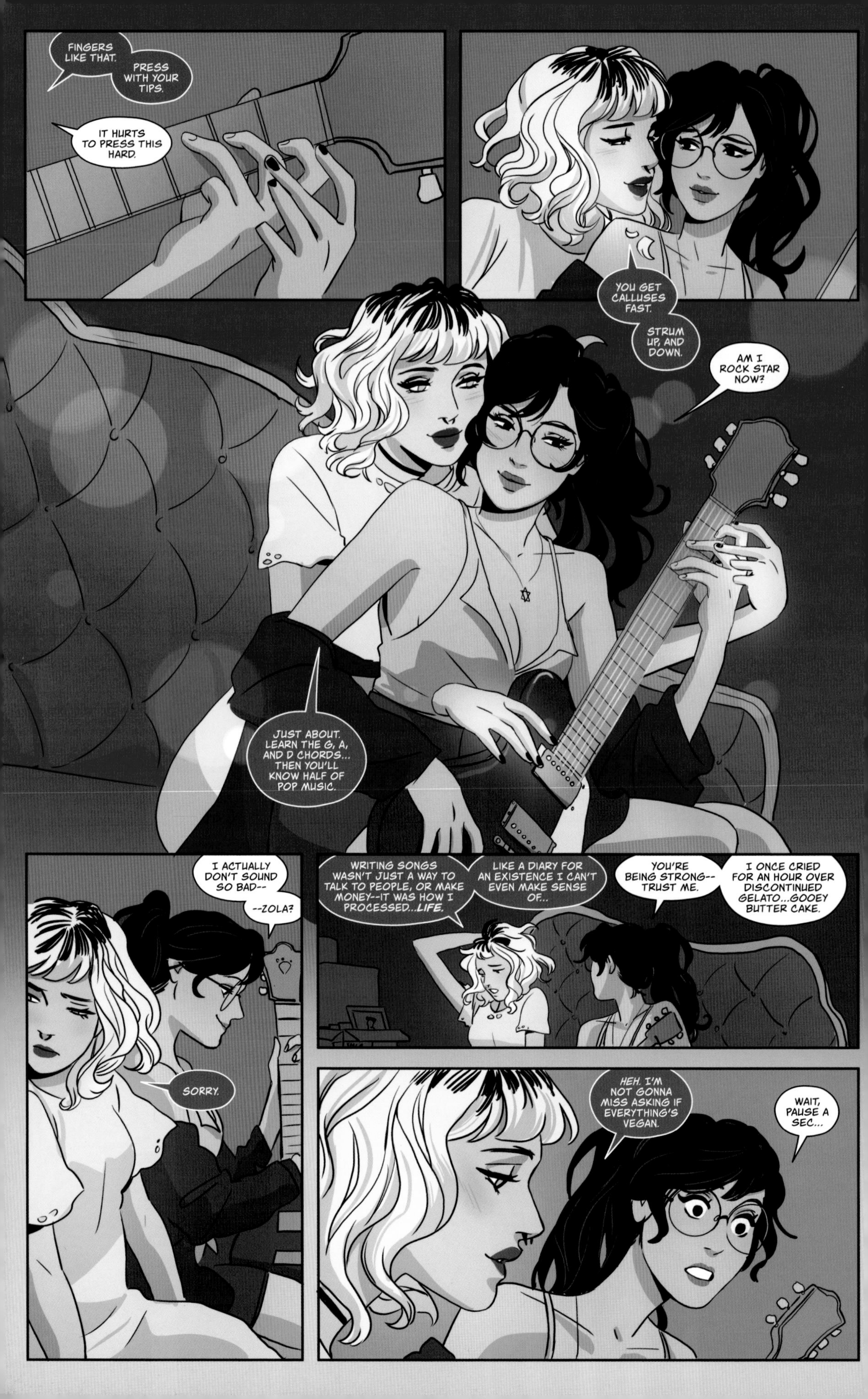

FINGERS LIKE THAT.
PRESS WITH YOUR TIPS.
IT HURTS TO PRESS THIS HARD.
YOU GET CALLUSES FAST.
STRUM UP, AND DOWN.
AM I ROCK STAR NOW?
JUST ABOUT. LEARN THE G, A, AND D CHORDS... THEN YOU'LL KNOW HALF OF POP MUSIC.
I ACTUALLY DON'T SOUND SO BAD--
--ZOLA?
SORRY.
WRITING SONGS WASN'T JUST A WAY TO TALK TO PEOPLE, OR MAKE MONEY--IT WAS HOW I PROCESSED...LIFE.
LIKE A DIARY FOR AN EXISTENCE I CAN'T EVEN MAKE SENSE OF...
YOU'RE BEING STRONG-- TRUST ME.
I ONCE CRIED FOR AN HOUR OVER DISCONTINUED GELATO...GOOEY BUTTER CAKE.
HEH. I'M NOT GONNA MISS ASKING IF EVERYTHING'S VEGAN.
WAIT, PAUSE A SEC...

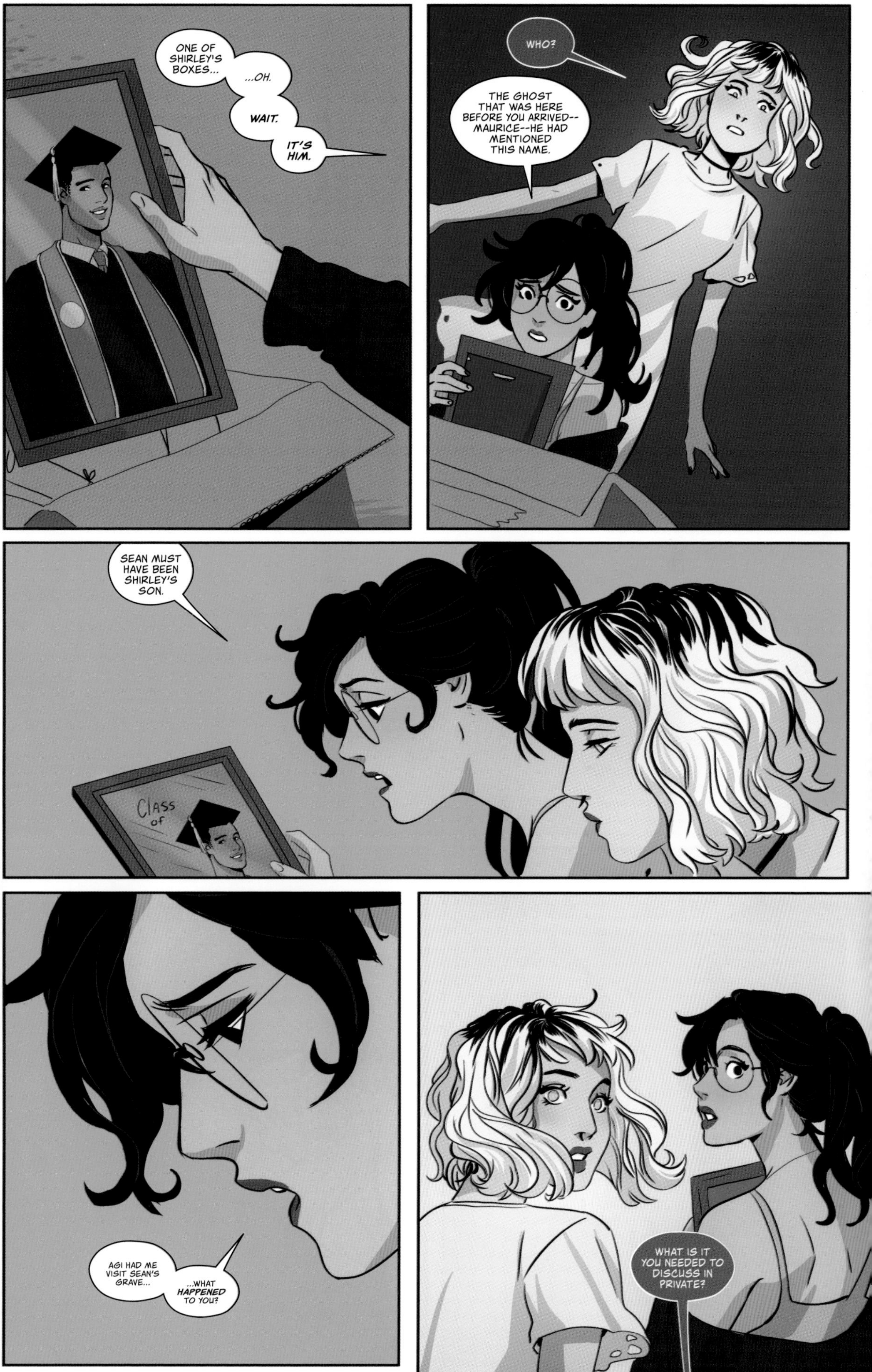
ONE OF SHIRLEY'S BOXES...
...OH.
WAIT.
IT'S HIM.
WHO?
THE GHOST THAT WAS HERE BEFORE YOU ARRIVED--MAURICE--HE HAD MENTIONED THIS NAME.
SEAN MUST HAVE BEEN SHIRLEY'S SON.
CLASS of
AGI HAD ME VISIT SEAN'S GRAVE...
...WHAT HAPPENED TO YOU?
WHAT IS IT YOU NEEDED TO DISCUSS IN PRIVATE?

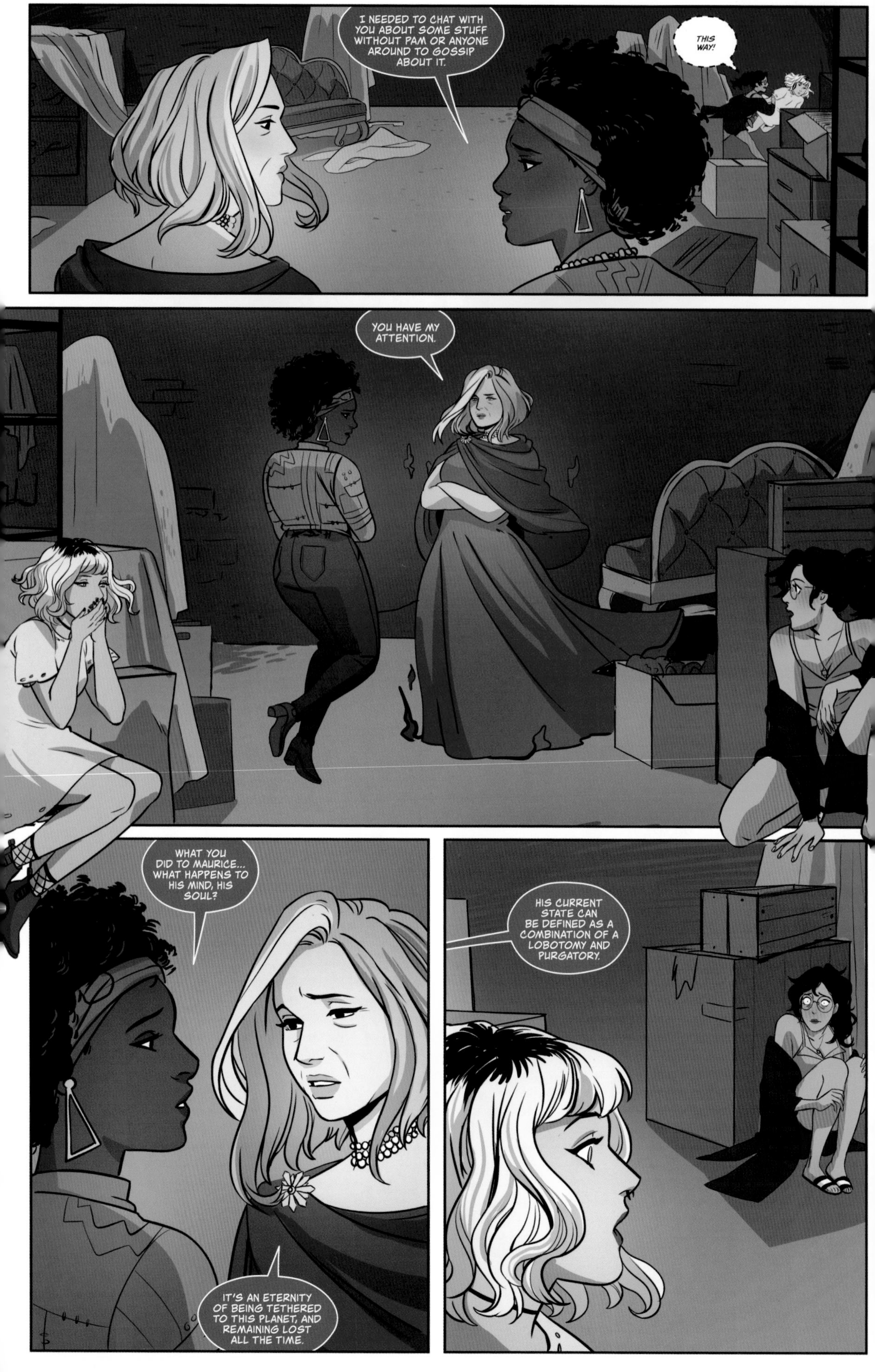
I NEEDED TO CHAT WITH YOU ABOUT SOME STUFF WITHOUT PAM OR ANYONE AROUND TO GOSSIP ABOUT IT.
THIS WAY!
YOU HAVE MY ATTENTION.
WHAT YOU DID TO MAURICE... WHAT HAPPENS TO HIS MIND, HIS SOUL?
IT'S AN ETERNITY OF BEING TETHERED TO THIS PLANET, AND REMAINING LOST ALL THE TIME.
HIS CURRENT STATE CAN BE DEFINED AS A COMBINATION OF A LOBOTOMY AND PURGATORY.

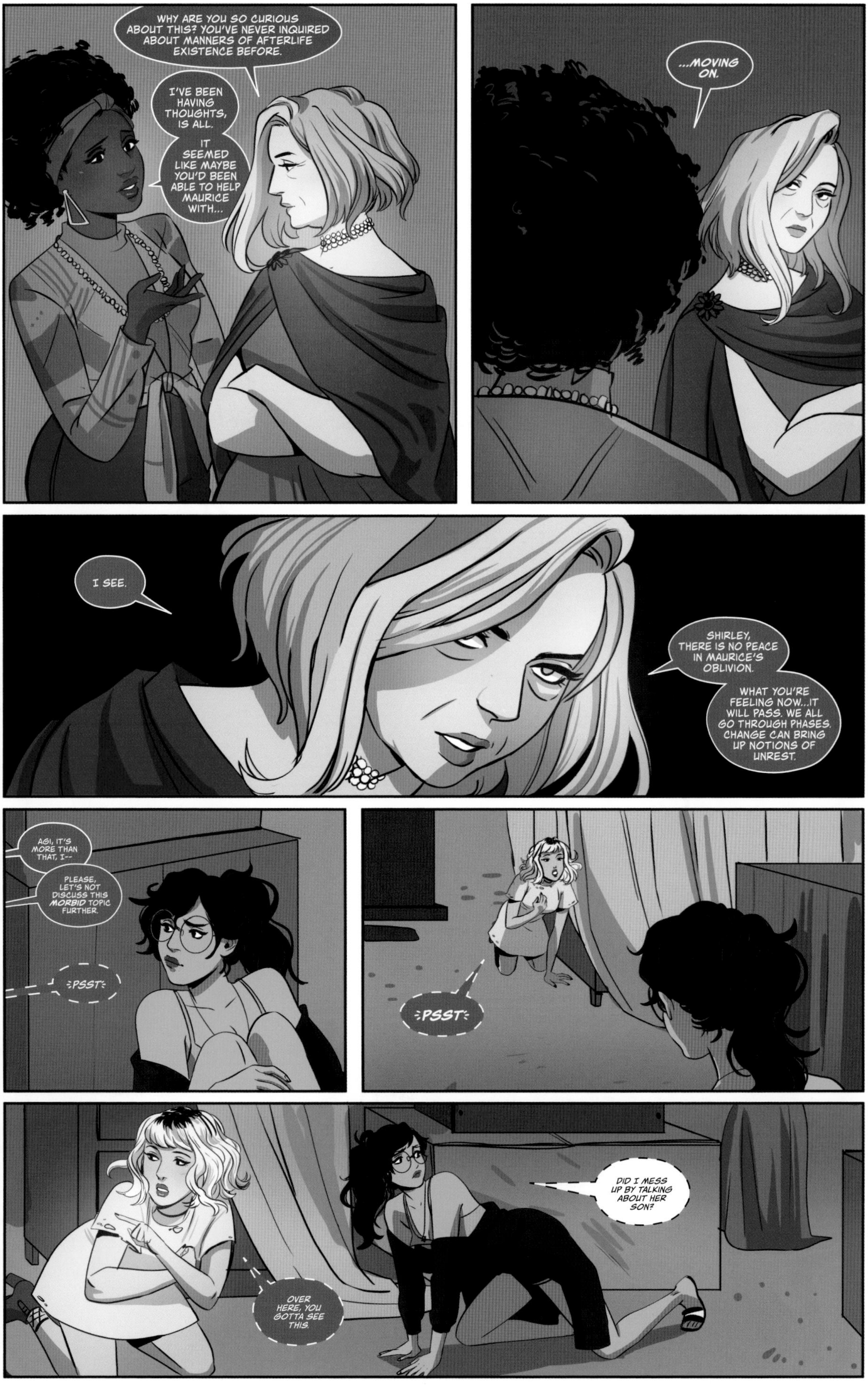
WHY ARE YOU SO CURIOUS ABOUT THIS? YOU'VE NEVER INQUIRED ABOUT MANNERS OF AFTERLIFE EXISTENCE BEFORE.
I'VE BEEN HAVING THOUGHTS, IS ALL.
IT SEEMED LIKE MAYBE YOU'D BEEN ABLE TO HELP MAURICE WITH...
...MOVING ON.
I SEE.
SHIRLEY, THERE IS NO PEACE IN MAURICE'S OBLIVION.
WHAT YOU'RE FEELING NOW...IT WILL PASS. WE ALL GO THROUGH PHASES. CHANGE CAN BRING UP NOTIONS OF UNREST.
AGI, IT'S MORE THAN THAT, I--
PLEASE, LET'S NOT DISCUSS THIS MORBID TOPIC FURTHER.
PSST
PSST
DID I MESS UP BY TALKING ABOUT HER SON?
OVER HERE, YOU GOTTA SEE THIS.

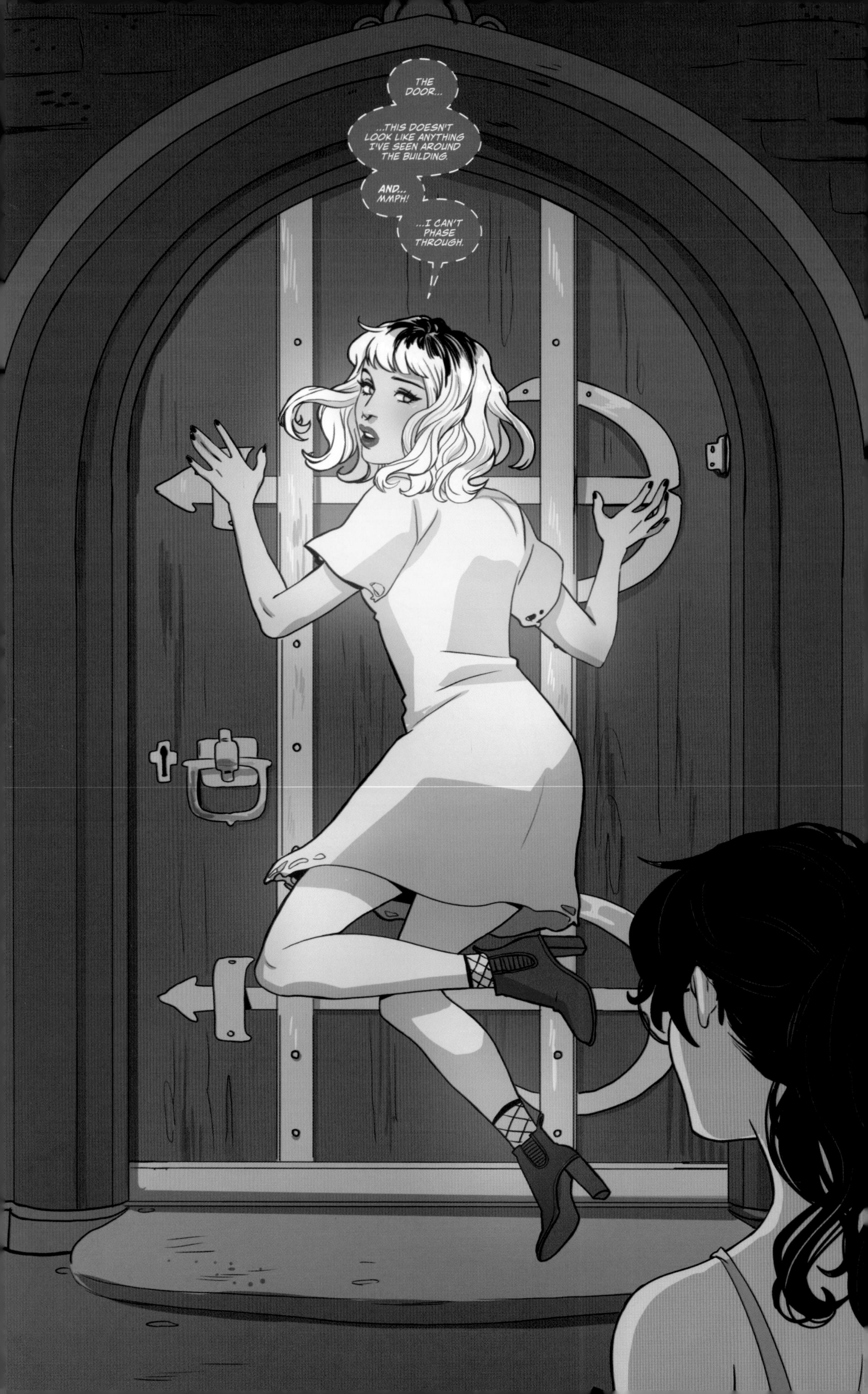
THE DOOR...
...THIS DOESN'T LOOK LIKE ANYTHING I'VE SEEN AROUND THE BUILDING.
AND... MMPH!
...I CAN'T PHASE THROUGH.

Chapter Six

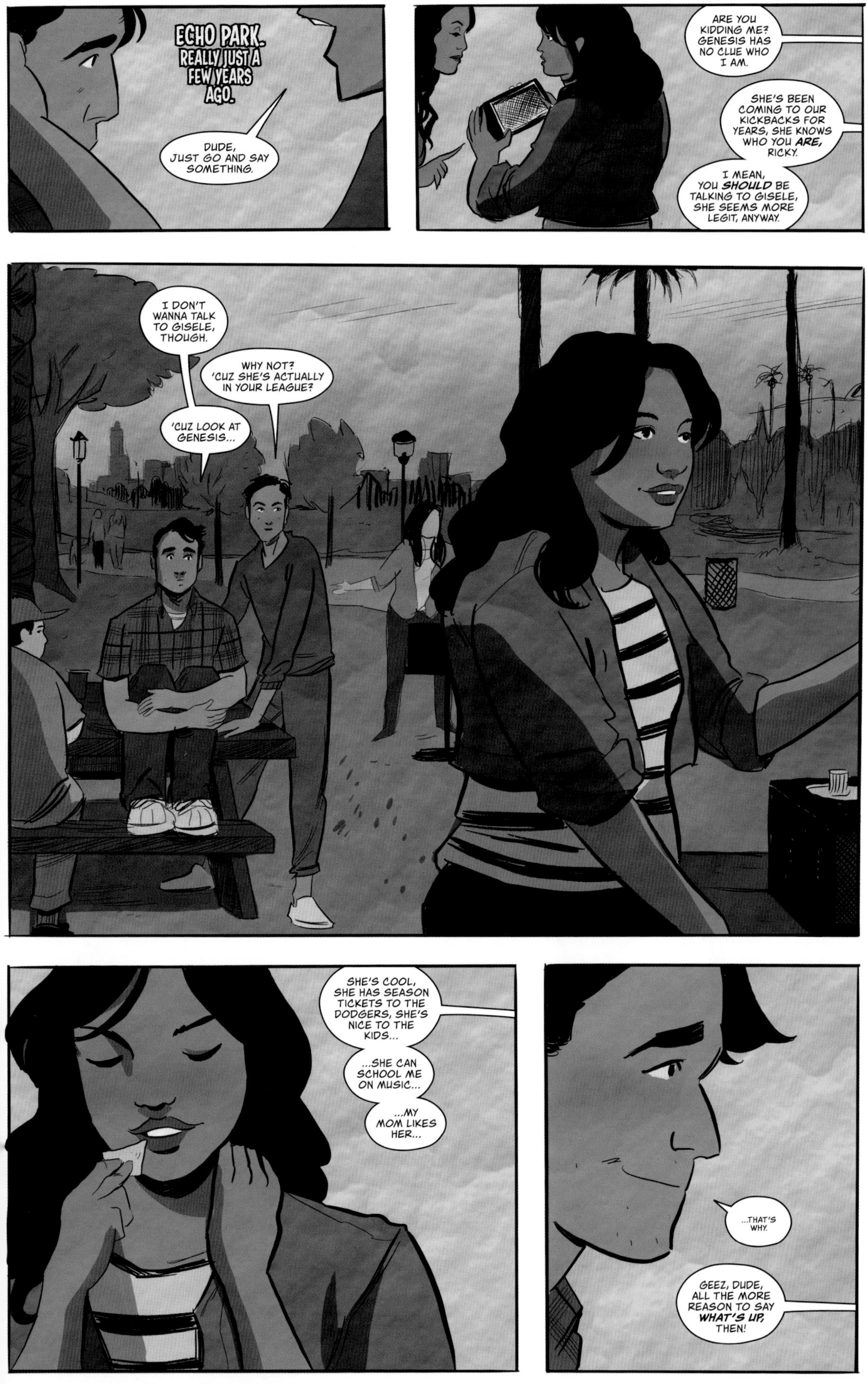
ECHO PARK. REALLY JUST A FEW YEARS AGO.
DUDE, JUST GO AND SAY SOMETHING.
ARE YOU KIDDING ME? GENESIS HAS NO CLUE WHO I AM.
SHE'S BEEN COMING TO OUR KICKBACKS FOR YEARS, SHE KNOWS WHO YOU *ARE,* RICKY.
I MEAN, YOU ***SHOULD*** BE TALKING TO GISELE, SHE SEEMS MORE LEGIT, ANYWAY.
I DON'T WANNA TALK TO GISELE, THOUGH.
WHY NOT? 'CUZ SHE'S ACTUALLY IN YOUR LEAGUE?
'CUZ LOOK AT GENESIS...
SHE'S COOL, SHE HAS SEASON TICKETS TO THE DODGERS, SHE'S NICE TO THE KIDS...
...SHE CAN SCHOOL ME ON MUSIC...
...MY MOM LIKES HER...
...THAT'S WHY.
GEEZ, DUDE, ALL THE MORE REASON TO SAY ***WHAT'S UP,*** THEN!

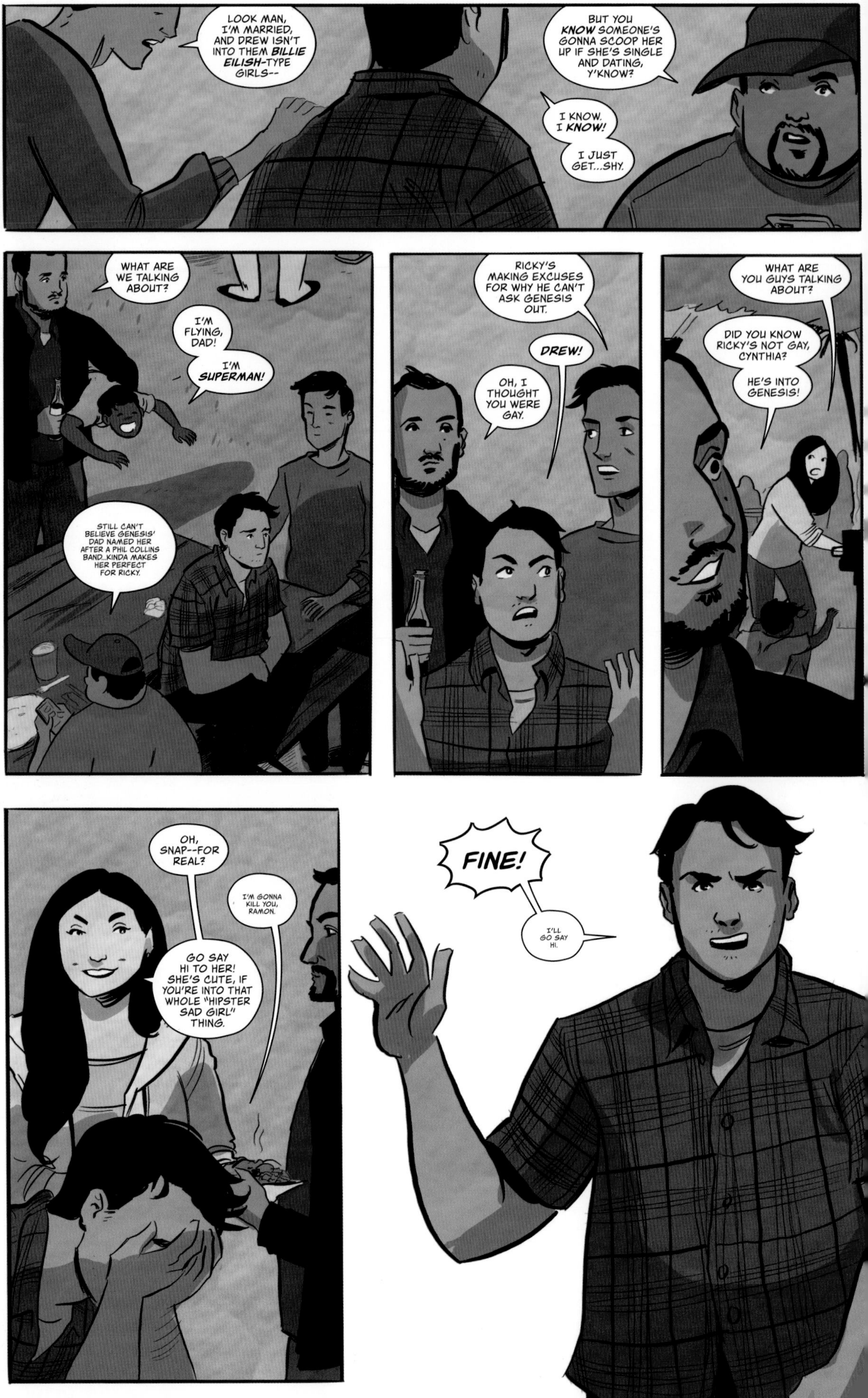
LOOK MAN, I'M MARRIED, AND DREW ISN'T INTO THEM BILLIE EILISH-TYPE GIRLS--
BUT YOU KNOW SOMEONE'S GONNA SCOOP HER UP IF SHE'S SINGLE AND DATING, Y'KNOW?
I KNOW. I KNOW!
I JUST GET...SHY.
WHAT ARE WE TALKING ABOUT?
I'M FLYING, DAD!
I'M SUPERMAN!
STILL CAN'T BELIEVE GENESIS' DAD NAMED HER AFTER A PHIL COLLINS BAND...KINDA MAKES HER PERFECT FOR RICKY.
RICKY'S MAKING EXCUSES FOR WHY HE CAN'T ASK GENESIS OUT.
DREW!
OH, I THOUGHT YOU WERE GAY.
WHAT ARE YOU GUYS TALKING ABOUT?
DID YOU KNOW RICKY'S NOT GAY, CYNTHIA?
HE'S INTO GENESIS!
OH, SNAP--FOR REAL?
GO SAY HI TO HER! SHE'S CUTE, IF YOU'RE INTO THAT WHOLE "HIPSTER SAD GIRL" THING.
I'M GONNA KILL YOU, RAMON.
FINE!
I'LL GO SAY HI.

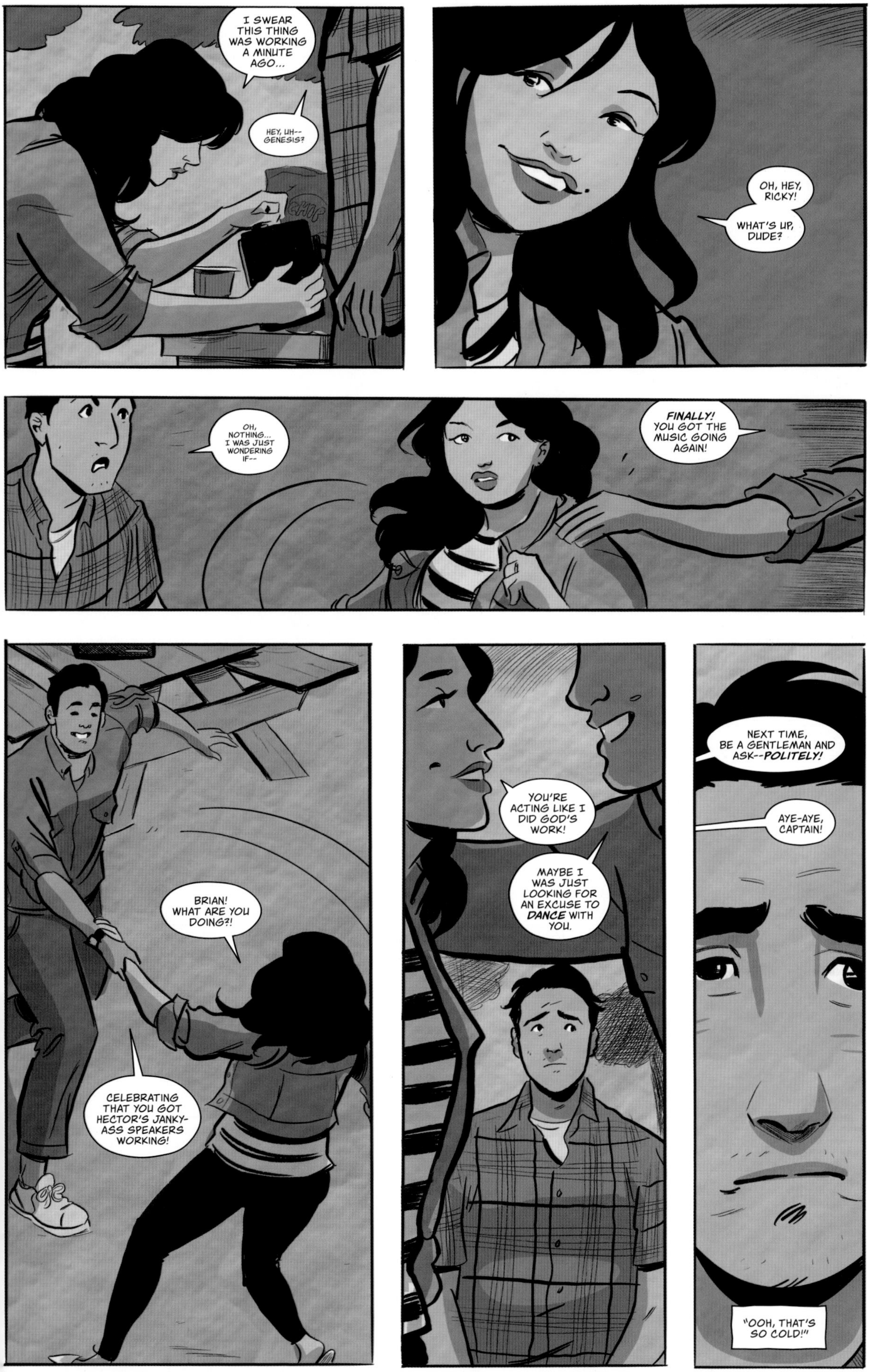
I SWEAR THIS THING WAS WORKING A MINUTE AGO...
HEY, UH-- GENESIS?
OH, HEY, RICKY!
WHAT'S UP, DUDE?
OH, NOTHING... I WAS JUST WONDERING IF--
FINALLY! YOU GOT THE MUSIC GOING AGAIN!
BRIAN! WHAT ARE YOU DOING?!
CELEBRATING THAT YOU GOT HECTOR'S JANKY-ASS SPEAKERS WORKING!
YOU'RE ACTING LIKE I DID GOD'S WORK!
MAYBE I WAS JUST LOOKING FOR AN EXCUSE TO DANCE WITH YOU.
NEXT TIME, BE A GENTLEMAN AND ASK--POLITELY!
AYE-AYE, CAPTAIN!
"OOH, THAT'S SO COLD!"

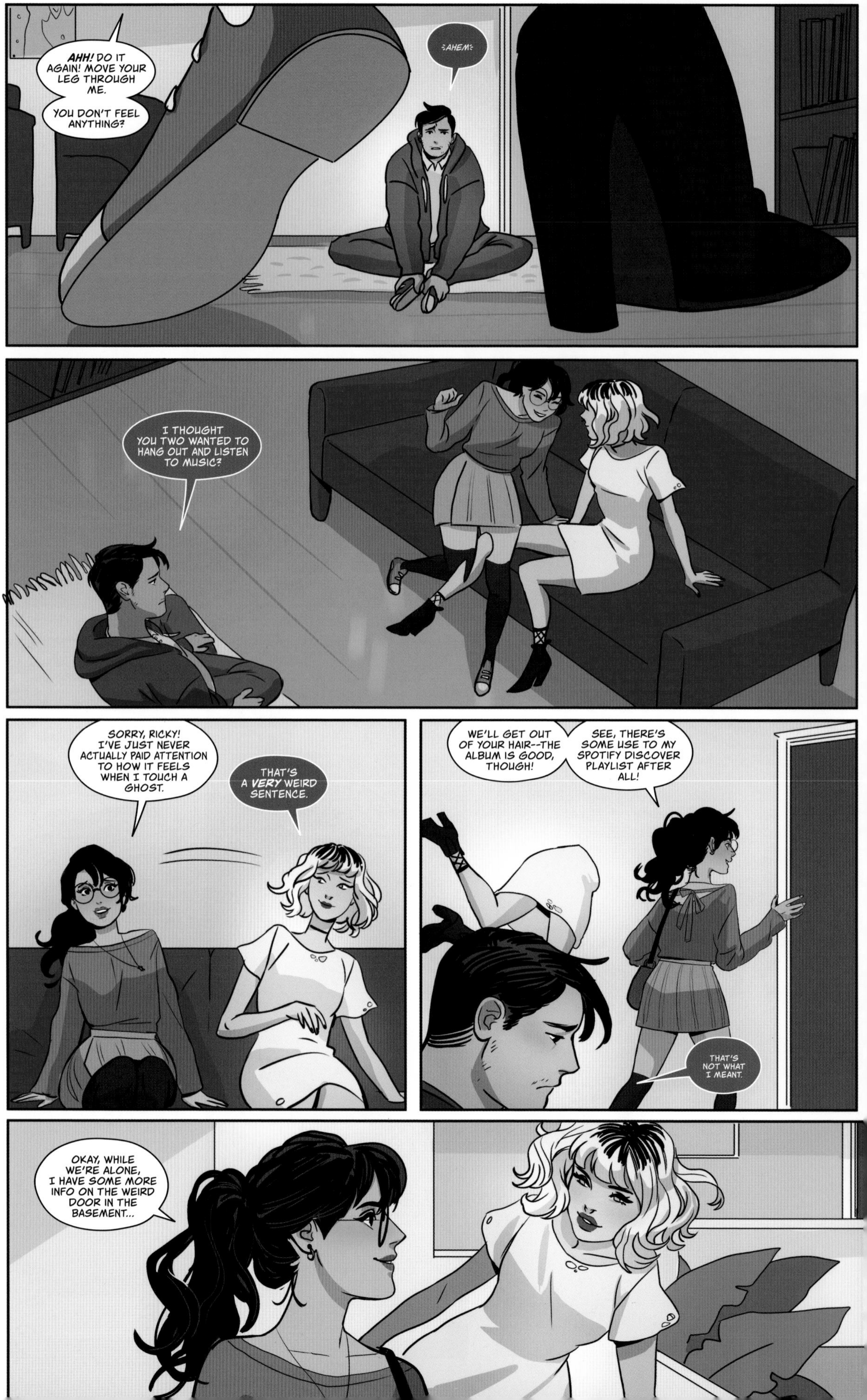
AHH! DO IT AGAIN! MOVE YOUR LEG THROUGH ME.
YOU DON'T FEEL ANYTHING?
AHEM
I THOUGHT YOU TWO WANTED TO HANG OUT AND LISTEN TO MUSIC?
SORRY, RICKY! I'VE JUST NEVER ACTUALLY PAID ATTENTION TO HOW IT FEELS WHEN I TOUCH A GHOST.
THAT'S A VERY WEIRD SENTENCE.
WE'LL GET OUT OF YOUR HAIR--THE ALBUM IS GOOD, THOUGH!
SEE, THERE'S SOME USE TO MY SPOTIFY DISCOVER PLAYLIST AFTER ALL!
THAT'S NOT WHAT I MEANT.
OKAY, WHILE WE'RE ALONE, I HAVE SOME MORE INFO ON THE WEIRD DOOR IN THE BASEMENT...

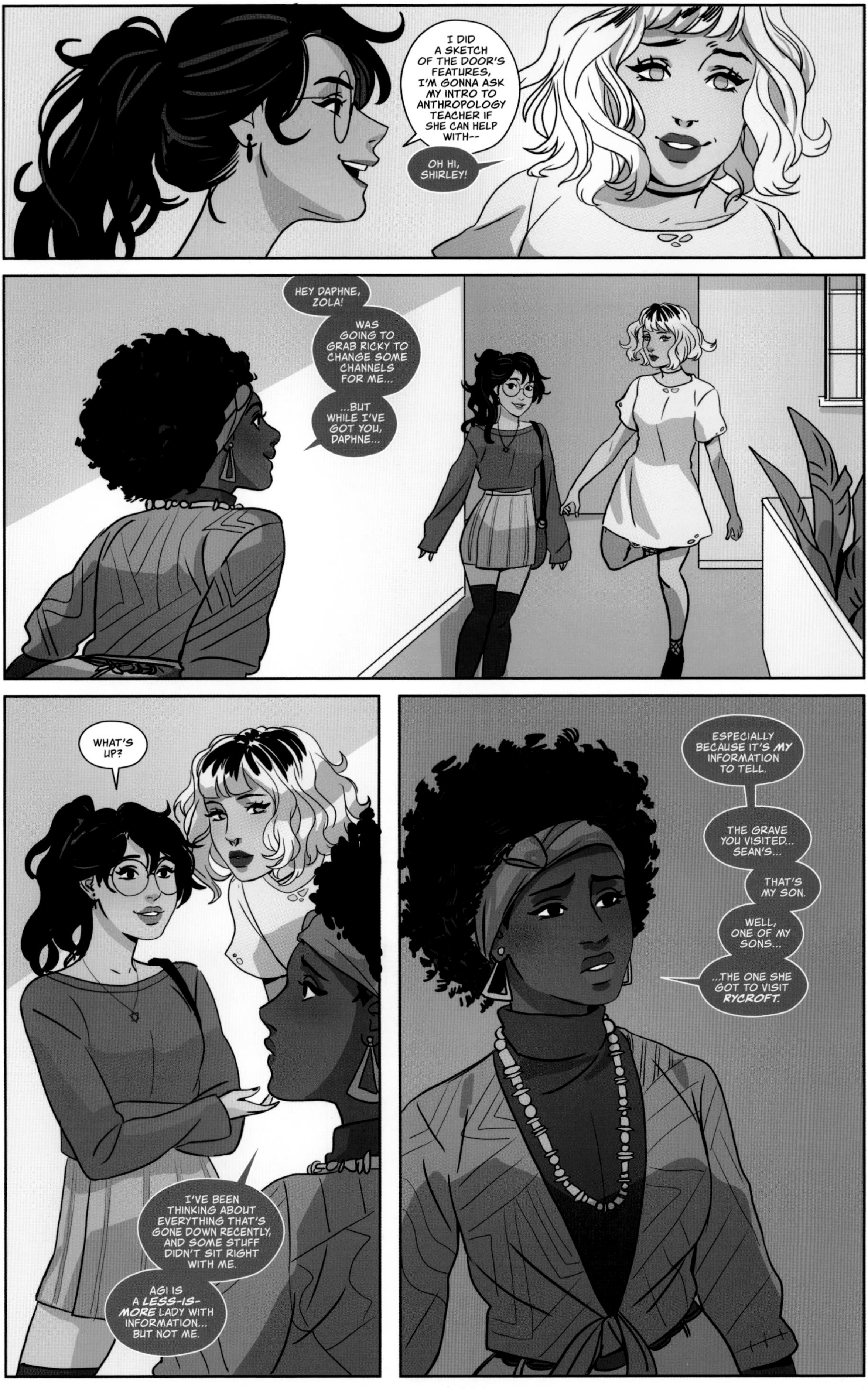
I DID A SKETCH OF THE DOOR'S FEATURES, I'M GONNA ASK MY INTRO TO ANTHROPOLOGY TEACHER IF SHE CAN HELP WITH--
OH HI, SHIRLEY!
HEY DAPHNE, ZOLA!
WAS GOING TO GRAB RICKY TO CHANGE SOME CHANNELS FOR ME...
...BUT WHILE I'VE GOT YOU, DAPHNE...
WHAT'S UP?
I'VE BEEN THINKING ABOUT EVERYTHING THAT'S GONE DOWN RECENTLY, AND SOME STUFF DIDN'T SIT RIGHT WITH ME.
AGI IS A LESS-IS-MORE LADY WITH INFORMATION... BUT NOT ME.
ESPECIALLY BECAUSE IT'S MY INFORMATION TO TELL.
THE GRAVE YOU VISITED... SEAN'S...
THAT'S MY SON.
WELL, ONE OF MY SONS...
...THE ONE SHE GOT TO VISIT RYCROFT.

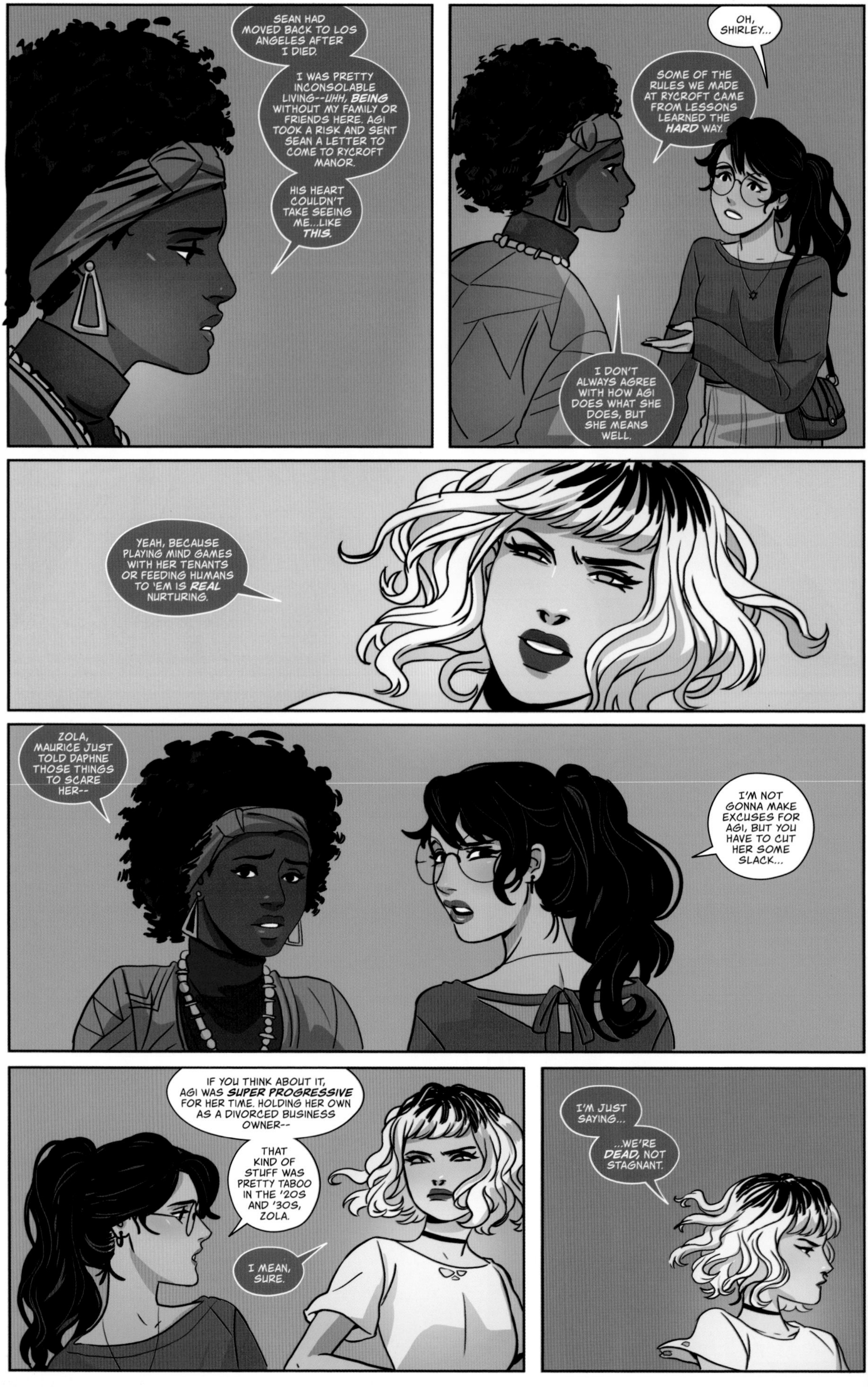
SEAN HAD MOVED BACK TO LOS ANGELES AFTER I DIED.
I WAS PRETTY INCONSOLABLE LIVING--*UHH,* ***BEING*** WITHOUT MY FAMILY OR FRIENDS HERE. AGI TOOK A RISK AND SENT SEAN A LETTER TO COME TO RYCROFT MANOR.
HIS HEART COULDN'T TAKE SEEING ME...LIKE ***THIS.***
OH, SHIRLEY...
SOME OF THE RULES WE MADE AT RYCROFT CAME FROM LESSONS LEARNED THE ***HARD*** WAY.
I DON'T ALWAYS AGREE WITH HOW AGI DOES WHAT SHE DOES, BUT SHE MEANS WELL.
YEAH, BECAUSE PLAYING MIND GAMES WITH HER TENANTS OR FEEDING HUMANS TO 'EM IS ***REAL*** NURTURING.
ZOLA, MAURICE JUST TOLD DAPHNE THOSE THINGS TO SCARE HER--
I'M NOT GONNA MAKE EXCUSES FOR AGI, BUT YOU HAVE TO CUT HER SOME SLACK...
IF YOU THINK ABOUT IT, AGI WAS ***SUPER PROGRESSIVE*** FOR HER TIME. HOLDING HER OWN AS A DIVORCED BUSINESS OWNER--
THAT KIND OF STUFF WAS PRETTY TABOO IN THE '20S AND '30S, ZOLA.
I MEAN, SURE.
I'M JUST SAYING...
...WE'RE ***DEAD,*** NOT STAGNANT.

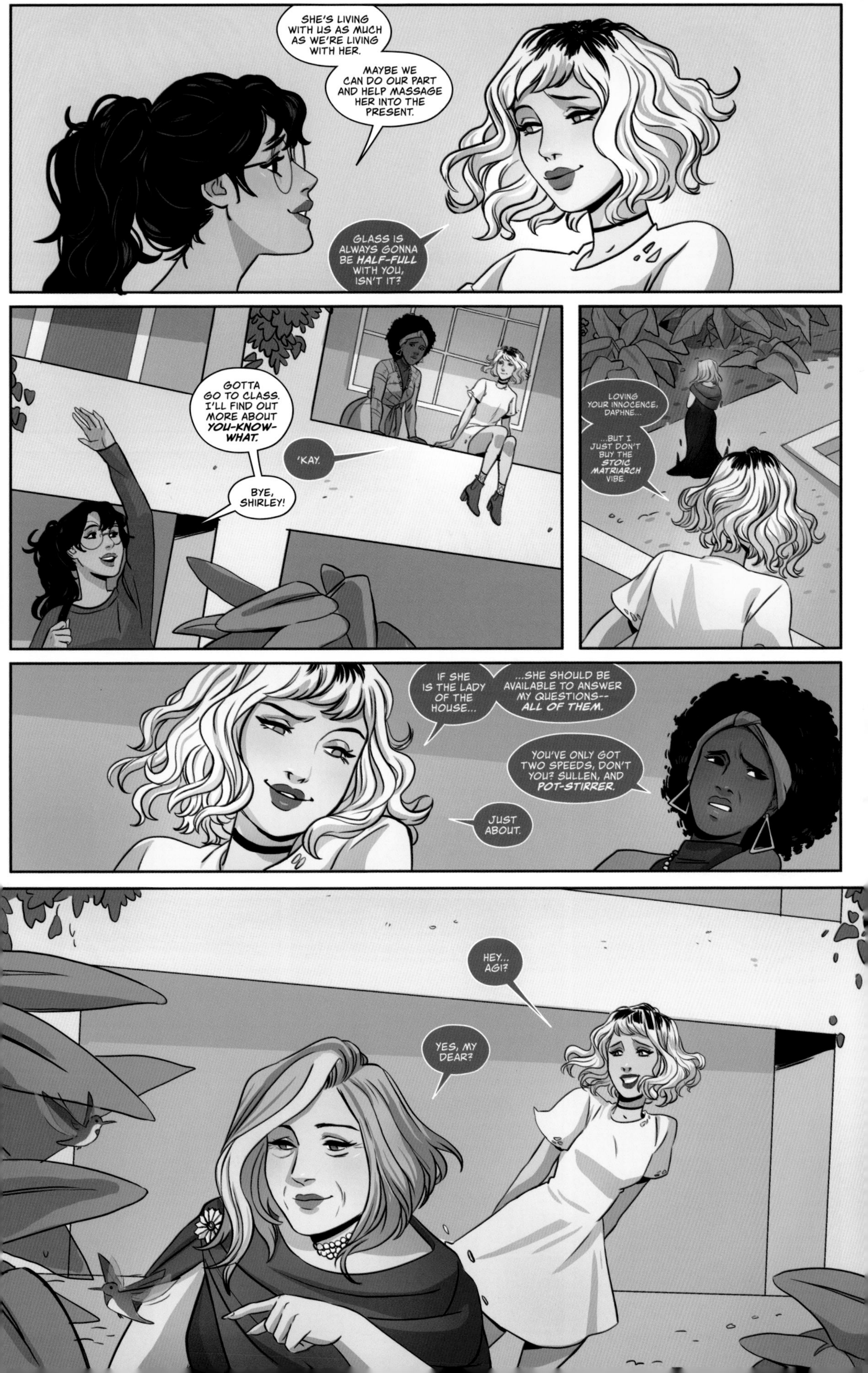
SHE'S LIVING WITH US AS MUCH AS WE'RE LIVING WITH HER.
MAYBE WE CAN DO OUR PART AND HELP MASSAGE HER INTO THE PRESENT.
GLASS IS ALWAYS GONNA BE *HALF-FULL* WITH YOU, ISN'T IT?
GOTTA GO TO CLASS. I'LL FIND OUT MORE ABOUT ***YOU-KNOW-WHAT.***
'KAY.
BYE, SHIRLEY!
LOVING YOUR INNOCENCE, DAPHNE...
...BUT I JUST DON'T BUY THE ***STOIC MATRIARCH*** VIBE.
IF SHE IS THE LADY OF THE HOUSE...
...SHE SHOULD BE AVAILABLE TO ANSWER MY QUESTIONS-- ***ALL OF THEM.***
YOU'VE ONLY GOT TWO SPEEDS, DON'T YOU? SULLEN, AND ***POT-STIRRER.***
JUST ABOUT.
HEY... AGI?
YES, MY DEAR?

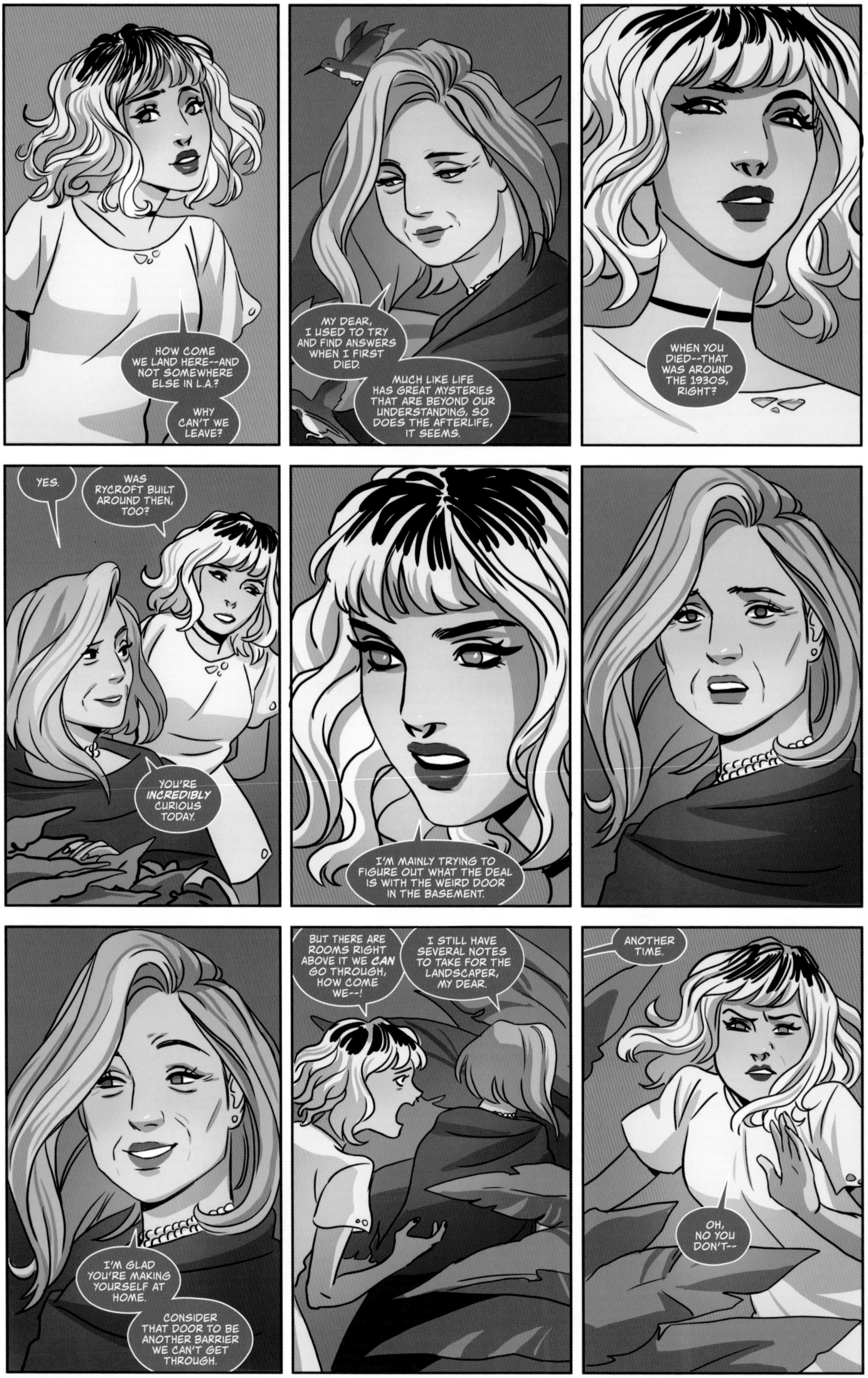
HOW COME WE LAND HERE--AND NOT SOMEWHERE ELSE IN L.A.?
WHY CAN'T WE LEAVE?
MY DEAR, I USED TO TRY AND FIND ANSWERS WHEN I FIRST DIED.
MUCH LIKE LIFE HAS GREAT MYSTERIES THAT ARE BEYOND OUR UNDERSTANDING, SO DOES THE AFTERLIFE, IT SEEMS.
WHEN YOU DIED--THAT WAS AROUND THE 1930S, RIGHT?
YES.
WAS RYCROFT BUILT AROUND THEN, TOO?
YOU'RE *INCREDIBLY* CURIOUS TODAY.
I'M MAINLY TRYING TO FIGURE OUT WHAT THE DEAL IS WITH THE WEIRD DOOR IN THE BASEMENT.
I'M GLAD YOU'RE MAKING YOURSELF AT HOME.
CONSIDER THAT DOOR TO BE ANOTHER BARRIER WE CAN'T GET THROUGH.
BUT THERE ARE ROOMS RIGHT ABOVE IT WE *CAN* GO THROUGH, HOW COME WE--!
I STILL HAVE SEVERAL NOTES TO TAKE FOR THE LANDSCAPER, MY DEAR.
ANOTHER TIME.
OH, NO YOU DON'T--

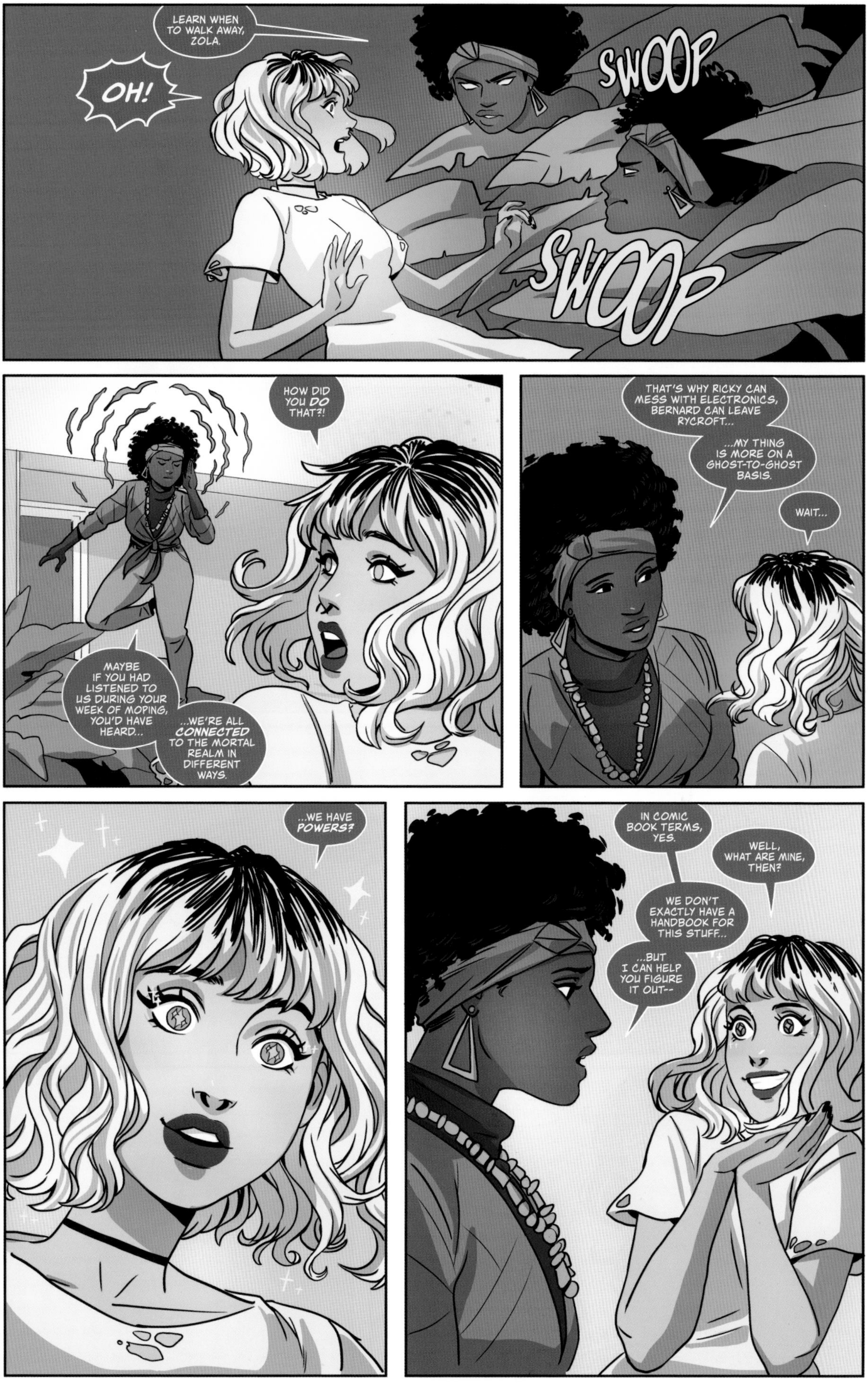

LEARN WHEN TO WALK AWAY, ZOLA.
OH!
SWOOP
SWOOP
HOW DID YOU DO THAT?!
MAYBE IF YOU HAD LISTENED TO US DURING YOUR WEEK OF MOPING, YOU'D HAVE HEARD...
...WE'RE ALL CONNECTED TO THE MORTAL REALM IN DIFFERENT WAYS.
THAT'S WHY RICKY CAN MESS WITH ELECTRONICS, BERNARD CAN LEAVE RYCROFT...
...MY THING IS MORE ON A GHOST-TO-GHOST BASIS.
WAIT...
...WE HAVE POWERS?
IN COMIC BOOK TERMS, YES.
WELL, WHAT ARE MINE, THEN?
WE DON'T EXACTLY HAVE A HANDBOOK FOR THIS STUFF...
...BUT I CAN HELP YOU FIGURE IT OUT--

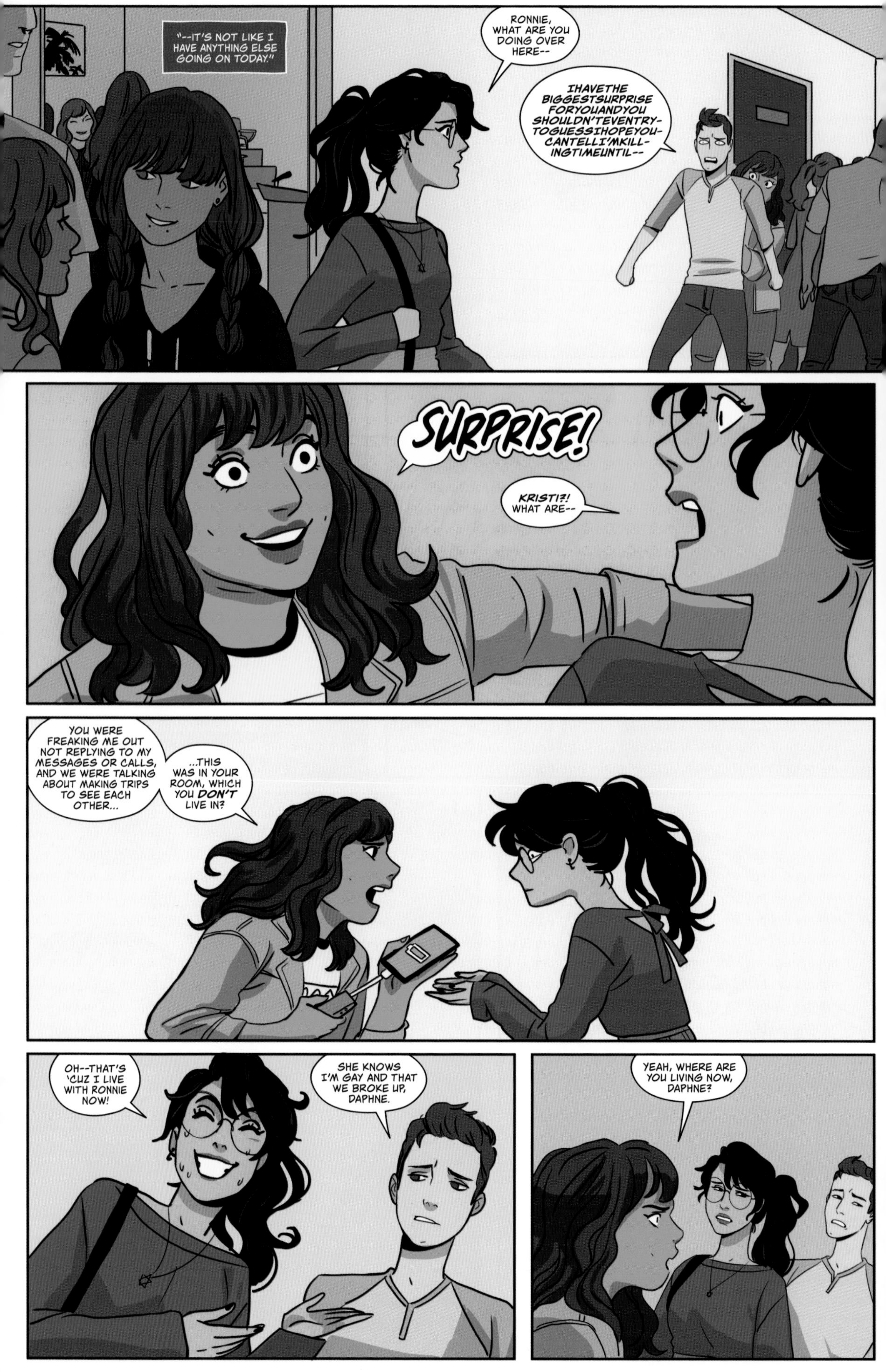
"--IT'S NOT LIKE I HAVE ANYTHING ELSE GOING ON TODAY."
RONNIE, WHAT ARE YOU DOING OVER HERE--
IHAVETHE BIGGESTSURPRISE FORYOUANDYOU SHOULDN'TEVENTRY-TOGUESSIHOPEYOU-CANTELLI'MKILL-INGTIMEUNTIL--
SURPRISE!
KRISTI?! WHAT ARE--
YOU WERE FREAKING ME OUT NOT REPLYING TO MY MESSAGES OR CALLS, AND WE WERE TALKING ABOUT MAKING TRIPS TO SEE EACH OTHER...
...THIS WAS IN YOUR ROOM, WHICH YOU DON'T LIVE IN?
OH--THAT'S 'CUZ I LIVE WITH RONNIE NOW!
SHE KNOWS I'M GAY AND THAT WE BROKE UP, DAPHNE.
YEAH, WHERE ARE YOU LIVING NOW, DAPHNE?

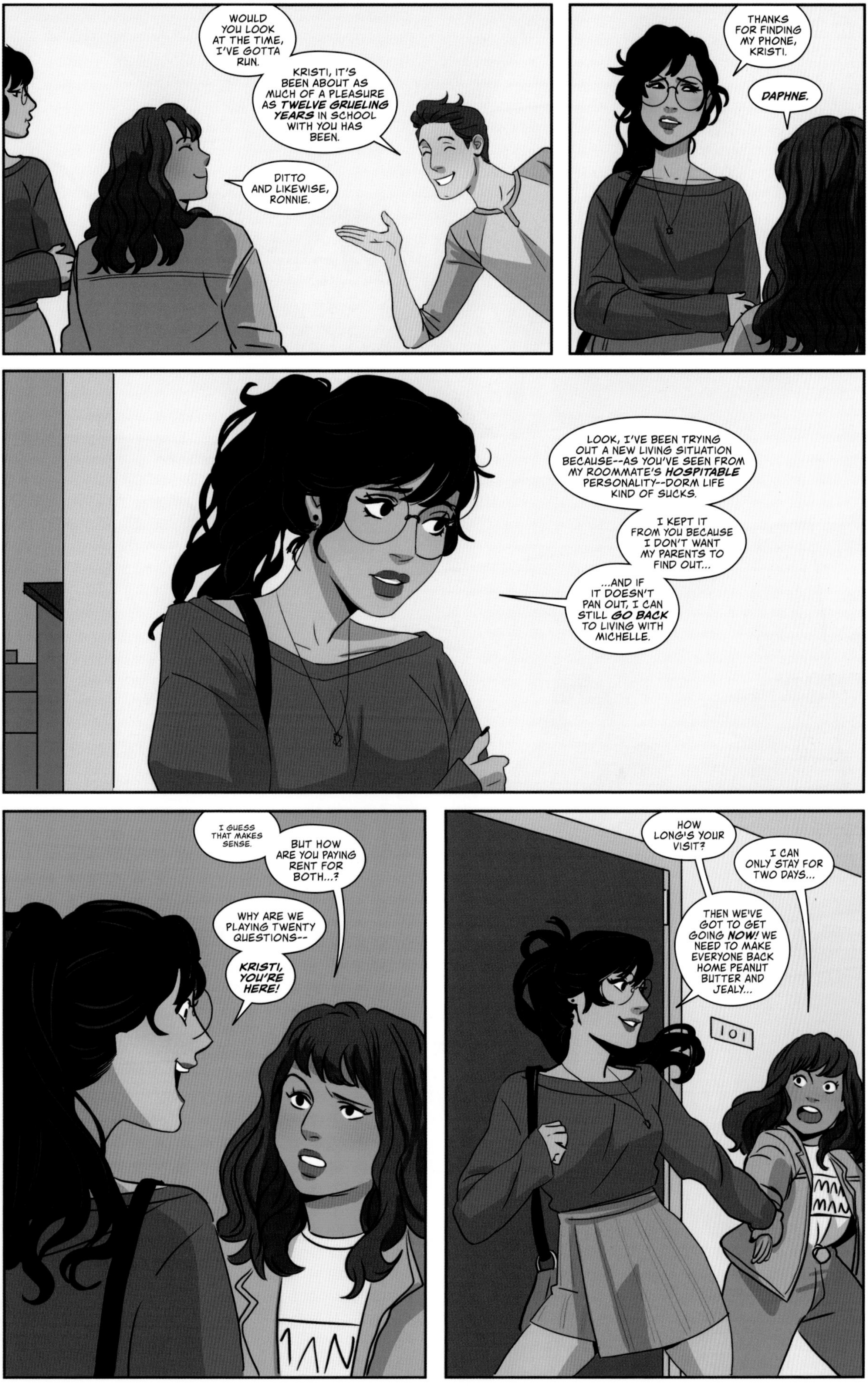
WOULD YOU LOOK AT THE TIME, I'VE GOTTA RUN.
KRISTI, IT'S BEEN ABOUT AS MUCH OF A PLEASURE AS TWELVE GRUELING YEARS IN SCHOOL WITH YOU HAS BEEN.
DITTO AND LIKEWISE, RONNIE.
THANKS FOR FINDING MY PHONE, KRISTI.
DAPHNE.
LOOK, I'VE BEEN TRYING OUT A NEW LIVING SITUATION BECAUSE--AS YOU'VE SEEN FROM MY ROOMMATE'S HOSPITABLE PERSONALITY--DORM LIFE KIND OF SUCKS.
I KEPT IT FROM YOU BECAUSE I DON'T WANT MY PARENTS TO FIND OUT...
...AND IF IT DOESN'T PAN OUT, I CAN STILL GO BACK TO LIVING WITH MICHELLE.
I GUESS THAT MAKES SENSE.
BUT HOW ARE YOU PAYING RENT FOR BOTH...?
WHY ARE WE PLAYING TWENTY QUESTIONS--
KRISTI, YOU'RE HERE!
HOW LONG'S YOUR VISIT?
I CAN ONLY STAY FOR TWO DAYS...
THEN WE'VE GOT TO GET GOING NOW! WE NEED TO MAKE EVERYONE BACK HOME PEANUT BUTTER AND JEALY...
101

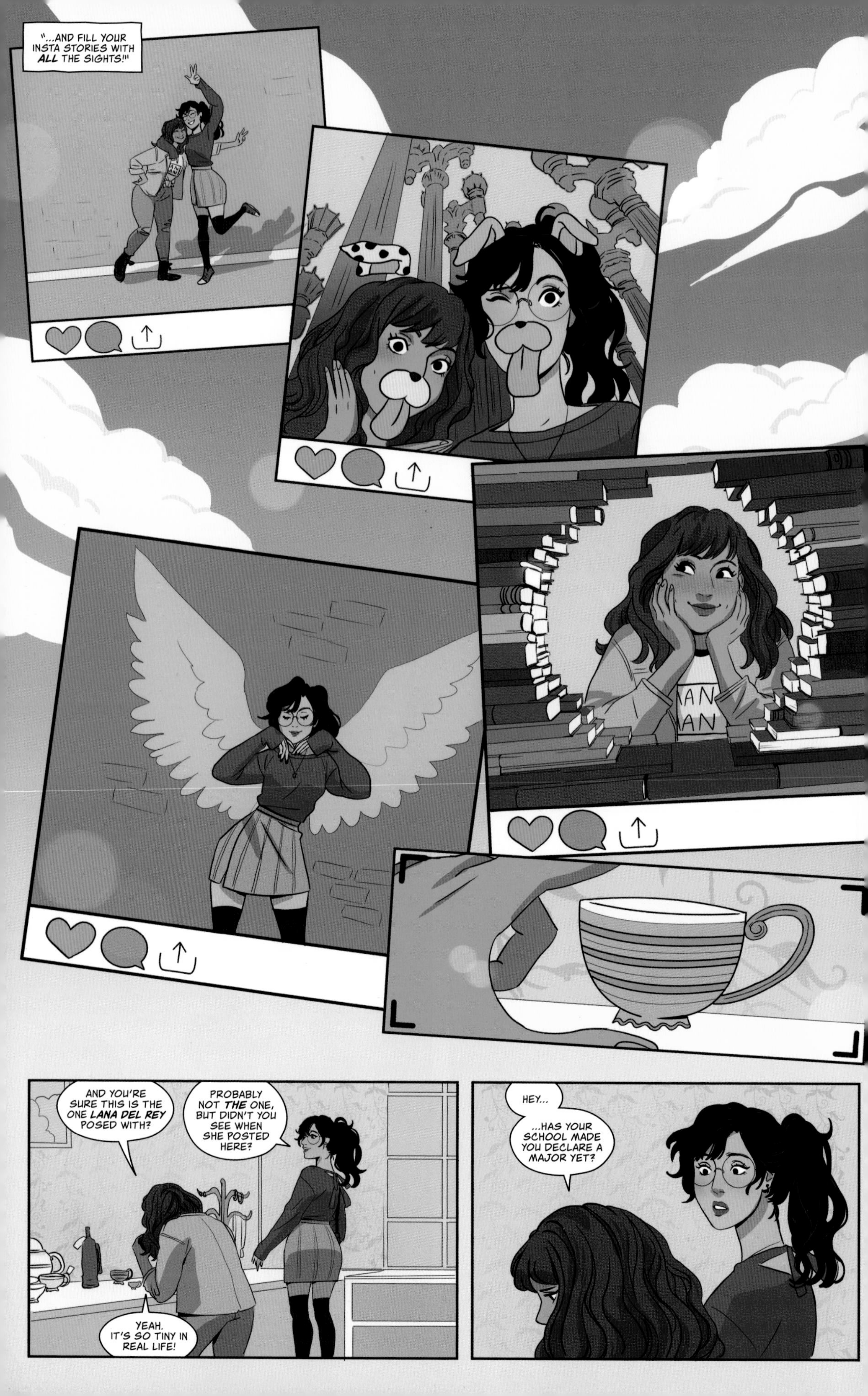
"...AND FILL YOUR INSTA STORIES WITH ALL THE SIGHTS!"
AND YOU'RE SURE THIS IS THE ONE LANA DEL REY POSED WITH?
PROBABLY NOT THE ONE, BUT DIDN'T YOU SEE WHEN SHE POSTED HERE?
YEAH. IT'S SO TINY IN REAL LIFE!
HEY...
...HAS YOUR SCHOOL MADE YOU DECLARE A MAJOR YET?

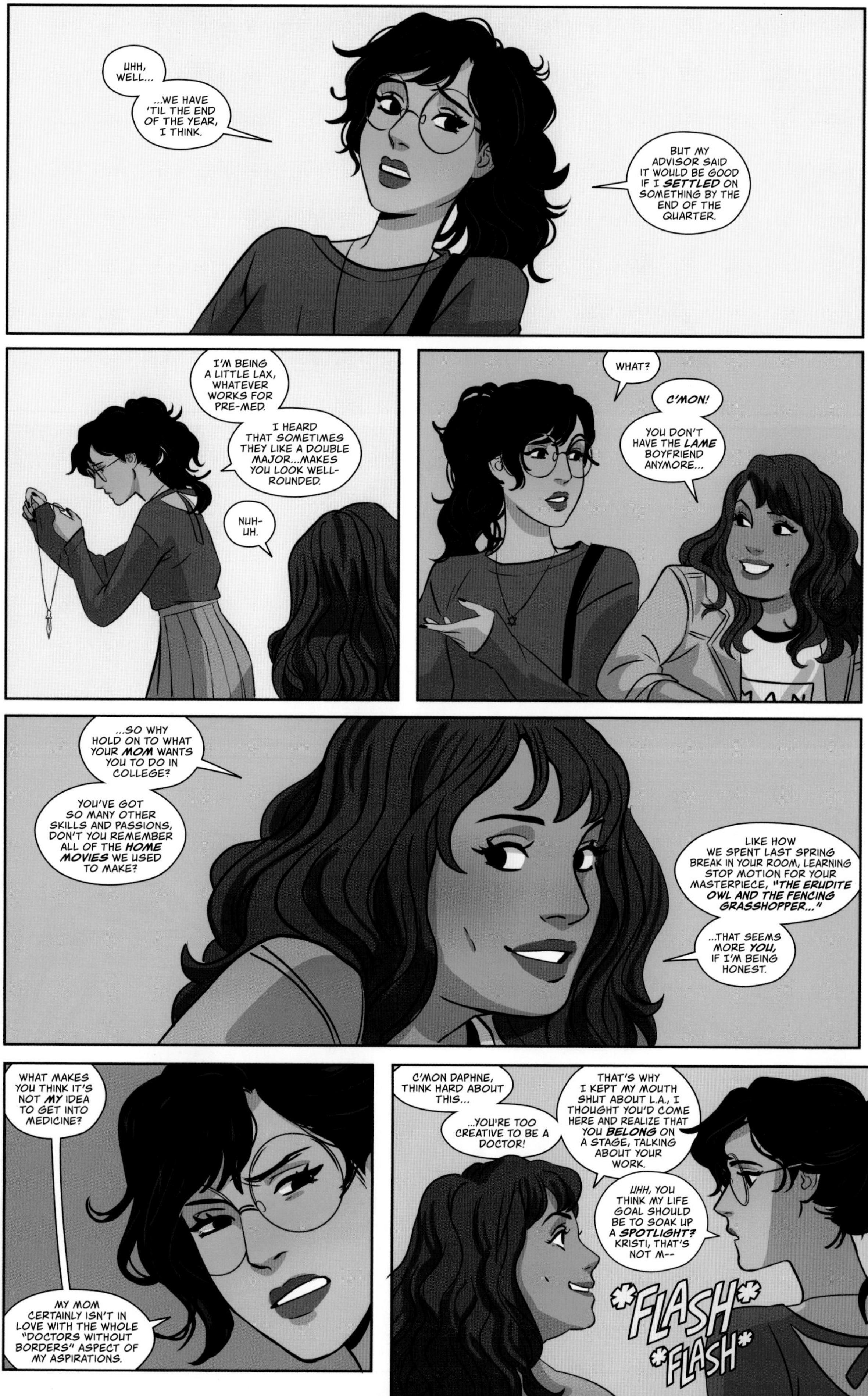
UHH, WELL...
...WE HAVE 'TIL THE END OF THE YEAR, I THINK.
BUT MY ADVISOR SAID IT WOULD BE GOOD IF I *SETTLED* ON SOMETHING BY THE END OF THE QUARTER.
I'M BEING A LITTLE LAX, WHATEVER WORKS FOR PRE-MED.
I HEARD THAT SOMETIMES THEY LIKE A DOUBLE MAJOR...MAKES YOU LOOK WELL-ROUNDED.
NUH-UH.
WHAT?
C'MON!
YOU DON'T HAVE THE *LAME* BOYFRIEND ANYMORE...
...SO WHY HOLD ON TO WHAT YOUR *MOM* WANTS YOU TO DO IN COLLEGE?
YOU'VE GOT SO MANY OTHER SKILLS AND PASSIONS, DON'T YOU REMEMBER ALL OF THE *HOME MOVIES* WE USED TO MAKE?
LIKE HOW WE SPENT LAST SPRING BREAK IN YOUR ROOM, LEARNING STOP MOTION FOR YOUR MASTERPIECE, *"THE ERUDITE OWL AND THE FENCING GRASSHOPPER..."*
...THAT SEEMS MORE *YOU,* IF I'M BEING HONEST.
WHAT MAKES YOU THINK IT'S NOT *MY* IDEA TO GET INTO MEDICINE?
MY MOM CERTAINLY ISN'T IN LOVE WITH THE WHOLE "DOCTORS WITHOUT BORDERS" ASPECT OF MY ASPIRATIONS.
C'MON DAPHNE, THINK HARD ABOUT THIS...
...YOU'RE TOO CREATIVE TO BE A DOCTOR!
THAT'S WHY I KEPT MY MOUTH SHUT ABOUT L.A., I THOUGHT YOU'D COME HERE AND REALIZE THAT YOU *BELONG* ON A STAGE, TALKING ABOUT YOUR WORK.
UHH, YOU THINK MY LIFE GOAL SHOULD BE TO SOAK UP A *SPOTLIGHT?* KRISTI, THAT'S NOT M--
FLASH
FLASH

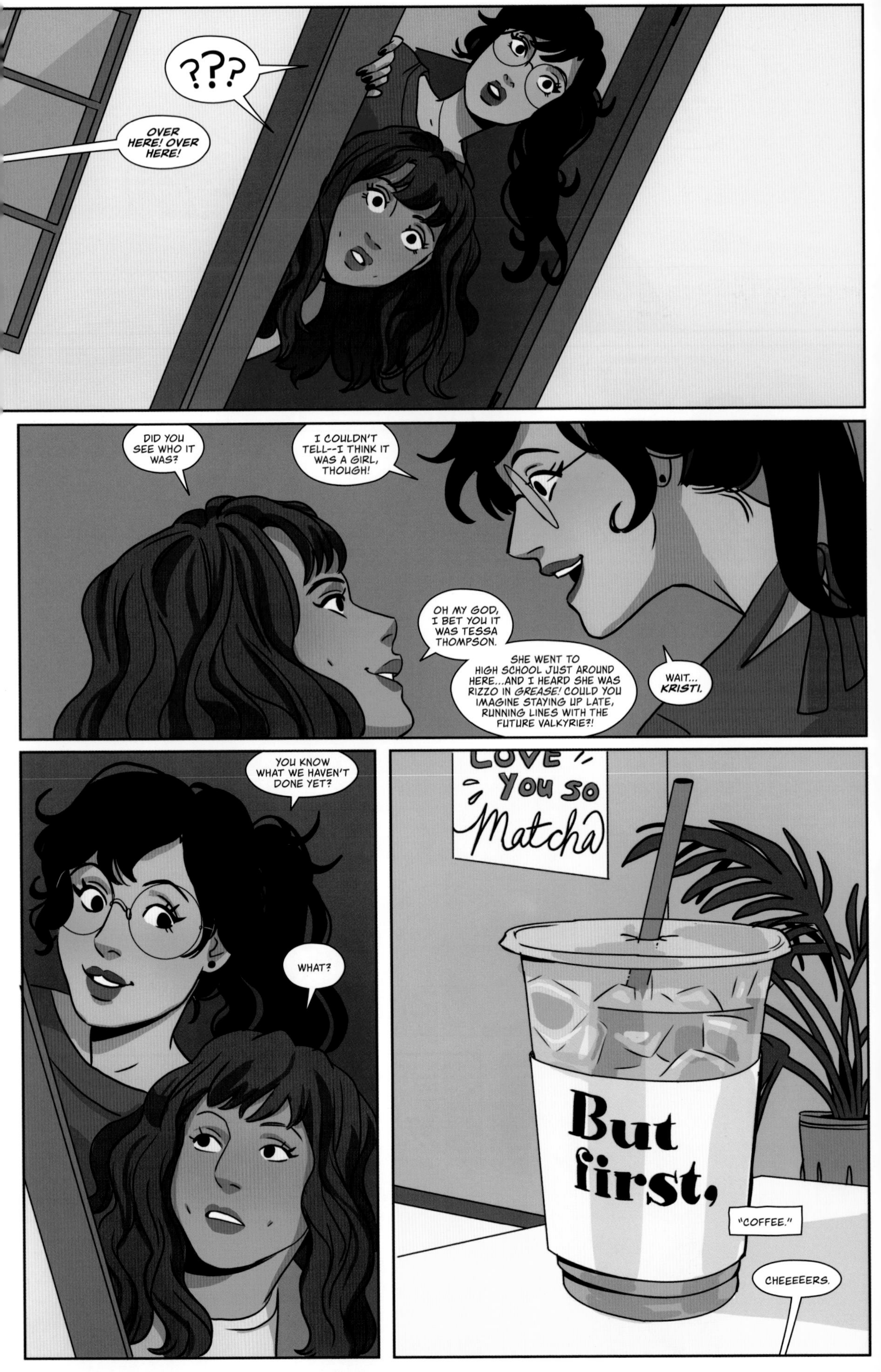
???
OVER HERE! OVER HERE!
DID YOU SEE WHO IT WAS?
I COULDN'T TELL--I THINK IT WAS A GIRL, THOUGH!
OH MY GOD, I BET YOU IT WAS TESSA THOMPSON.
SHE WENT TO HIGH SCHOOL JUST AROUND HERE...AND I HEARD SHE WAS RIZZO IN GREASE! COULD YOU IMAGINE STAYING UP LATE, RUNNING LINES WITH THE FUTURE VALKYRIE?!
WAIT... KRISTI.
YOU KNOW WHAT WE HAVEN'T DONE YET?
WHAT?
LOVE You so Matcha
But first,
"COFFEE."
CHEEEEERS.

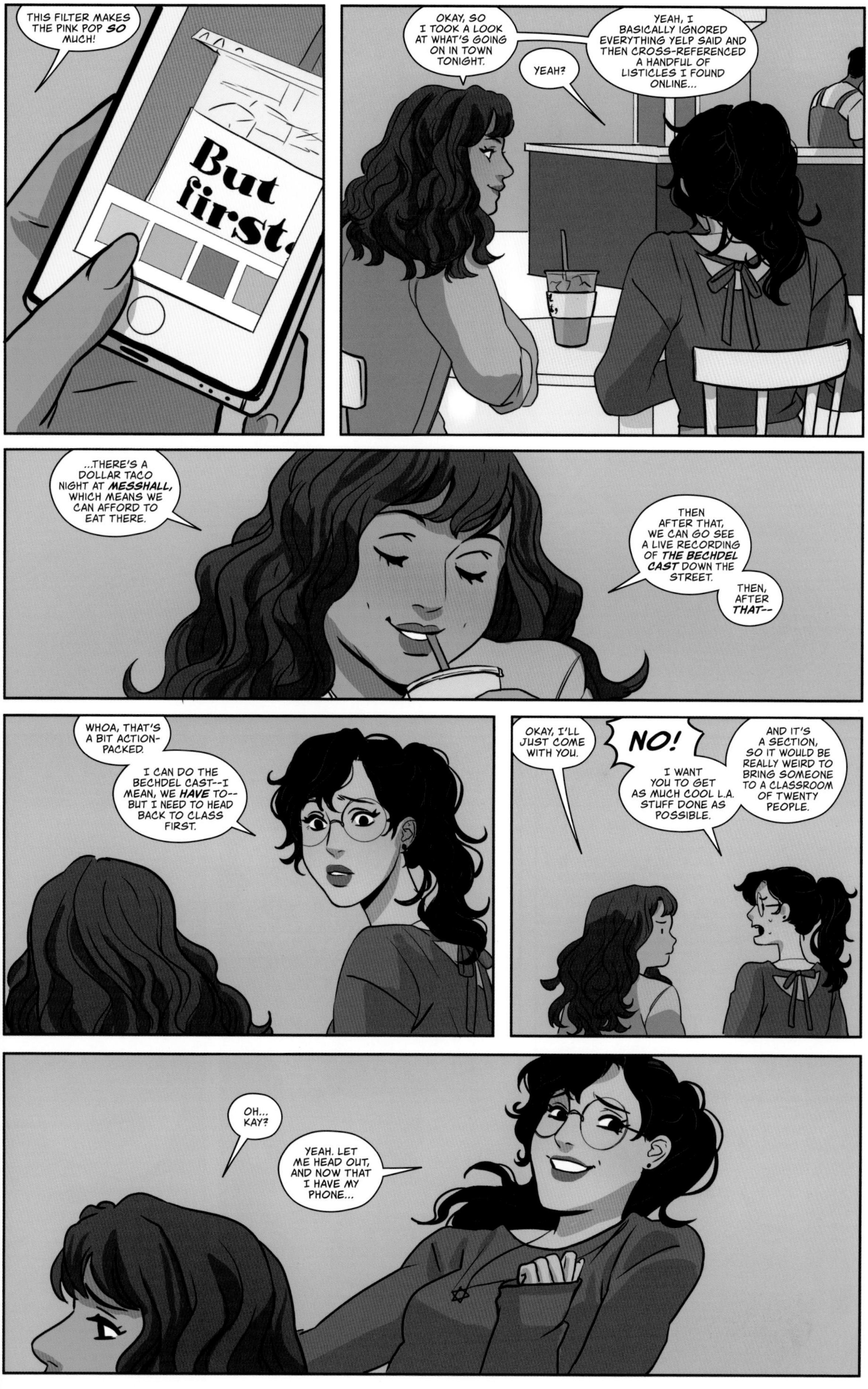
THIS FILTER MAKES THE PINK POP SO MUCH!
But first.
OKAY, SO I TOOK A LOOK AT WHAT'S GOING ON IN TOWN TONIGHT.
YEAH?
YEAH, I BASICALLY IGNORED EVERYTHING YELP SAID AND THEN CROSS-REFERENCED A HANDFUL OF LISTICLES I FOUND ONLINE...
...THERE'S A DOLLAR TACO NIGHT AT MESSHALL, WHICH MEANS WE CAN AFFORD TO EAT THERE.
THEN AFTER THAT, WE CAN GO SEE A LIVE RECORDING OF THE BECHDEL CAST DOWN THE STREET.
THEN, AFTER THAT--
WHOA, THAT'S A BIT ACTION-PACKED.
I CAN DO THE BECHDEL CAST--I MEAN, WE HAVE TO--BUT I NEED TO HEAD BACK TO CLASS FIRST.
OKAY, I'LL JUST COME WITH YOU.
NO!
I WANT YOU TO GET AS MUCH COOL L.A. STUFF DONE AS POSSIBLE.
AND IT'S A SECTION, SO IT WOULD BE REALLY WEIRD TO BRING SOMEONE TO A CLASSROOM OF TWENTY PEOPLE.
OH... KAY?
YEAH. LET ME HEAD OUT, AND NOW THAT I HAVE MY PHONE...

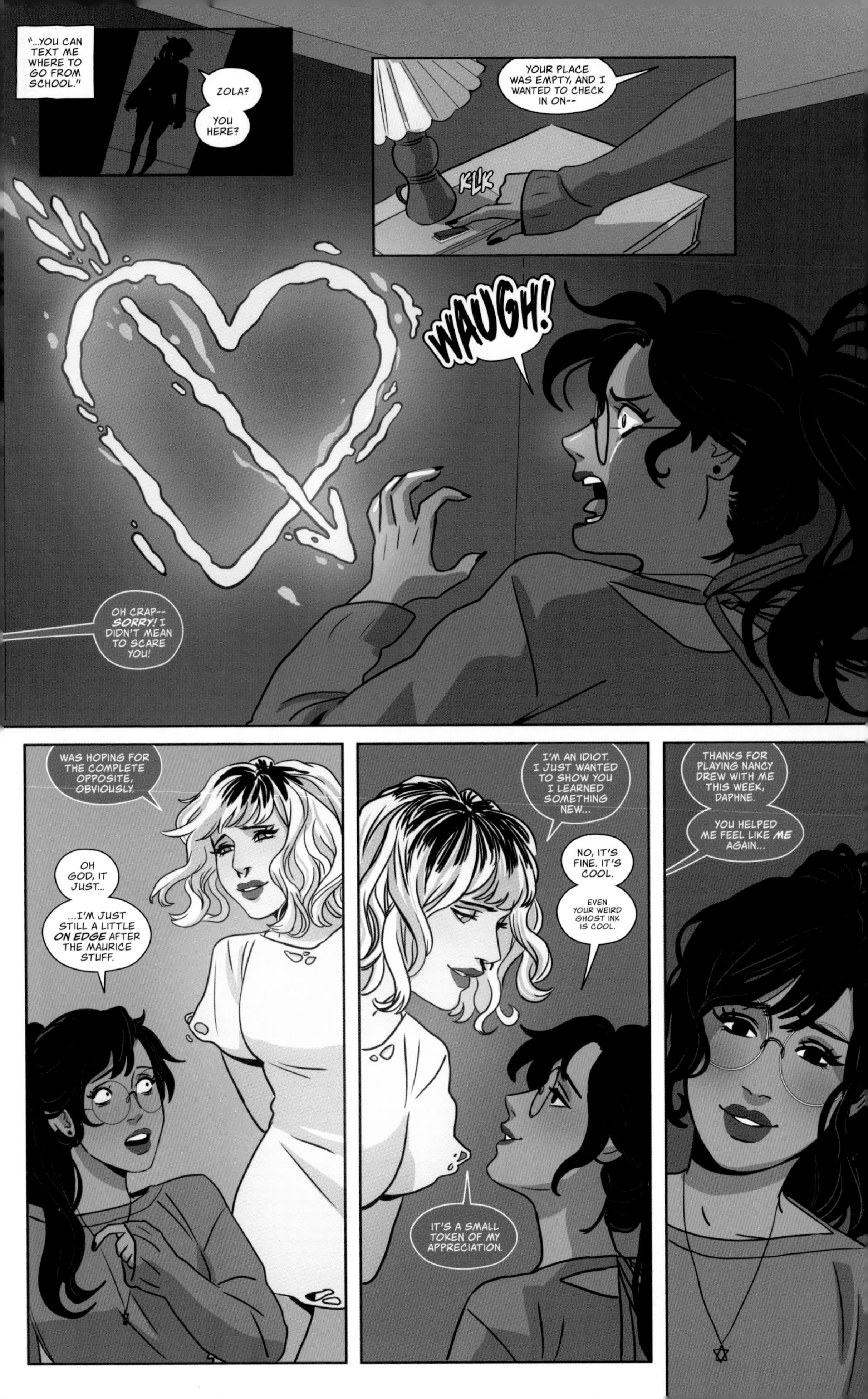
"...YOU CAN TEXT ME WHERE TO GO FROM SCHOOL."
ZOLA?
YOU HERE?
YOUR PLACE WAS EMPTY, AND I WANTED TO CHECK IN ON--
KLIK
WAUGH!
OH CRAP-- SORRY! I DIDN'T MEAN TO SCARE YOU!
WAS HOPING FOR THE COMPLETE OPPOSITE, OBVIOUSLY.
OH GOD, IT JUST...
...I'M JUST STILL A LITTLE ON EDGE AFTER THE MAURICE STUFF.
I'M AN IDIOT. I JUST WANTED TO SHOW YOU I LEARNED SOMETHING NEW...
NO, IT'S FINE. IT'S COOL.
EVEN YOUR WEIRD GHOST INK IS COOL.
IT'S A SMALL TOKEN OF MY APPRECIATION.
THANKS FOR PLAYING NANCY DREW WITH ME THIS WEEK, DAPHNE.
YOU HELPED ME FEEL LIKE ME AGAIN...

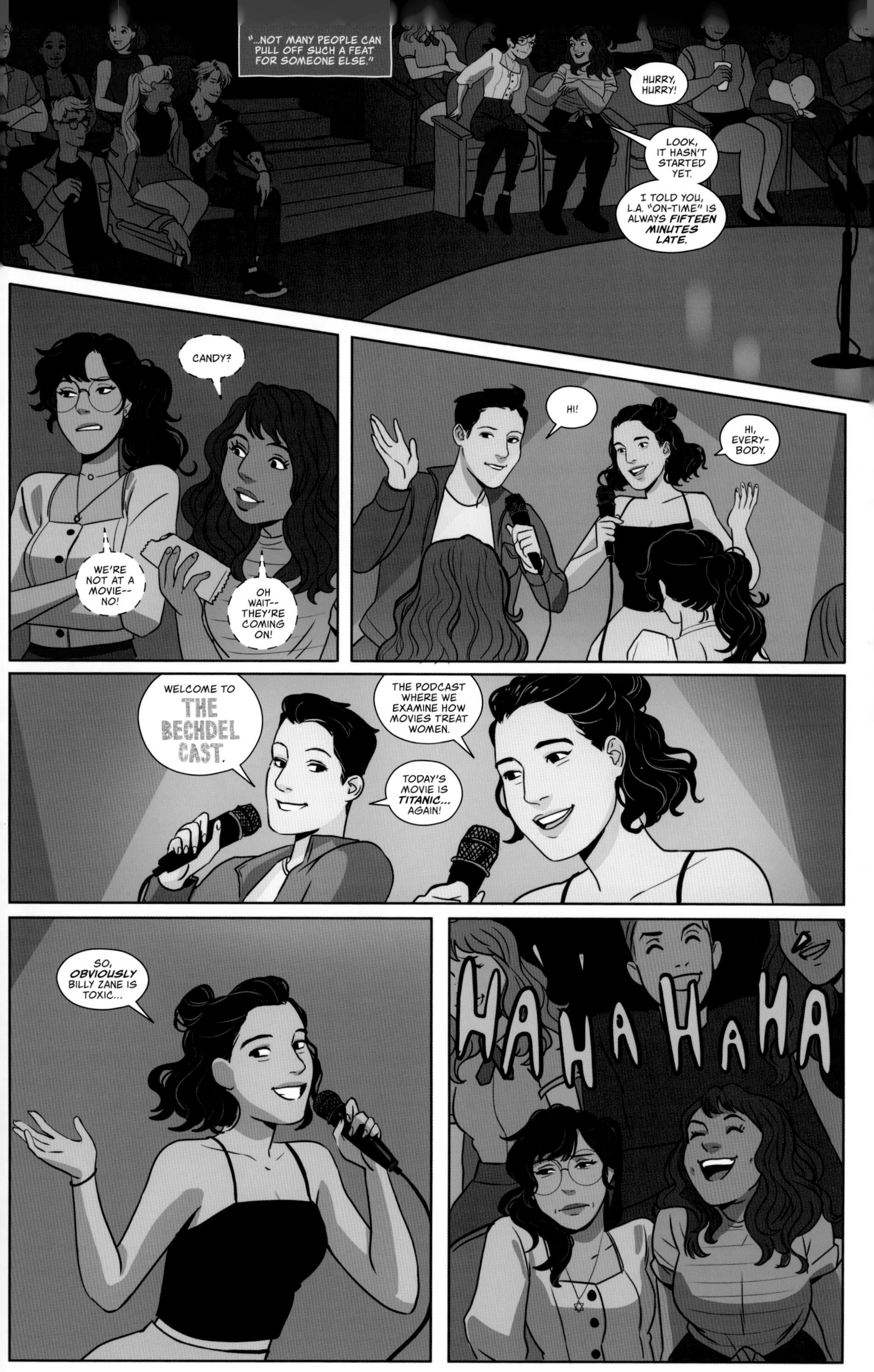
"...NOT MANY PEOPLE CAN PULL OFF SUCH A FEAT FOR SOMEONE ELSE."
HURRY, HURRY!
LOOK, IT HASN'T STARTED YET.
I TOLD YOU, L.A. "ON-TIME" IS ALWAYS FIFTEEN MINUTES LATE.
CANDY?
WE'RE NOT AT A MOVIE-- NO!
OH WAIT-- THEY'RE COMING ON!
HI!
HI, EVERY-BODY.
WELCOME TO THE BECHDEL CAST.
THE PODCAST WHERE WE EXAMINE HOW MOVIES TREAT WOMEN.
TODAY'S MOVIE IS TITANIC... AGAIN!
SO, OBVIOUSLY BILLY ZANE IS TOXIC...
HAHAHAHA

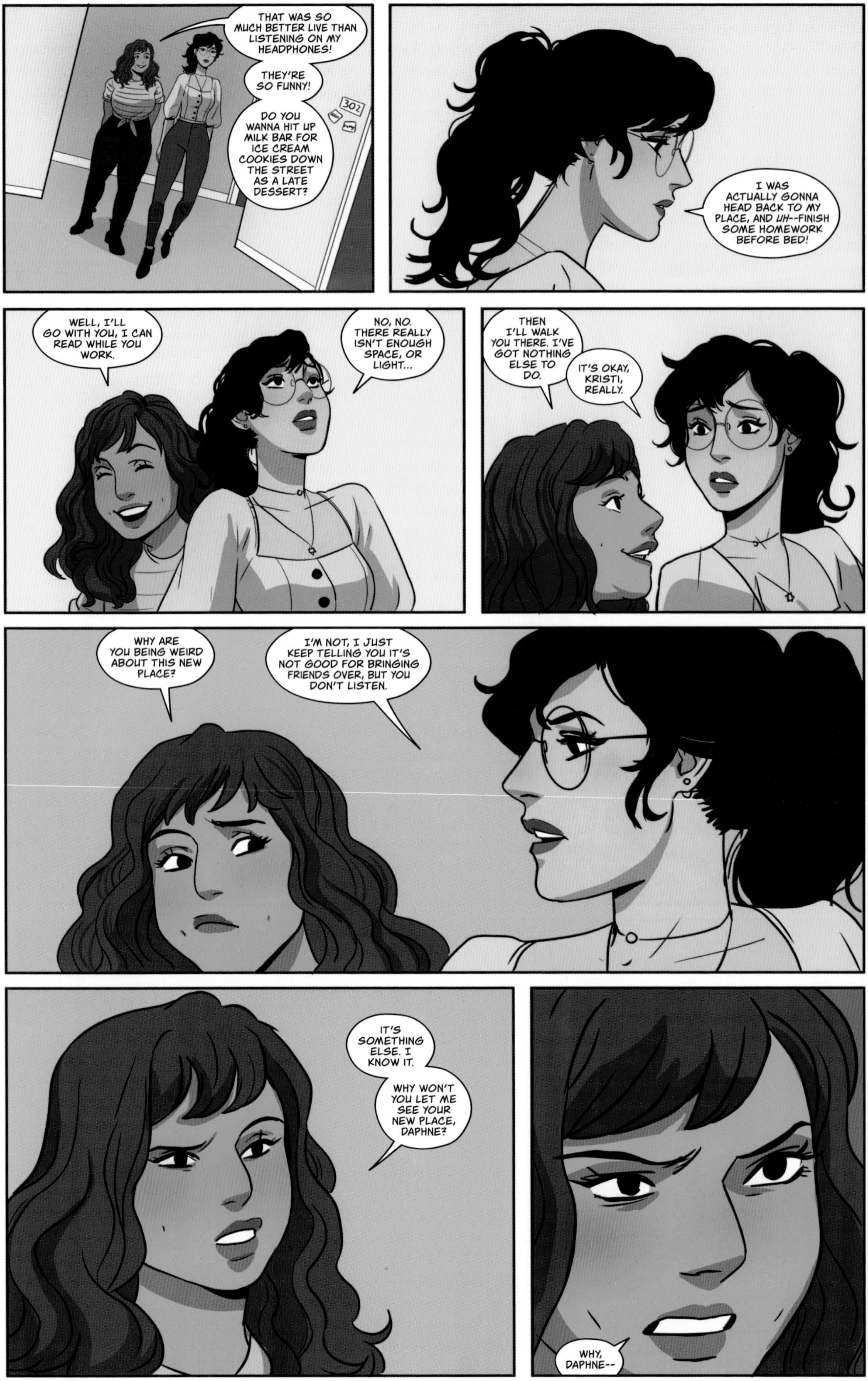
THAT WAS SO MUCH BETTER LIVE THAN LISTENING ON MY HEADPHONES!
THEY'RE SO FUNNY!
DO YOU WANNA HIT UP MILK BAR FOR ICE CREAM COOKIES DOWN THE STREET AS A LATE DESSERT?
302
I WAS ACTUALLY GONNA HEAD BACK TO MY PLACE, AND UH--FINISH SOME HOMEWORK BEFORE BED!
WELL, I'LL GO WITH YOU, I CAN READ WHILE YOU WORK.
NO, NO. THERE REALLY ISN'T ENOUGH SPACE, OR LIGHT...
THEN I'LL WALK YOU THERE. I'VE GOT NOTHING ELSE TO DO.
IT'S OKAY, KRISTI, REALLY.
WHY ARE YOU BEING WEIRD ABOUT THIS NEW PLACE?
I'M NOT, I JUST KEEP TELLING YOU IT'S NOT GOOD FOR BRINGING FRIENDS OVER, BUT YOU DON'T LISTEN.
IT'S SOMETHING ELSE. I KNOW IT.
WHY WON'T YOU LET ME SEE YOUR NEW PLACE, DAPHNE?
WHY, DAPHNE--

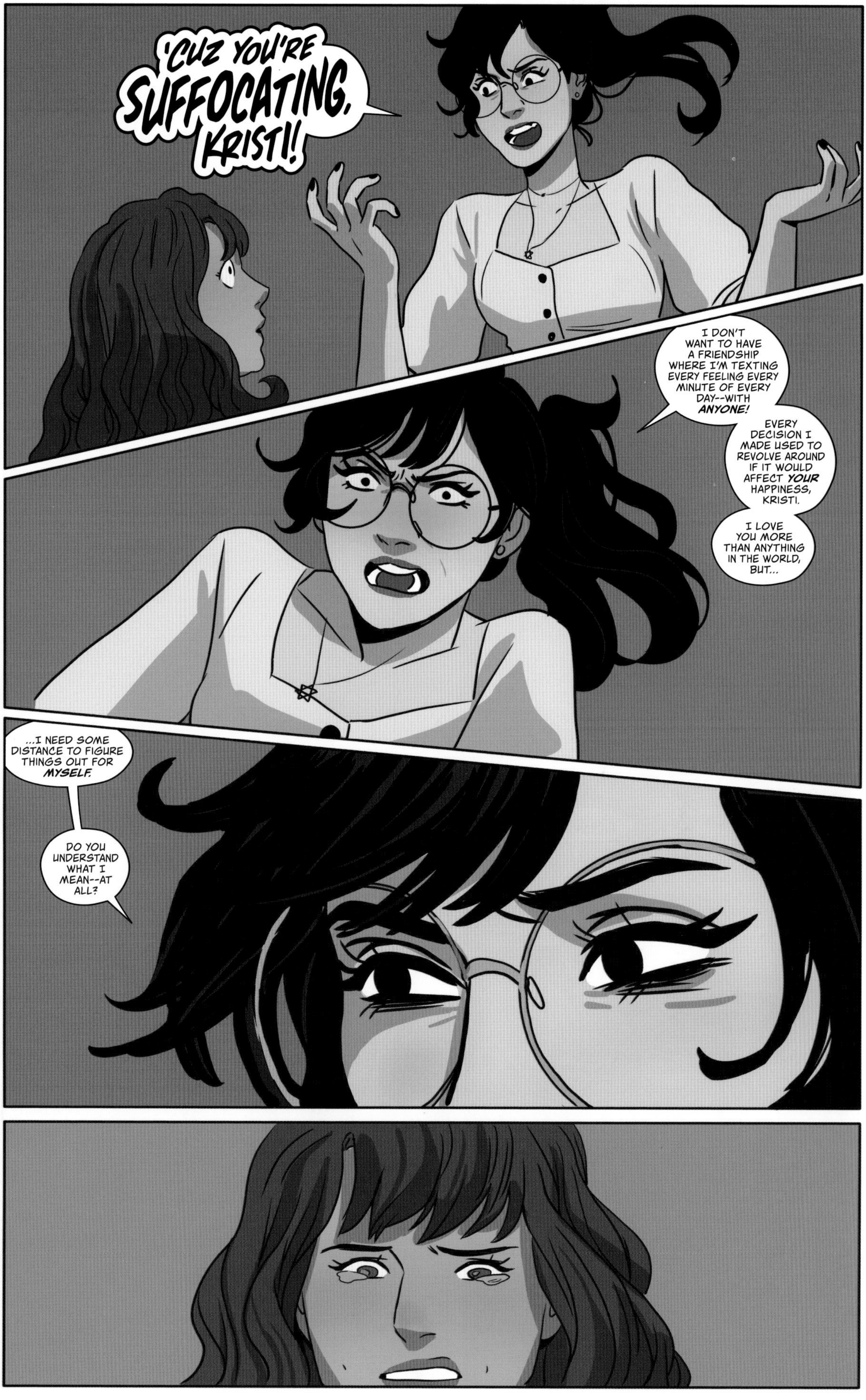
'CUZ YOU'RE SUFFOCATING, KRISTI!
I DON'T WANT TO HAVE A FRIENDSHIP WHERE I'M TEXTING EVERY FEELING EVERY MINUTE OF EVERY DAY--WITH ANYONE!
EVERY DECISION I MADE USED TO REVOLVE AROUND IF IT WOULD AFFECT YOUR HAPPINESS, KRISTI.
I LOVE YOU MORE THAN ANYTHING IN THE WORLD, BUT...
...I NEED SOME DISTANCE TO FIGURE THINGS OUT FOR MYSELF.
DO YOU UNDERSTAND WHAT I MEAN--AT ALL?

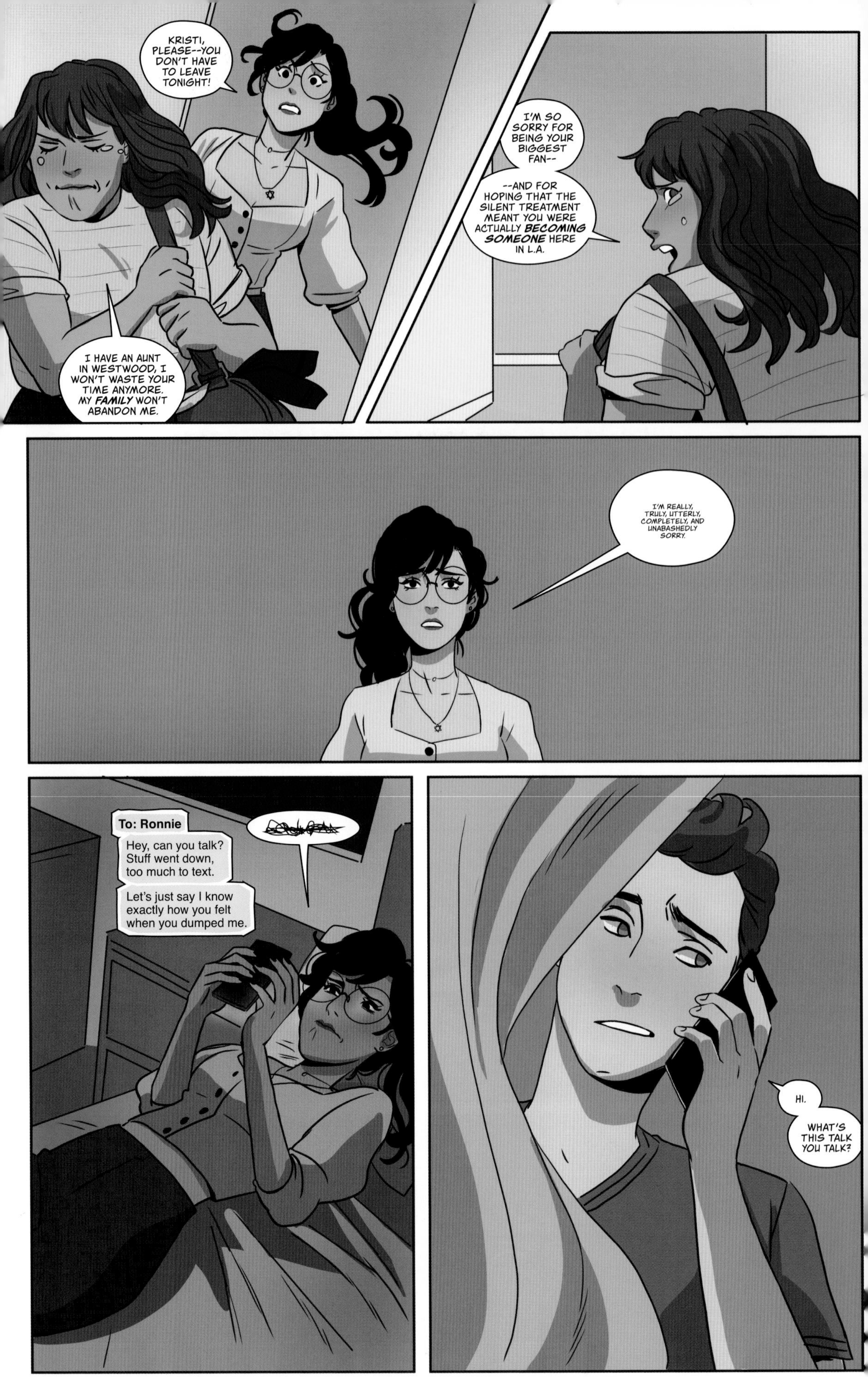
KRISTI, PLEASE--YOU DON'T HAVE TO LEAVE TONIGHT!
I HAVE AN AUNT IN WESTWOOD, I WON'T WASTE YOUR TIME ANYMORE. MY ***FAMILY*** WON'T ABANDON ME.
I'M SO SORRY FOR BEING YOUR BIGGEST FAN--
--AND FOR HOPING THAT THE SILENT TREATMENT MEANT YOU WERE ACTUALLY ***BECOMING SOMEONE*** HERE IN L.A.
I'M REALLY, TRULY, UTTERLY, COMPLETELY, AND UNABASHEDLY SORRY.
To: Ronnie
Hey, can you talk? Stuff went down, too much to text.
Let's just say I know exactly how you felt when you dumped me.
HI.
WHAT'S THIS TALK YOU TALK?

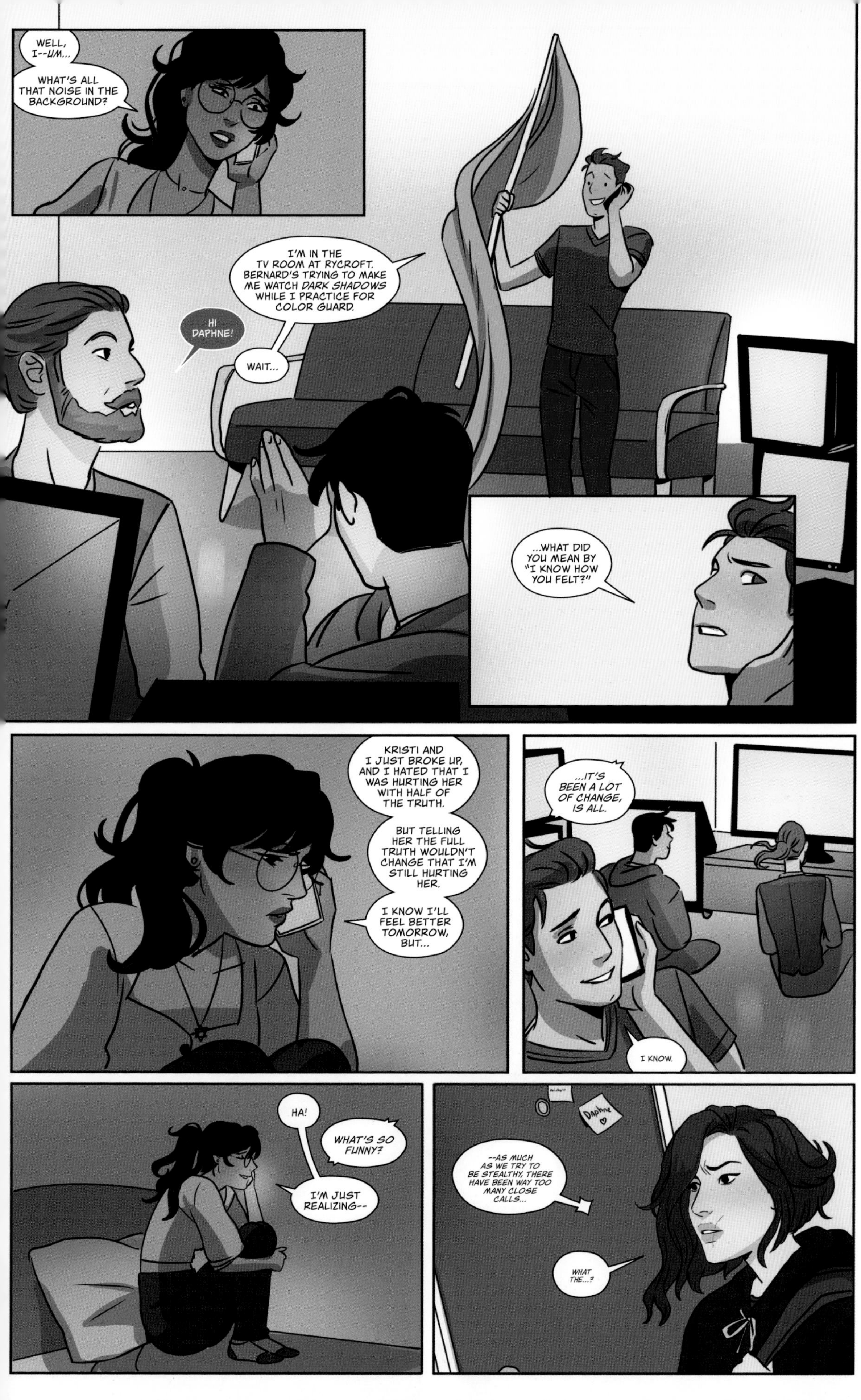
WELL, I--UM...
WHAT'S ALL THAT NOISE IN THE BACKGROUND?
I'M IN THE TV ROOM AT RYCROFT. BERNARD'S TRYING TO MAKE ME WATCH DARK SHADOWS WHILE I PRACTICE FOR COLOR GUARD.
HI DAPHNE!
WAIT...
...WHAT DID YOU MEAN BY "I KNOW HOW YOU FELT?"
KRISTI AND I JUST BROKE UP, AND I HATED THAT I WAS HURTING HER WITH HALF OF THE TRUTH.
BUT TELLING HER THE FULL TRUTH WOULDN'T CHANGE THAT I'M STILL HURTING HER.
I KNOW I'LL FEEL BETTER TOMORROW, BUT...
...IT'S BEEN A LOT OF CHANGE, IS ALL.
I KNOW.
HA!
WHAT'S SO FUNNY?
I'M JUST REALIZING--
--AS MUCH AS WE TRY TO BE STEALTHY, THERE HAVE BEEN WAY TOO MANY CLOSE CALLS...
Daphne
WHAT THE...?

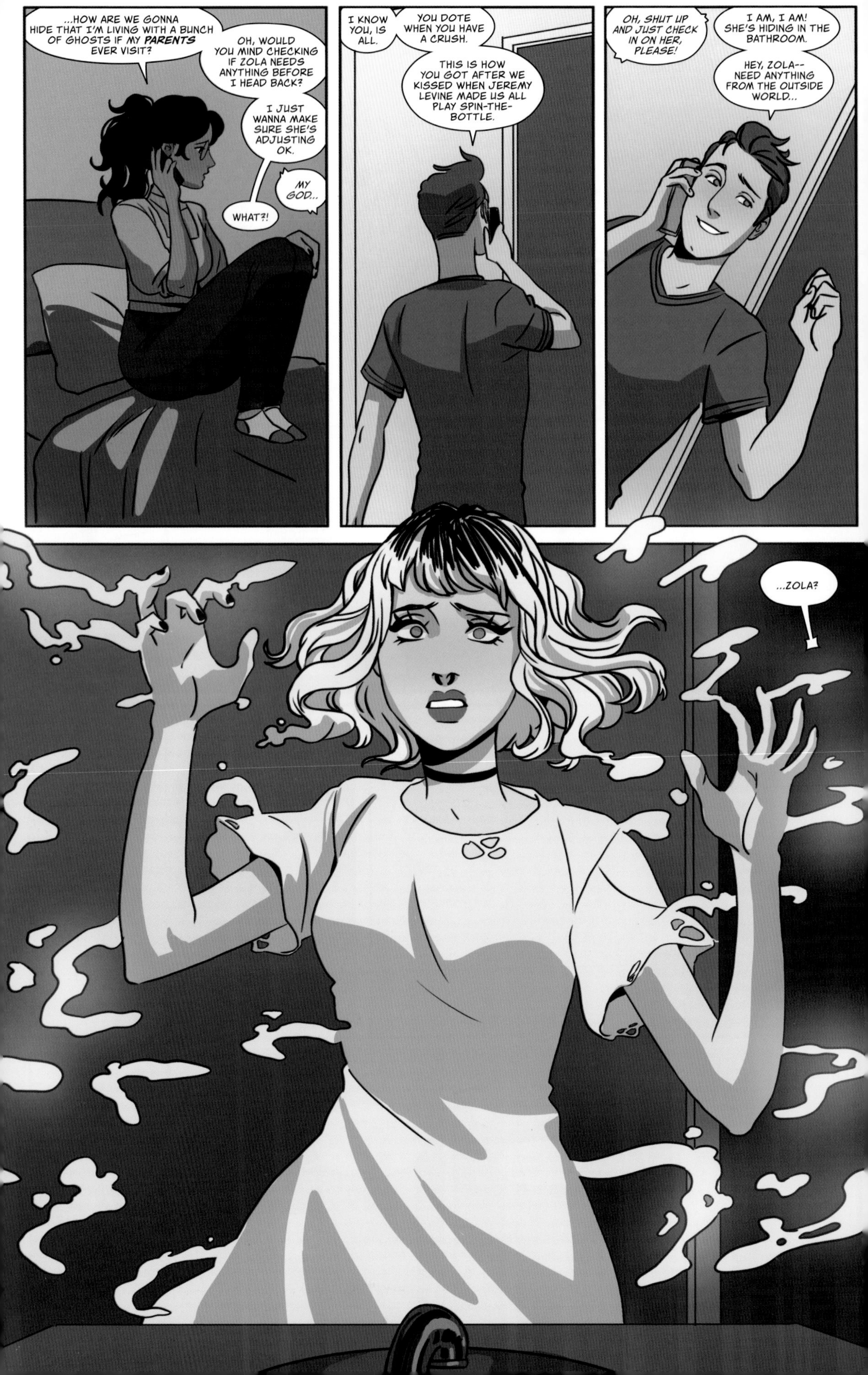
...HOW ARE WE GONNA HIDE THAT I'M LIVING WITH A BUNCH OF GHOSTS IF MY **PARENTS** EVER VISIT?
OH, WOULD YOU MIND CHECKING IF ZOLA NEEDS ANYTHING BEFORE I HEAD BACK?
I JUST WANNA MAKE SURE SHE'S ADJUSTING OK.
MY GOD...
WHAT?!
I KNOW YOU, IS ALL.
YOU DOTE WHEN YOU HAVE A CRUSH.
THIS IS HOW YOU GOT AFTER WE KISSED WHEN JEREMY LEVINE MADE US ALL PLAY SPIN-THE-BOTTLE.
OH, SHUT UP AND JUST CHECK IN ON HER, PLEASE!
I AM, I AM! SHE'S HIDING IN THE BATHROOM.
HEY, ZOLA-- NEED ANYTHING FROM THE OUTSIDE WORLD...
...ZOLA?

Chapter Seven

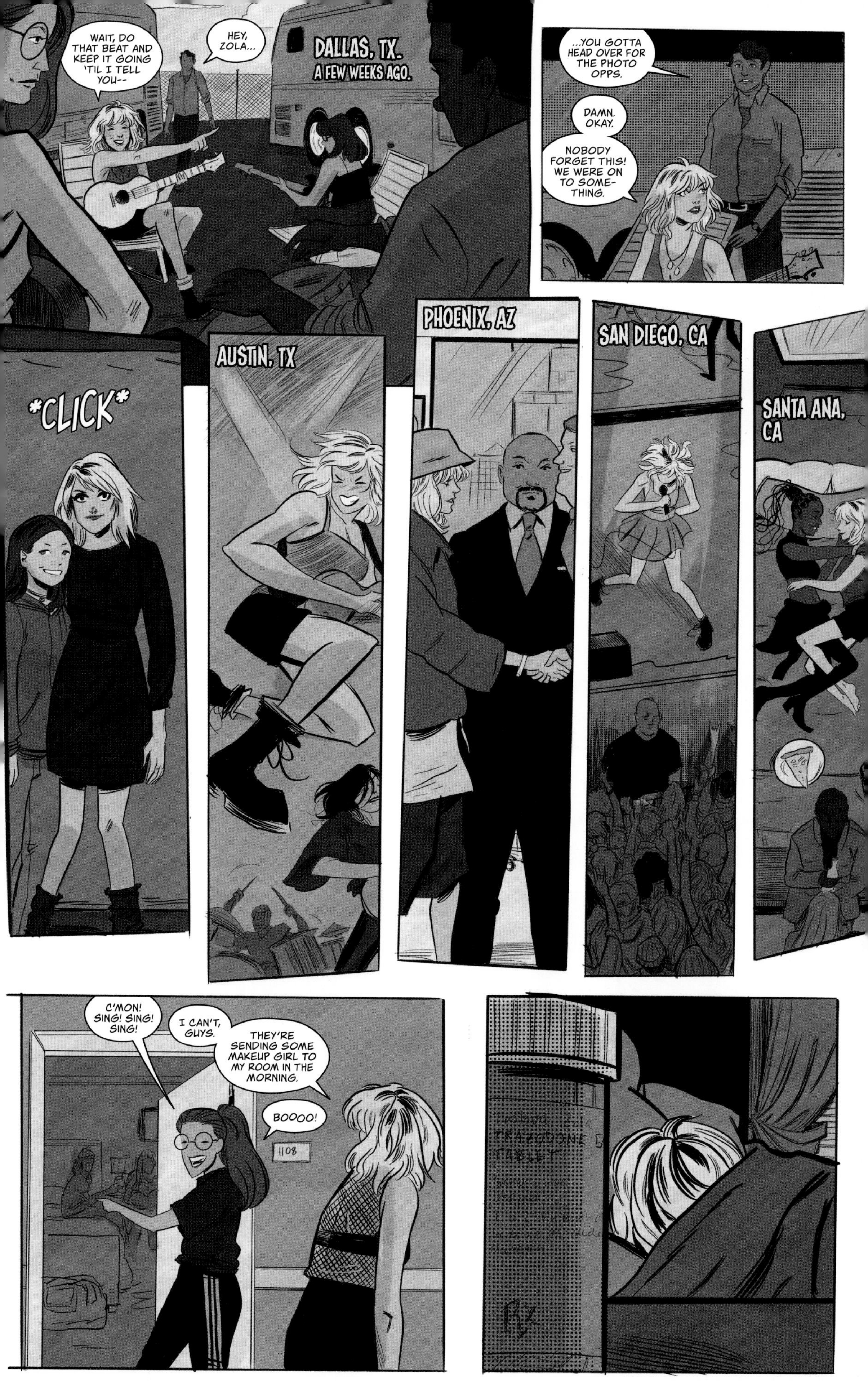
WAIT, DO THAT BEAT AND KEEP IT GOING 'TIL I TELL YOU--
HEY, ZOLA...
DALLAS, TX. A FEW WEEKS AGO.
...YOU GOTTA HEAD OVER FOR THE PHOTO OPPS.
DAMN. OKAY.
NOBODY FORGET THIS! WE WERE ON TO SOME-THING.
CLICK
AUSTIN, TX
PHOENIX, AZ
SAN DIEGO, CA
SANTA ANA, CA
C'MON! SING! SING! SING!
I CAN'T, GUYS.
THEY'RE SENDING SOME MAKEUP GIRL TO MY ROOM IN THE MORNING.
BOOOO!
1108
TRAZODONE
TABLET

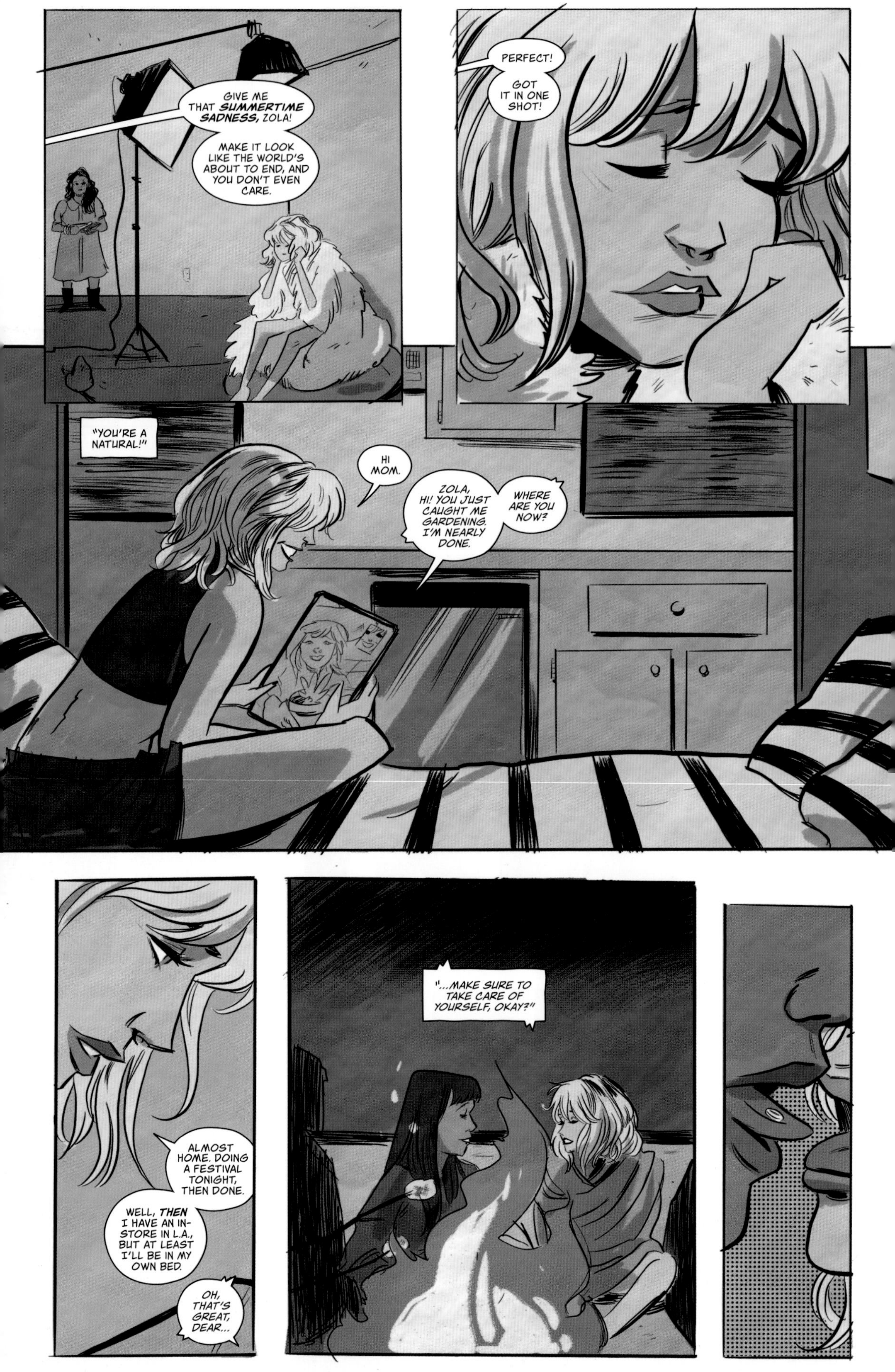
GIVE ME THAT SUMMERTIME SADNESS, ZOLA!
MAKE IT LOOK LIKE THE WORLD'S ABOUT TO END, AND YOU DON'T EVEN CARE.
PERFECT!
GOT IT IN ONE SHOT!
"YOU'RE A NATURAL!"
HI MOM.
ZOLA, HI! YOU JUST CAUGHT ME GARDENING. I'M NEARLY DONE.
WHERE ARE YOU NOW?
ALMOST HOME. DOING A FESTIVAL TONIGHT, THEN DONE.
WELL, THEN I HAVE AN IN-STORE IN L.A., BUT AT LEAST I'LL BE IN MY OWN BED.
OH, THAT'S GREAT, DEAR...
"...MAKE SURE TO TAKE CARE OF YOURSELF, OKAY?"

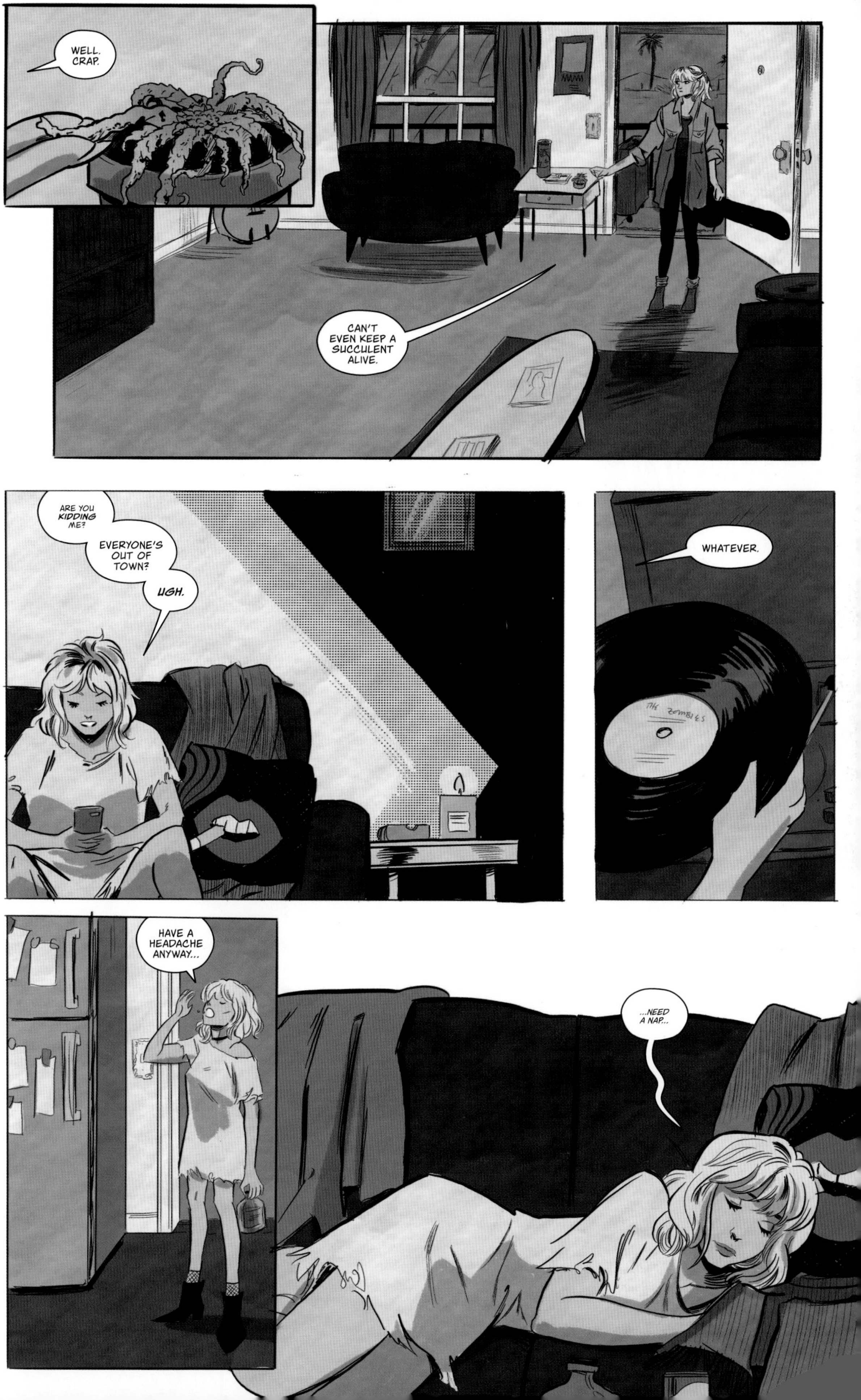
WELL. CRAP.
CAN'T EVEN KEEP A SUCCULENT ALIVE.
ARE YOU *KIDDING* ME?
EVERYONE'S OUT OF TOWN?
UGH.
WHATEVER.
THE ZOMBIES
HAVE A HEADACHE ANYWAY...
...NEED A NAP...

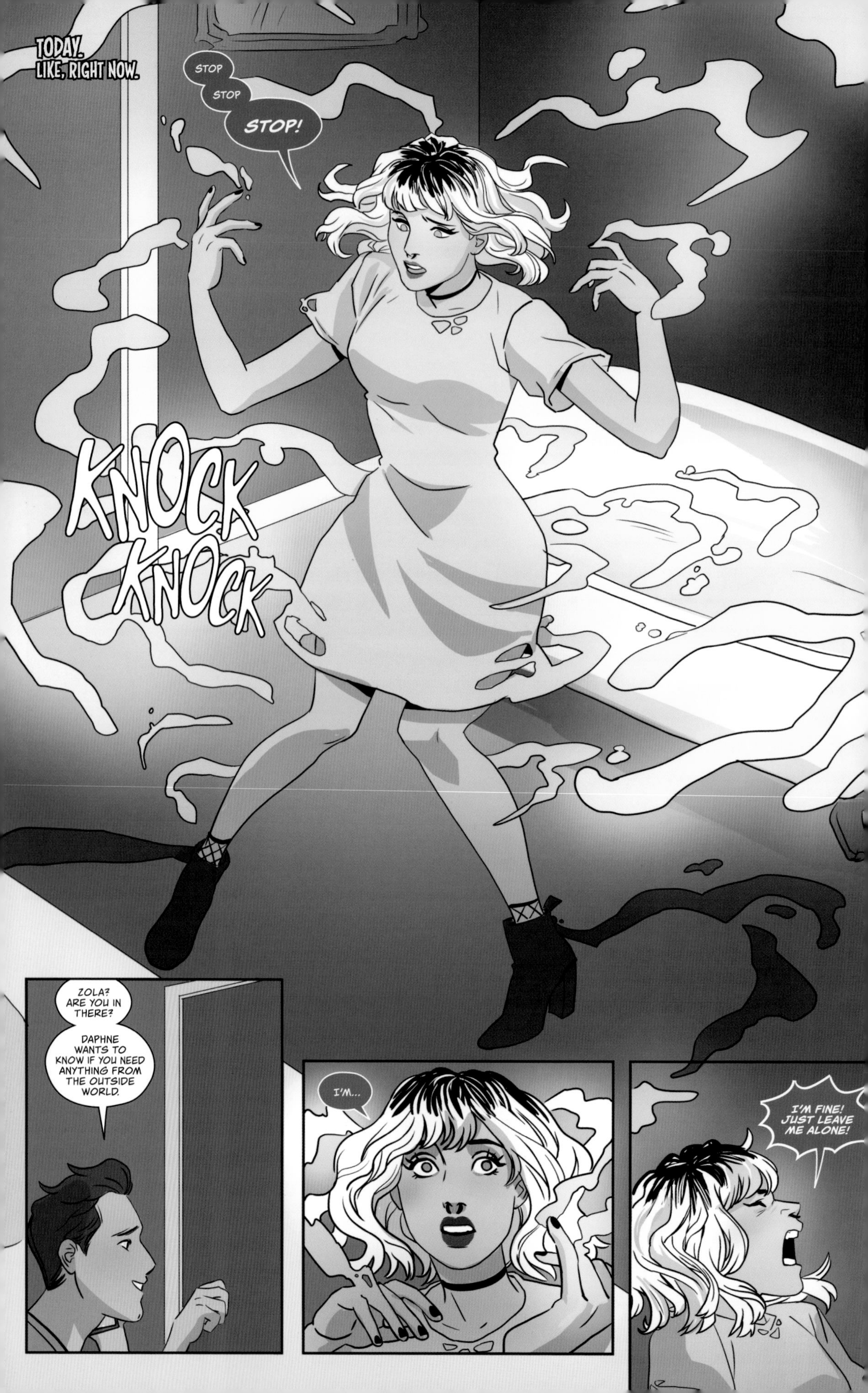
TODAY.
LIKE, RIGHT NOW.
STOP
STOP
STOP!
KNOCK KNOCK
ZOLA? ARE YOU IN THERE?
DAPHNE WANTS TO KNOW IF YOU NEED ANYTHING FROM THE OUTSIDE WORLD.
I'M...
I'M FINE! JUST LEAVE ME ALONE!

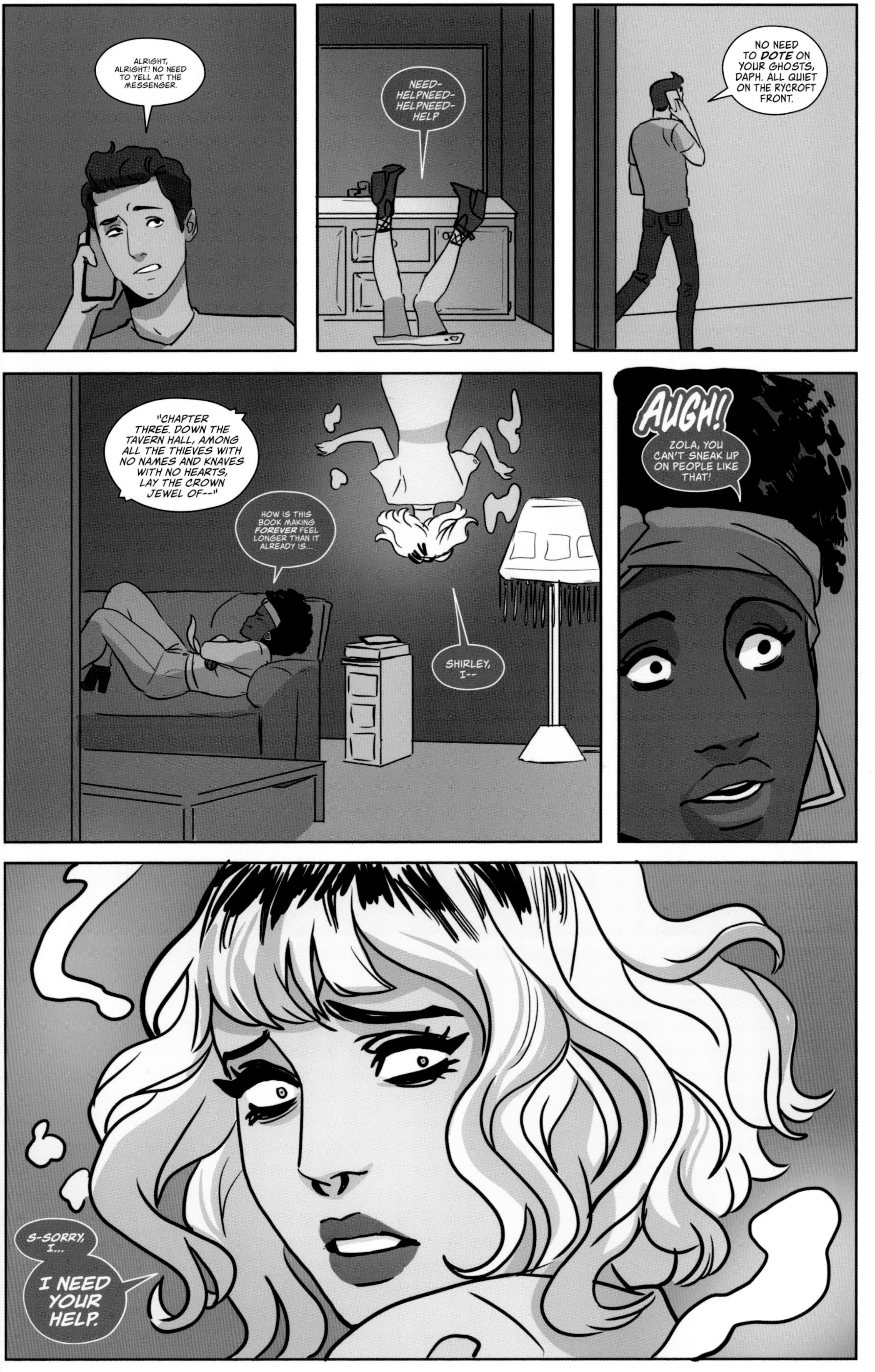
ALRIGHT, ALRIGHT! NO NEED TO YELL AT THE MESSENGER.
NEED-HELPNEED-HELPNEED-HELP
NO NEED TO DOTE ON YOUR GHOSTS, DAPH. ALL QUIET ON THE RYCROFT FRONT.
"CHAPTER THREE. DOWN THE TAVERN HALL, AMONG ALL THE THIEVES WITH NO NAMES AND KNAVES WITH NO HEARTS, LAY THE CROWN JEWEL OF--"
HOW IS THIS BOOK MAKING FOREVER FEEL LONGER THAN IT ALREADY IS...
SHIRLEY, I--
AUGH!
ZOLA, YOU CAN'T SNEAK UP ON PEOPLE LIKE THAT!
S-SORRY, I...
I NEED YOUR HELP.

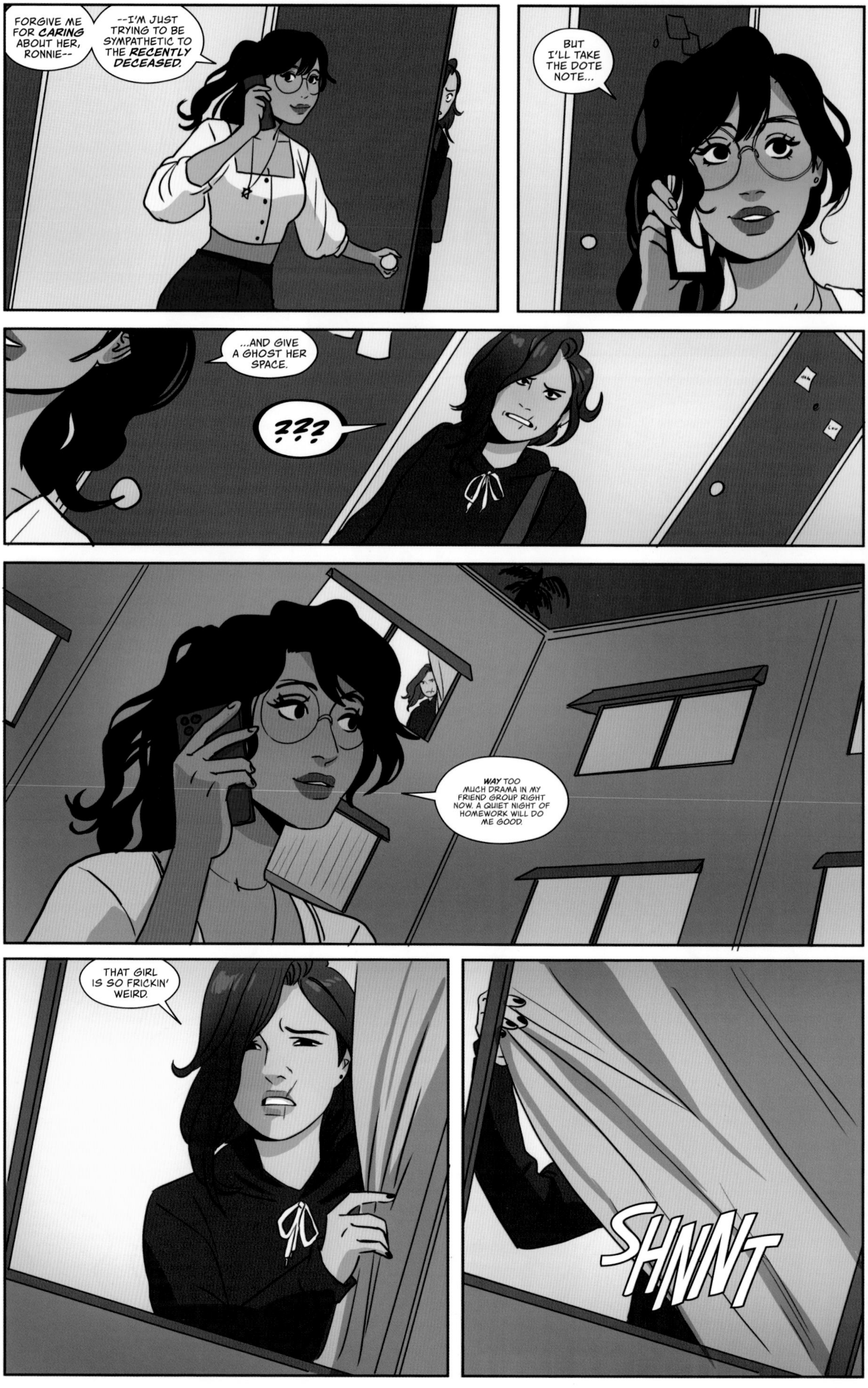
FORGIVE ME FOR CARING ABOUT HER, RONNIE--
--I'M JUST TRYING TO BE SYMPATHETIC TO THE RECENTLY DECEASED.
BUT I'LL TAKE THE DOTE NOTE...
...AND GIVE A GHOST HER SPACE.
???
WAY TOO MUCH DRAMA IN MY FRIEND GROUP RIGHT NOW. A QUIET NIGHT OF HOMEWORK WILL DO ME GOOD.
THAT GIRL IS SO FRICKIN' WEIRD.
SHNNT

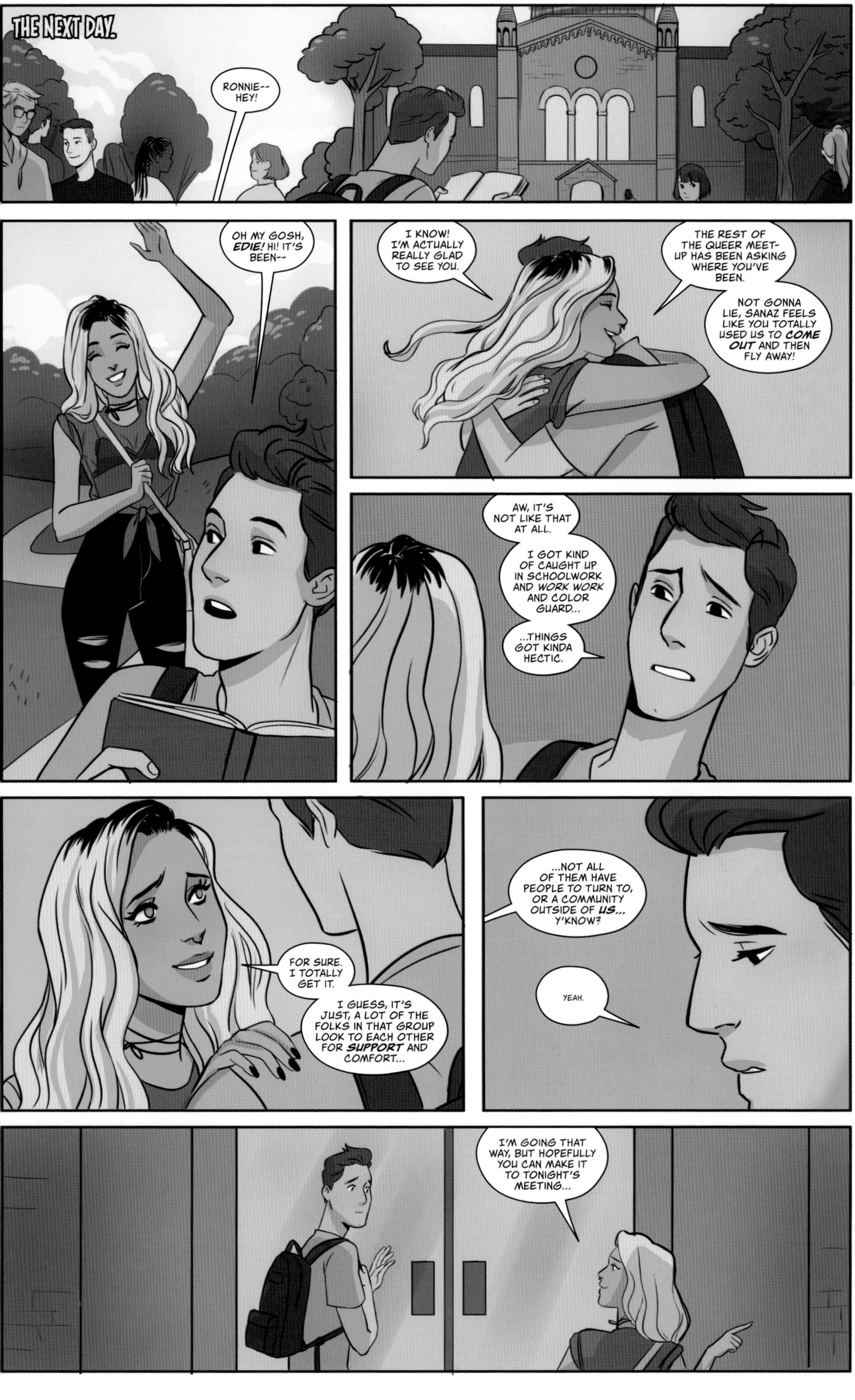
THE NEXT DAY.
RONNIE-- HEY!
OH MY GOSH, EDIE! HI! IT'S BEEN--
I KNOW! I'M ACTUALLY REALLY GLAD TO SEE YOU.
THE REST OF THE QUEER MEET-UP HAS BEEN ASKING WHERE YOU'VE BEEN.
NOT GONNA LIE, SANAZ FEELS LIKE YOU TOTALLY USED US TO COME OUT AND THEN FLY AWAY!
AW, IT'S NOT LIKE THAT AT ALL.
I GOT KIND OF CAUGHT UP IN SCHOOLWORK AND WORK WORK AND COLOR GUARD...
...THINGS GOT KINDA HECTIC.
FOR SURE. I TOTALLY GET IT.
I GUESS, IT'S JUST, A LOT OF THE FOLKS IN THAT GROUP LOOK TO EACH OTHER FOR SUPPORT AND COMFORT...
...NOT ALL OF THEM HAVE PEOPLE TO TURN TO, OR A COMMUNITY OUTSIDE OF US... Y'KNOW?
YEAH.
I'M GOING THAT WAY, BUT HOPEFULLY YOU CAN MAKE IT TO TONIGHT'S MEETING...

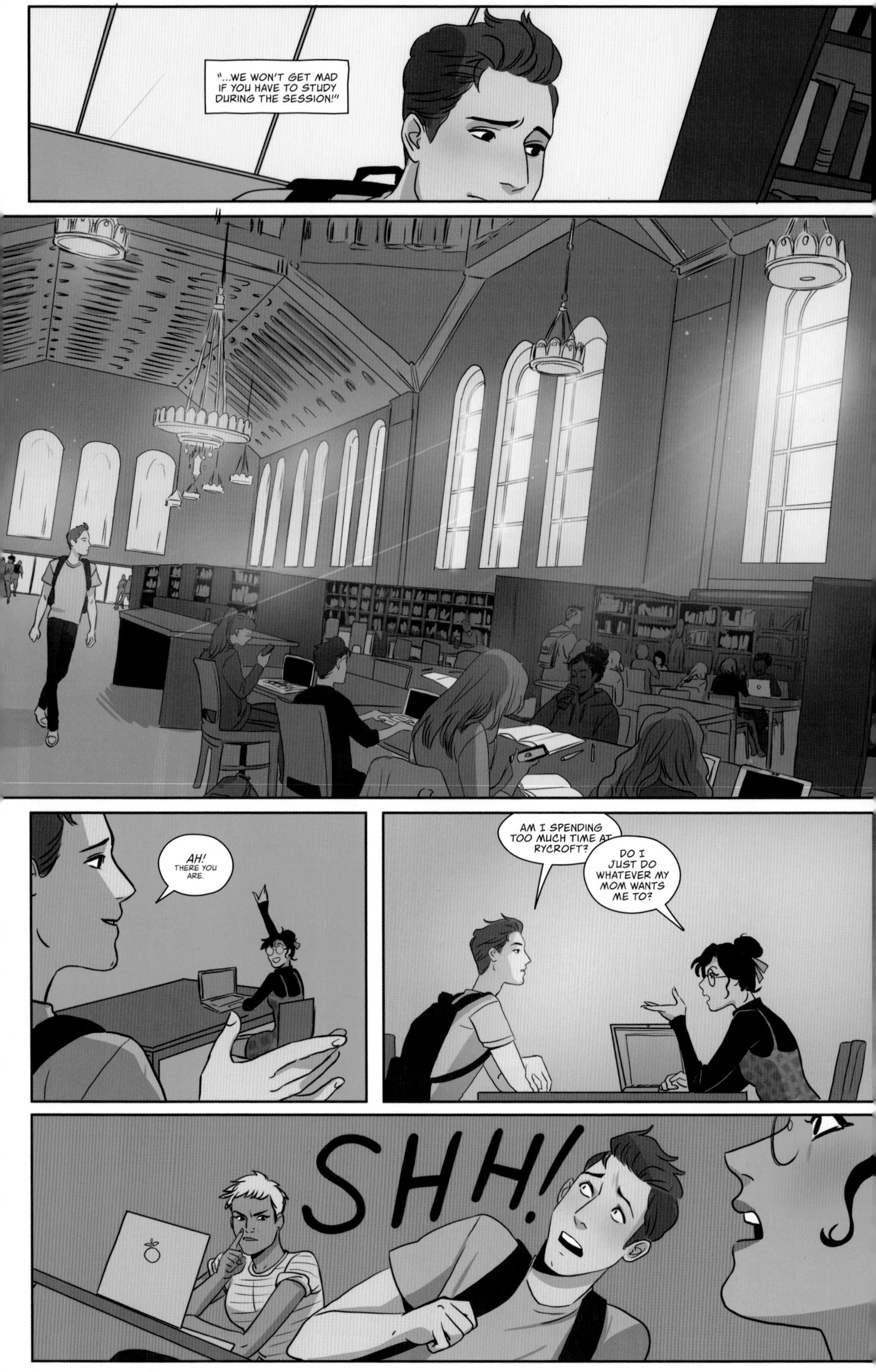
"...WE WON'T GET MAD IF YOU HAVE TO STUDY DURING THE SESSION!"
AH! THERE YOU ARE.
AM I SPENDING TOO MUCH TIME AT RYCROFT?
DO I JUST DO WHATEVER MY MOM WANTS ME TO?
SHH!

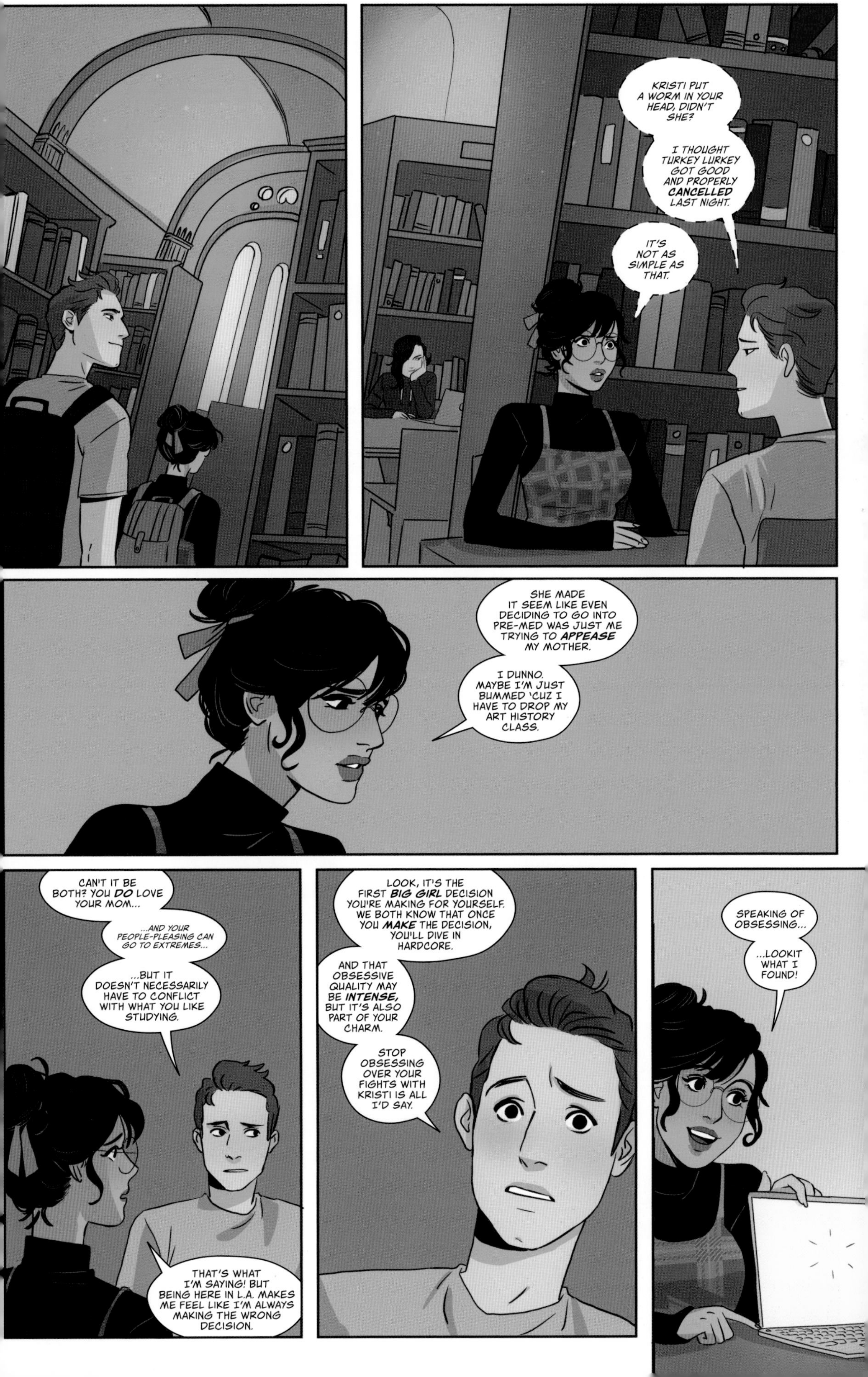
KRISTI PUT A WORM IN YOUR HEAD, DIDN'T SHE?
I THOUGHT TURKEY LURKEY GOT GOOD AND PROPERLY CANCELLED LAST NIGHT.
IT'S NOT AS SIMPLE AS THAT.
SHE MADE IT SEEM LIKE EVEN DECIDING TO GO INTO PRE-MED WAS JUST ME TRYING TO APPEASE MY MOTHER.
I DUNNO. MAYBE I'M JUST BUMMED 'CUZ I HAVE TO DROP MY ART HISTORY CLASS.
CAN'T IT BE BOTH? YOU DO LOVE YOUR MOM...
...AND YOUR PEOPLE-PLEASING CAN GO TO EXTREMES...
...BUT IT DOESN'T NECESSARILY HAVE TO CONFLICT WITH WHAT YOU LIKE STUDYING.
THAT'S WHAT I'M SAYING! BUT BEING HERE IN L.A. MAKES ME FEEL LIKE I'M ALWAYS MAKING THE WRONG DECISION.
LOOK, IT'S THE FIRST BIG GIRL DECISION YOU'RE MAKING FOR YOURSELF. WE BOTH KNOW THAT ONCE YOU MAKE THE DECISION, YOU'LL DIVE IN HARDCORE.
AND THAT OBSESSIVE QUALITY MAY BE INTENSE, BUT IT'S ALSO PART OF YOUR CHARM.
STOP OBSESSING OVER YOUR FIGHTS WITH KRISTI IS ALL I'D SAY.
SPEAKING OF OBSESSING...
...LOOKIT WHAT I FOUND!

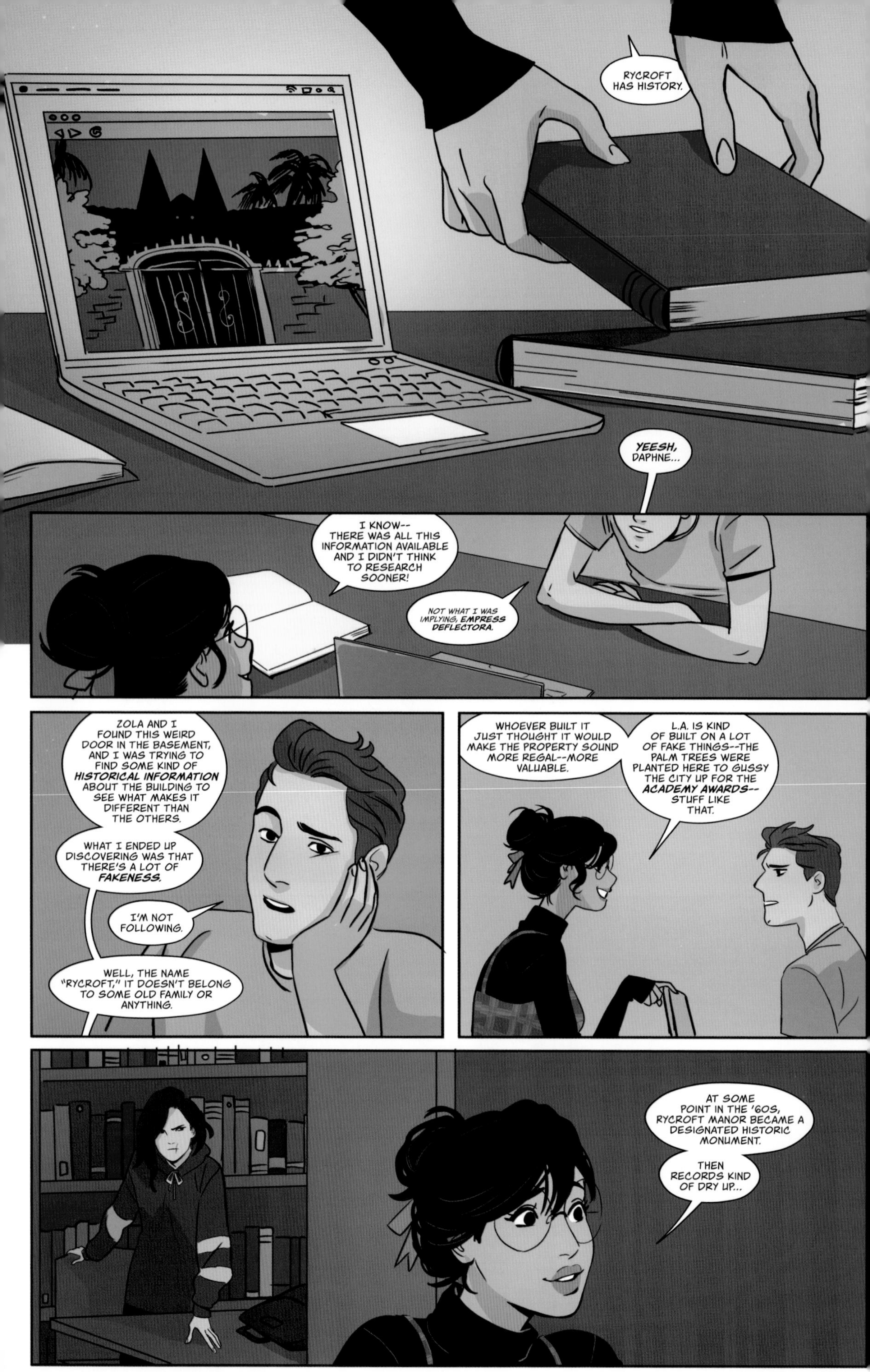
RYCROFT HAS HISTORY.
YEESH, DAPHNE...
I KNOW-- THERE WAS ALL THIS INFORMATION AVAILABLE AND I DIDN'T THINK TO RESEARCH SOONER!
NOT WHAT I WAS IMPLYING, EMPRESS DEFLECTORA.
ZOLA AND I FOUND THIS WEIRD DOOR IN THE BASEMENT, AND I WAS TRYING TO FIND SOME KIND OF HISTORICAL INFORMATION ABOUT THE BUILDING TO SEE WHAT MAKES IT DIFFERENT THAN THE OTHERS.
WHAT I ENDED UP DISCOVERING WAS THAT THERE'S A LOT OF FAKENESS.
I'M NOT FOLLOWING.
WELL, THE NAME "RYCROFT," IT DOESN'T BELONG TO SOME OLD FAMILY OR ANYTHING.
WHOEVER BUILT IT JUST THOUGHT IT WOULD MAKE THE PROPERTY SOUND MORE REGAL--MORE VALUABLE.
L.A. IS KIND OF BUILT ON A LOT OF FAKE THINGS--THE PALM TREES WERE PLANTED HERE TO GUSSY THE CITY UP FOR THE ACADEMY AWARDS-- STUFF LIKE THAT.
AT SOME POINT IN THE '60S, RYCROFT MANOR BECAME A DESIGNATED HISTORIC MONUMENT.
THEN RECORDS KIND OF DRY UP...

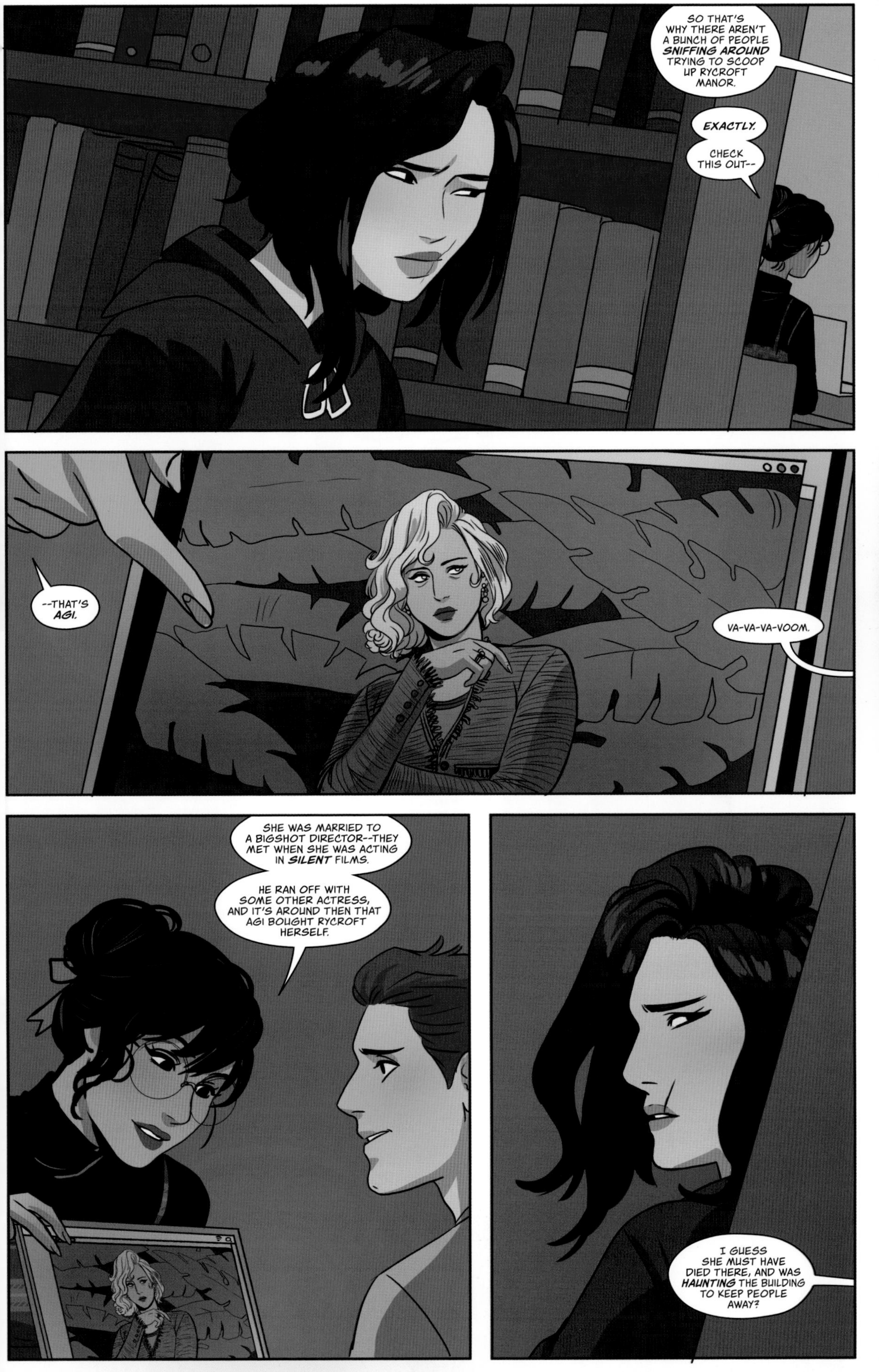
SO THAT'S WHY THERE AREN'T A BUNCH OF PEOPLE SNIFFING AROUND TRYING TO SCOOP UP RYCROFT MANOR.
EXACTLY.
CHECK THIS OUT--
--THAT'S AGI.
VA-VA-VA-VOOM.
SHE WAS MARRIED TO A BIGSHOT DIRECTOR--THEY MET WHEN SHE WAS ACTING IN SILENT FILMS.
HE RAN OFF WITH SOME OTHER ACTRESS, AND IT'S AROUND THEN THAT AGI BOUGHT RYCROFT HERSELF.
I GUESS SHE MUST HAVE DIED THERE, AND WAS HAUNTING THE BUILDING TO KEEP PEOPLE AWAY?

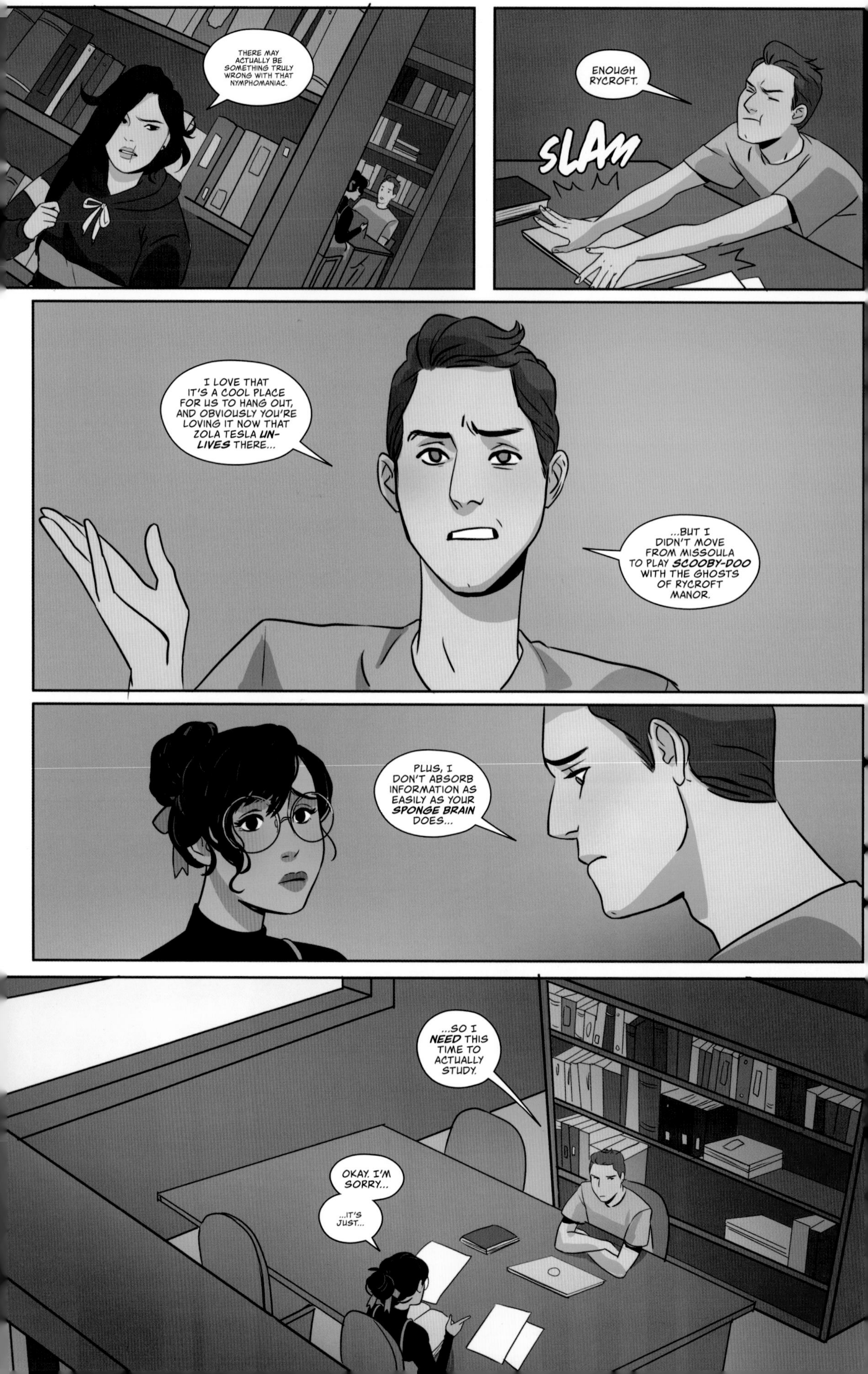
THERE MAY ACTUALLY BE SOMETHING TRULY WRONG WITH THAT NYMPHOMANIAC.
ENOUGH RYCROFT.
SLAM
I LOVE THAT IT'S A COOL PLACE FOR US TO HANG OUT, AND OBVIOUSLY YOU'RE LOVING IT NOW THAT ZOLA TESLA UN-LIVES THERE...
...BUT I DIDN'T MOVE FROM MISSOULA TO PLAY SCOOBY-DOO WITH THE GHOSTS OF RYCROFT MANOR.
PLUS, I DON'T ABSORB INFORMATION AS EASILY AS YOUR SPONGE BRAIN DOES...
...SO I NEED THIS TIME TO ACTUALLY STUDY.
OKAY. I'M SORRY...
...IT'S JUST...

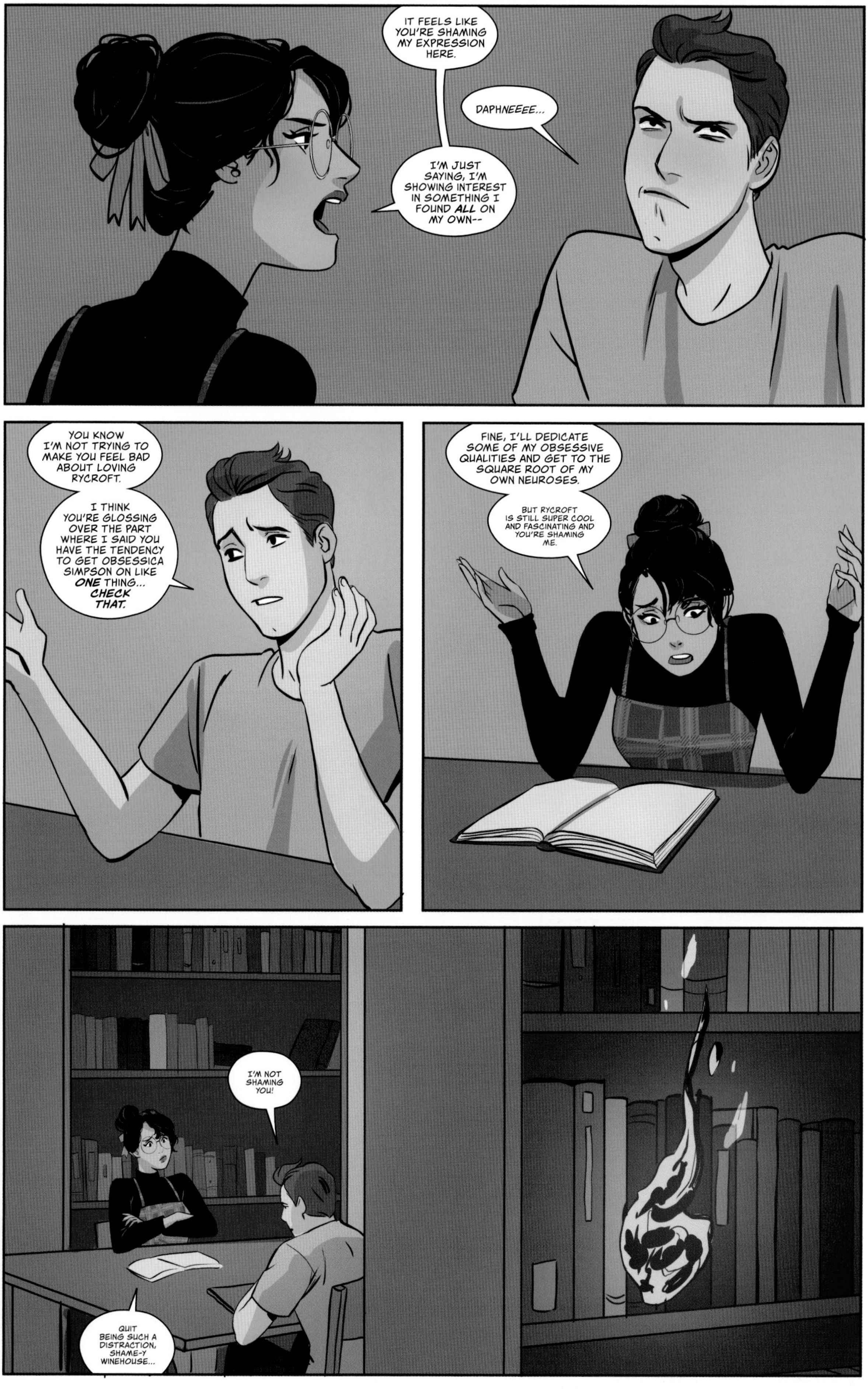
IT FEELS LIKE YOU'RE SHAMING MY EXPRESSION HERE.
I'M JUST SAYING, I'M SHOWING INTEREST IN SOMETHING I FOUND ALL ON MY OWN--
DAPHNEEEE...
YOU KNOW I'M NOT TRYING TO MAKE YOU FEEL BAD ABOUT LOVING RYCROFT.
I THINK YOU'RE GLOSSING OVER THE PART WHERE I SAID YOU HAVE THE TENDENCY TO GET OBSESSICA SIMPSON ON LIKE ONE THING... CHECK THAT.
FINE, I'LL DEDICATE SOME OF MY OBSESSIVE QUALITIES AND GET TO THE SQUARE ROOT OF MY OWN NEUROSES.
BUT RYCROFT IS STILL SUPER COOL AND FASCINATING AND YOU'RE SHAMING ME.
I'M NOT SHAMING YOU!
QUIT BEING SUCH A DISTRACTION, SHAME-Y WINEHOUSE...

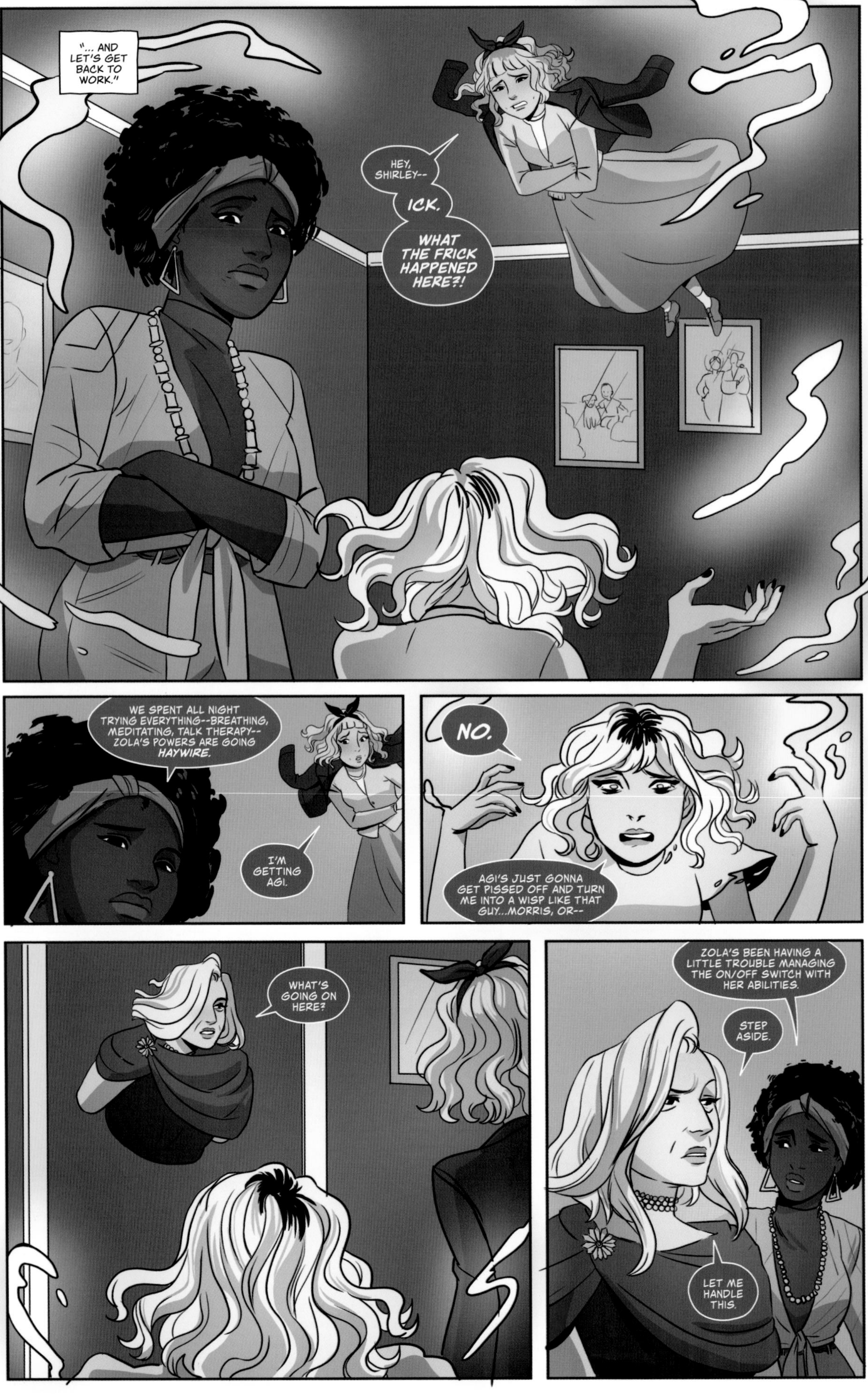
"... AND LET'S GET BACK TO WORK."
HEY, SHIRLEY--
ICK.
WHAT THE FRICK HAPPENED HERE?!
WE SPENT ALL NIGHT TRYING EVERYTHING--BREATHING, MEDITATING, TALK THERAPY-- ZOLA'S POWERS ARE GOING HAYWIRE.
I'M GETTING AGI.
NO.
AGI'S JUST GONNA GET PISSED OFF AND TURN ME INTO A WISP LIKE THAT GUY...MORRIS, OR--
WHAT'S GOING ON HERE?
ZOLA'S BEEN HAVING A LITTLE TROUBLE MANAGING THE ON/OFF SWITCH WITH HER ABILITIES.
STEP ASIDE.
LET ME HANDLE THIS.

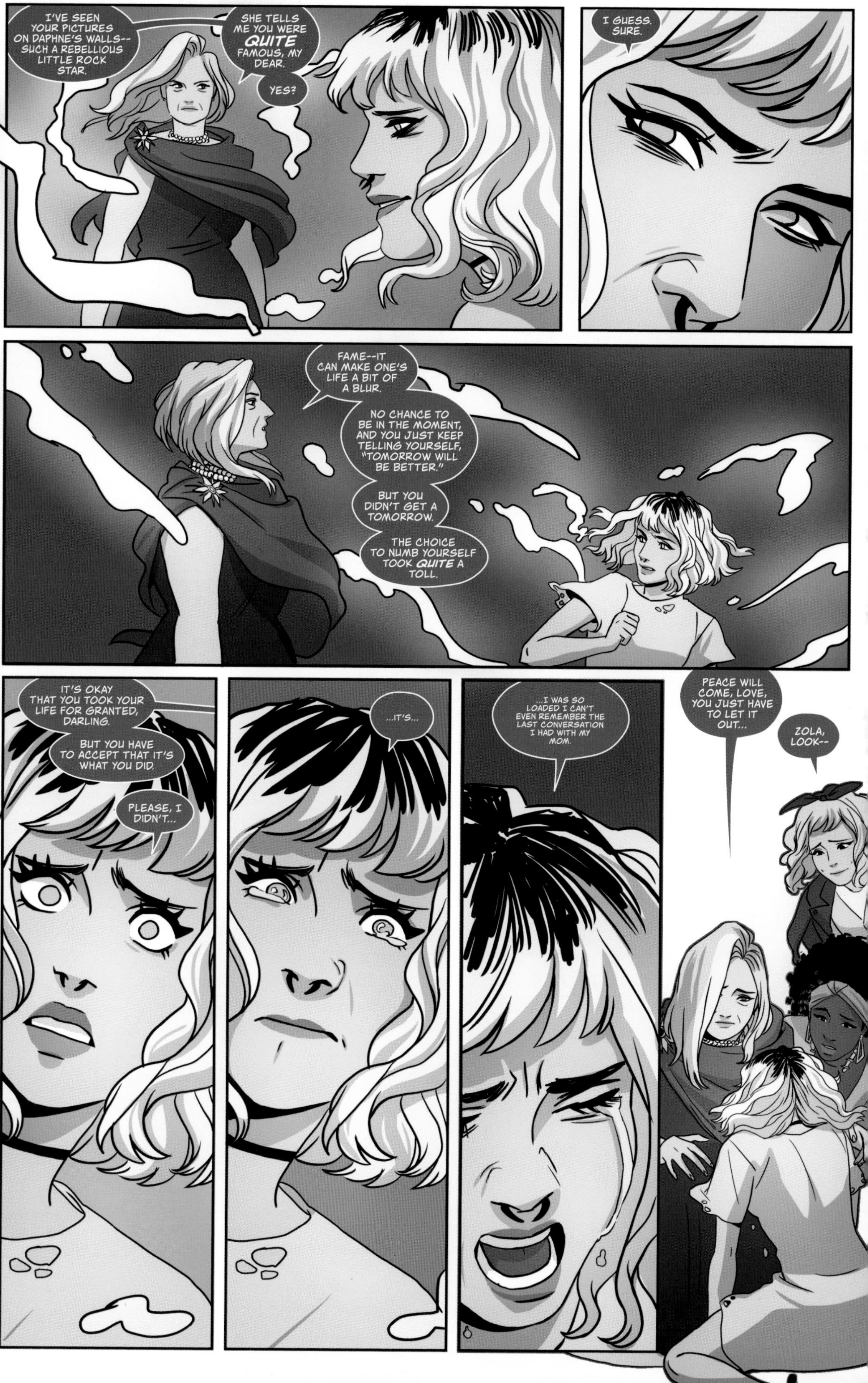
I'VE SEEN YOUR PICTURES ON DAPHNE'S WALLS-- SUCH A REBELLIOUS LITTLE ROCK STAR.
SHE TELLS ME YOU WERE QUITE FAMOUS, MY DEAR.
YES?
I GUESS. SURE.
FAME--IT CAN MAKE ONE'S LIFE A BIT OF A BLUR.
NO CHANCE TO BE IN THE MOMENT, AND YOU JUST KEEP TELLING YOURSELF, "TOMORROW WILL BE BETTER."
BUT YOU DIDN'T GET A TOMORROW.
THE CHOICE TO NUMB YOURSELF TOOK QUITE A TOLL.
IT'S OKAY THAT YOU TOOK YOUR LIFE FOR GRANTED, DARLING.
BUT YOU HAVE TO ACCEPT THAT IT'S WHAT YOU DID.
PLEASE, I DIDN'T...
...IT'S...
...I WAS SO LOADED I CAN'T EVEN REMEMBER THE LAST CONVERSATION I HAD WITH MY MOM.
PEACE WILL COME, LOVE, YOU JUST HAVE TO LET IT OUT...
ZOLA, LOOK--

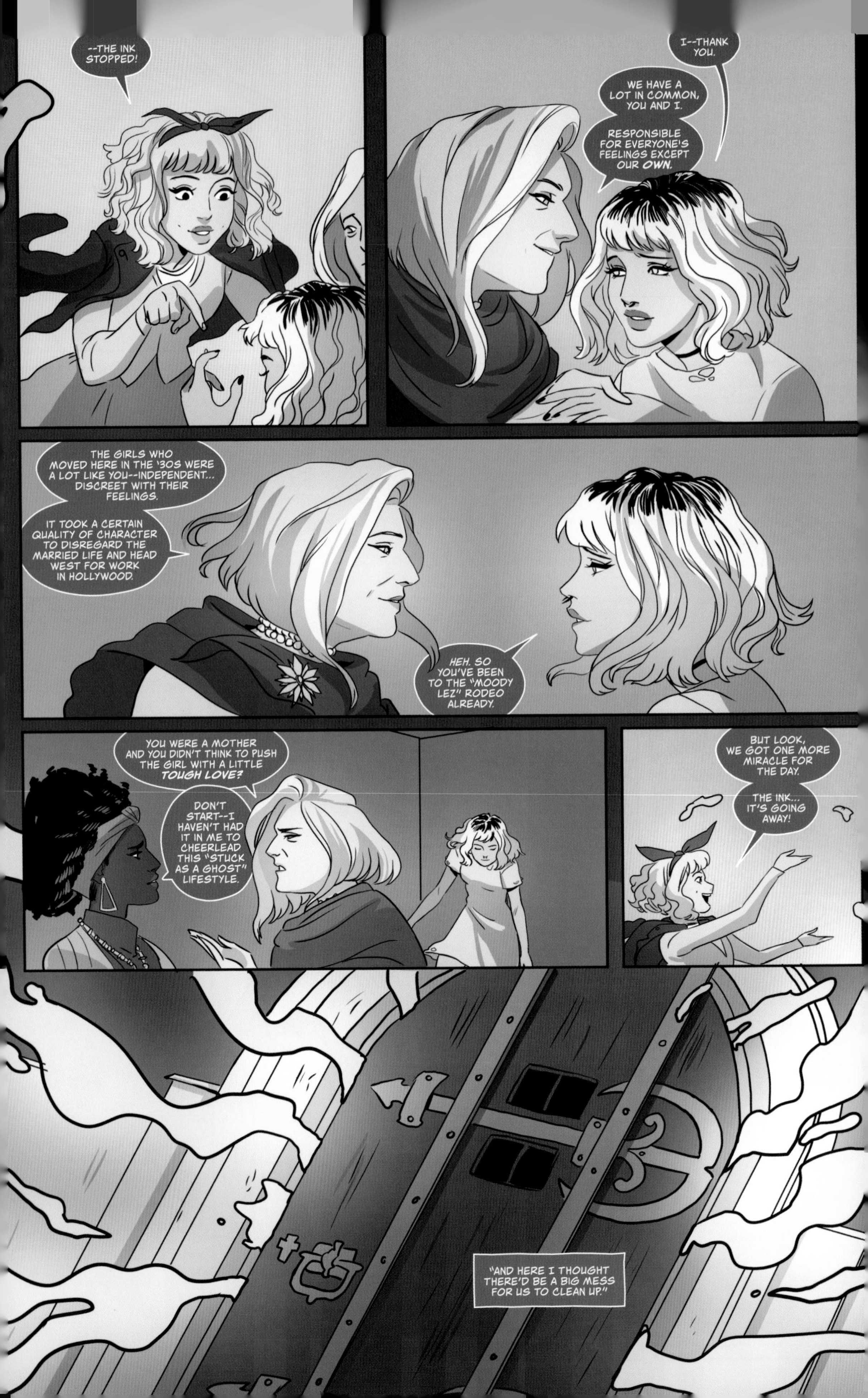
--THE INK STOPPED!
WE HAVE A LOT IN COMMON, YOU AND I.
RESPONSIBLE FOR EVERYONE'S FEELINGS EXCEPT OUR *OWN*.
I--THANK YOU.
THE GIRLS WHO MOVED HERE IN THE '30S WERE A LOT LIKE YOU--INDEPENDENT... DISCREET WITH THEIR FEELINGS.
IT TOOK A CERTAIN QUALITY OF CHARACTER TO DISREGARD THE MARRIED LIFE AND HEAD WEST FOR WORK IN HOLLYWOOD.
HEH. SO YOU'VE BEEN TO THE "MOODY LEZ" RODEO ALREADY.
YOU WERE A MOTHER AND YOU DIDN'T THINK TO PUSH THE GIRL WITH A LITTLE *TOUGH LOVE?*
DON'T START--I HAVEN'T HAD IT IN ME TO CHEERLEAD THIS "STUCK AS A GHOST" LIFESTYLE.
BUT LOOK, WE GOT ONE MORE MIRACLE FOR THE DAY.
THE INK... IT'S GOING AWAY!
"AND HERE I THOUGHT THERE'D BE A BIG MESS FOR US TO CLEAN UP."

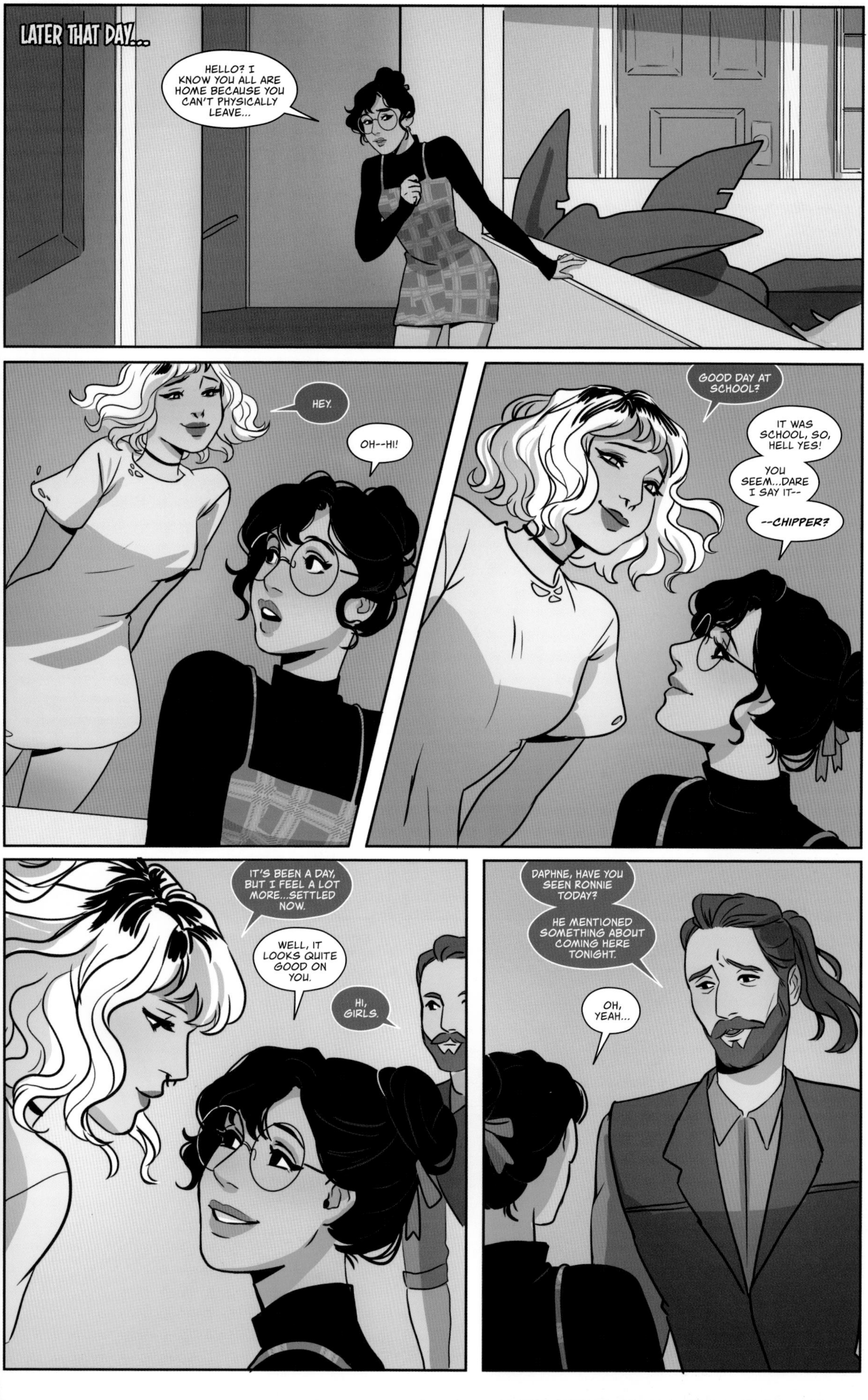
LATER THAT DAY...
HELLO? I KNOW YOU ALL ARE HOME BECAUSE YOU CAN'T PHYSICALLY LEAVE...
HEY.
OH--HI!
GOOD DAY AT SCHOOL?
IT WAS SCHOOL, SO, HELL YES!
YOU SEEM...DARE I SAY IT--
--CHIPPER?
IT'S BEEN A DAY, BUT I FEEL A LOT MORE...SETTLED NOW.
WELL, IT LOOKS QUITE GOOD ON YOU.
HI, GIRLS.
DAPHNE, HAVE YOU SEEN RONNIE TODAY?
HE MENTIONED SOMETHING ABOUT COMING HERE TONIGHT.
OH, YEAH...

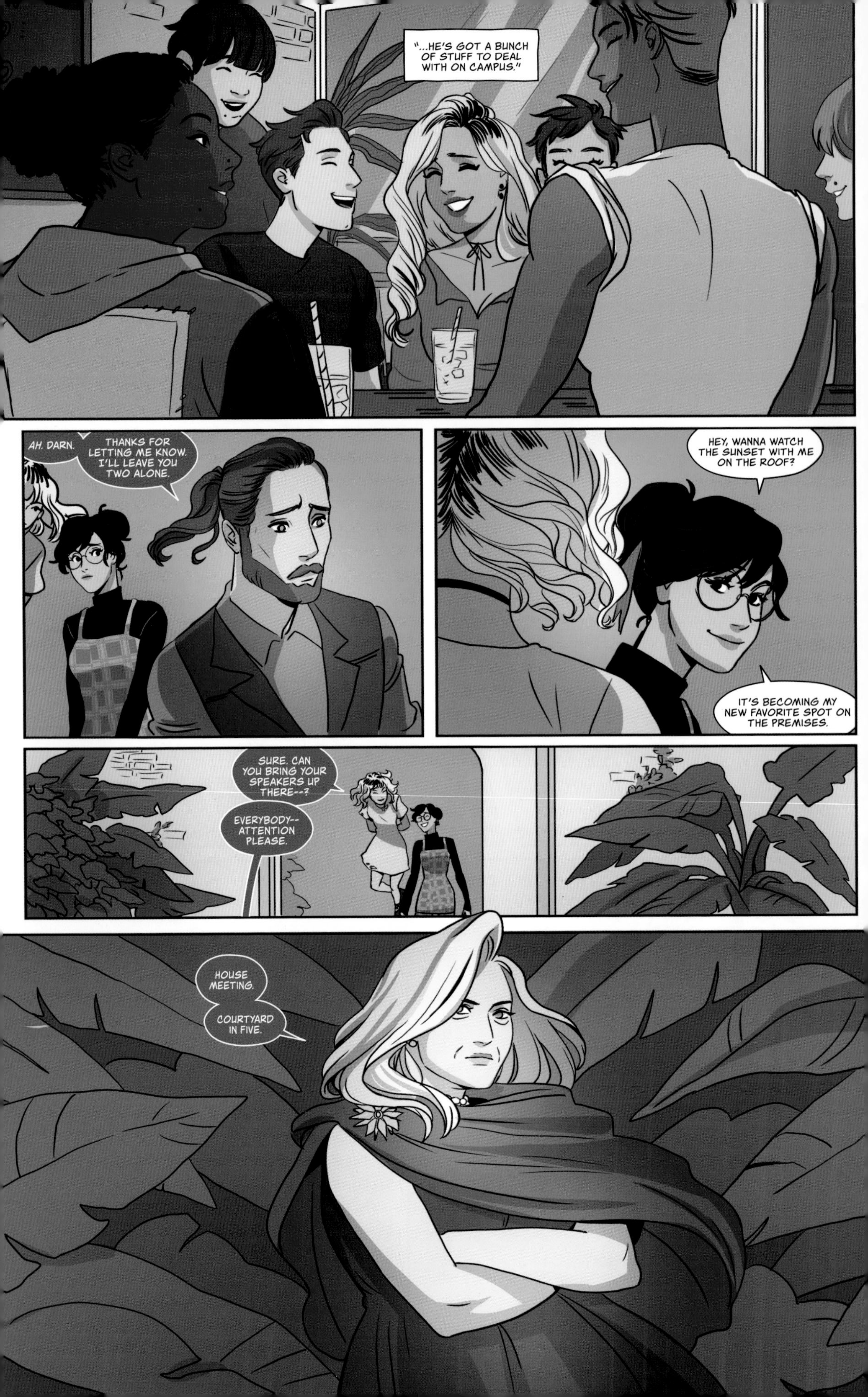
"...HE'S GOT A BUNCH OF STUFF TO DEAL WITH ON CAMPUS."
AH. DARN.
THANKS FOR LETTING ME KNOW. I'LL LEAVE YOU TWO ALONE.
HEY, WANNA WATCH THE SUNSET WITH ME ON THE ROOF?
IT'S BECOMING MY NEW FAVORITE SPOT ON THE PREMISES.
SURE. CAN YOU BRING YOUR SPEAKERS UP THERE--?
EVERYBODY-- ATTENTION PLEASE.
HOUSE MEETING.
COURTYARD IN FIVE.

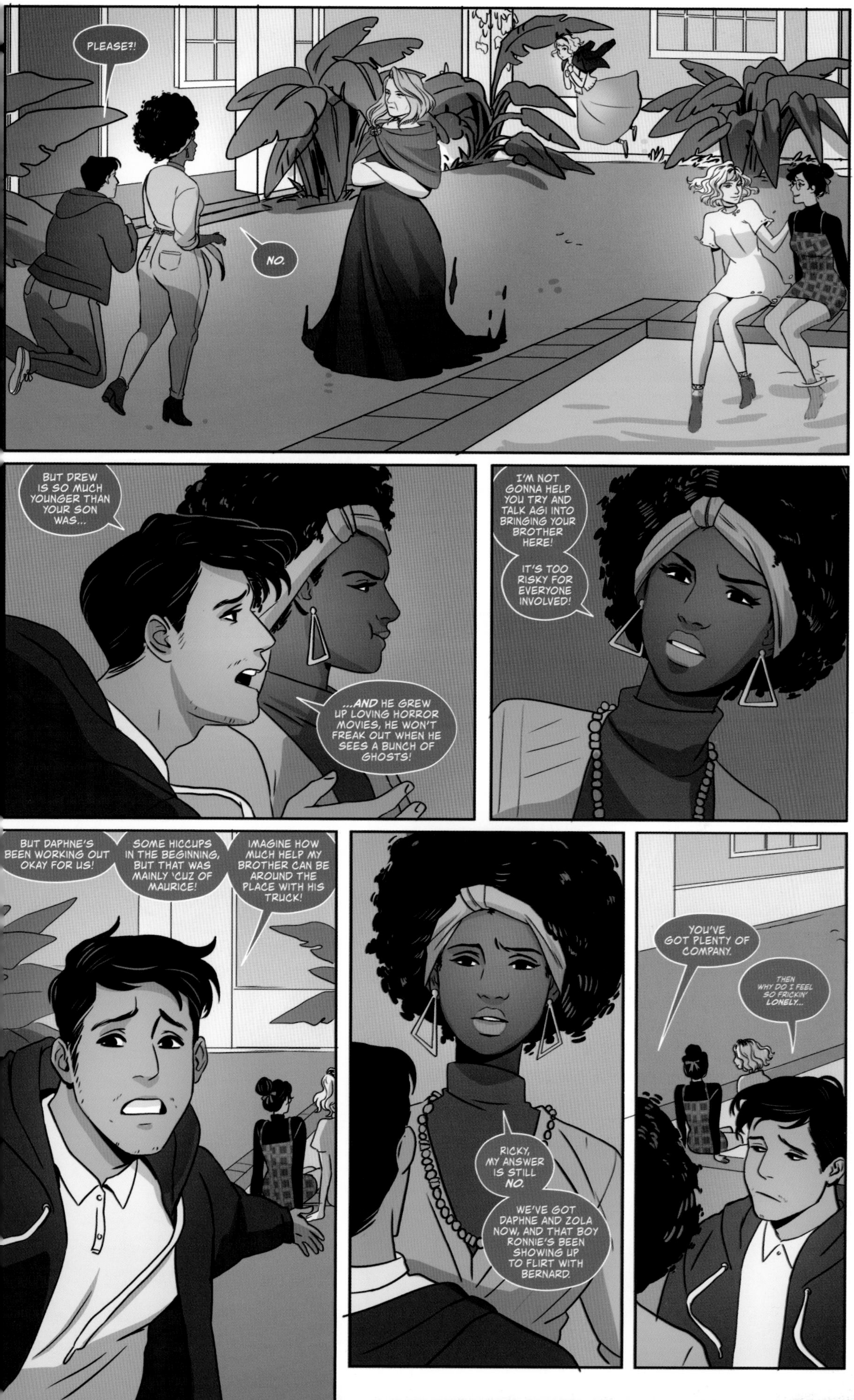
PLEASE?!
NO.
BUT DREW IS SO MUCH YOUNGER THAN YOUR SON WAS...
...AND HE GREW UP LOVING HORROR MOVIES, HE WON'T FREAK OUT WHEN HE SEES A BUNCH OF GHOSTS!
I'M NOT GONNA HELP YOU TRY AND TALK AGI INTO BRINGING YOUR BROTHER HERE!
IT'S TOO RISKY FOR EVERYONE INVOLVED!
BUT DAPHNE'S BEEN WORKING OUT OKAY FOR US!
SOME HICCUPS IN THE BEGINNING, BUT THAT WAS MAINLY 'CUZ OF MAURICE!
IMAGINE HOW MUCH HELP MY BROTHER CAN BE AROUND THE PLACE WITH HIS TRUCK!
RICKY, MY ANSWER IS STILL NO.
WE'VE GOT DAPHNE AND ZOLA NOW, AND THAT BOY RONNIE'S BEEN SHOWING UP TO FLIRT WITH BERNARD.
YOU'VE GOT PLENTY OF COMPANY.
THEN WHY DO I FEEL SO FRICKIN' LONELY...

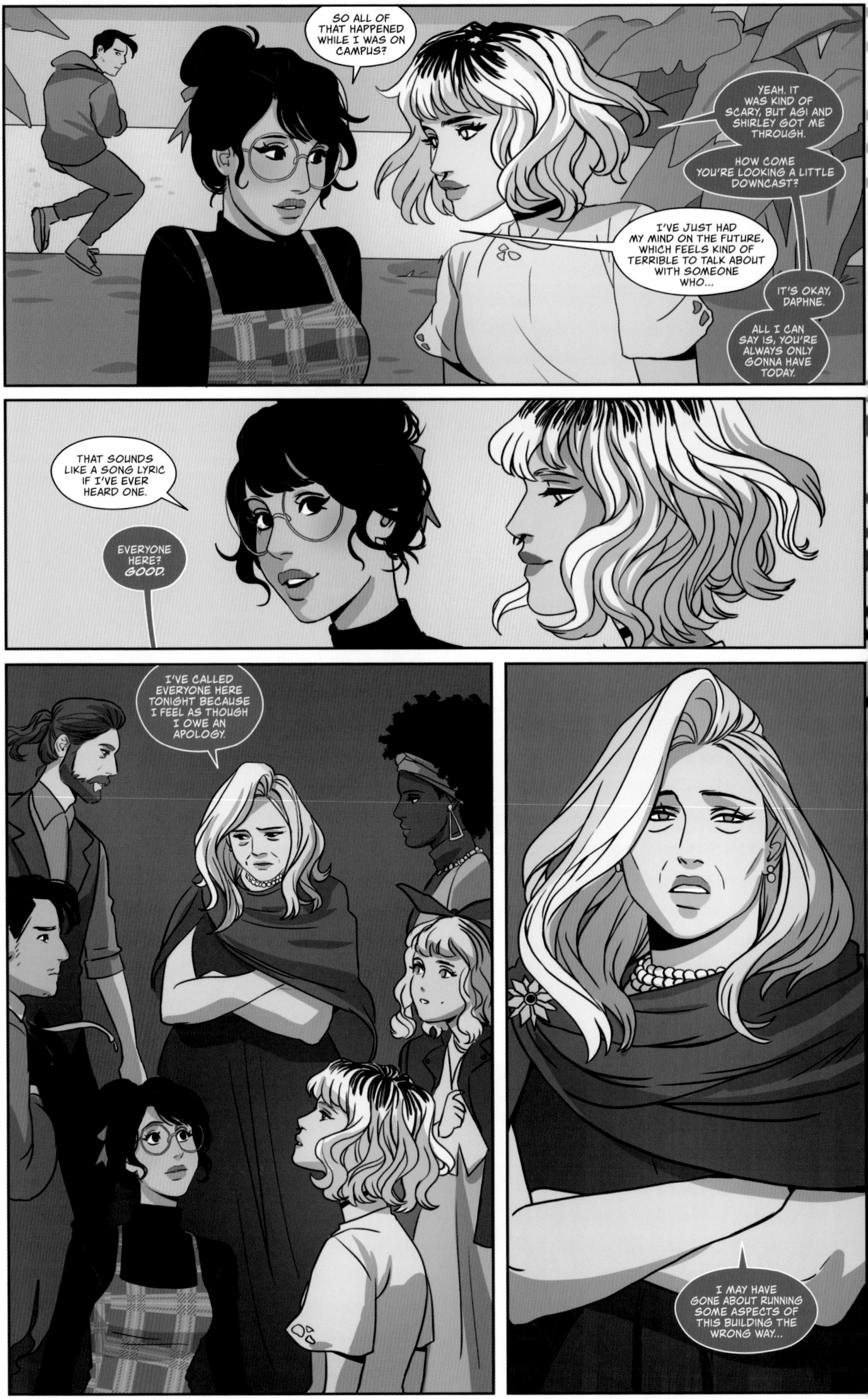
SO ALL OF THAT HAPPENED WHILE I WAS ON CAMPUS?
YEAH. IT WAS KIND OF SCARY, BUT AGI AND SHIRLEY GOT ME THROUGH.
HOW COME YOU'RE LOOKING A LITTLE DOWNCAST?
I'VE JUST HAD MY MIND ON THE FUTURE, WHICH FEELS KIND OF TERRIBLE TO TALK ABOUT WITH SOMEONE WHO...
IT'S OKAY, DAPHNE.
ALL I CAN SAY IS, YOU'RE ALWAYS ONLY GONNA HAVE TODAY.
THAT SOUNDS LIKE A SONG LYRIC IF I'VE EVER HEARD ONE.
EVERYONE HERE? GOOD.
I'VE CALLED EVERYONE HERE TONIGHT BECAUSE I FEEL AS THOUGH I OWE AN APOLOGY.
I MAY HAVE GONE ABOUT RUNNING SOME ASPECTS OF THIS BUILDING THE WRONG WAY...

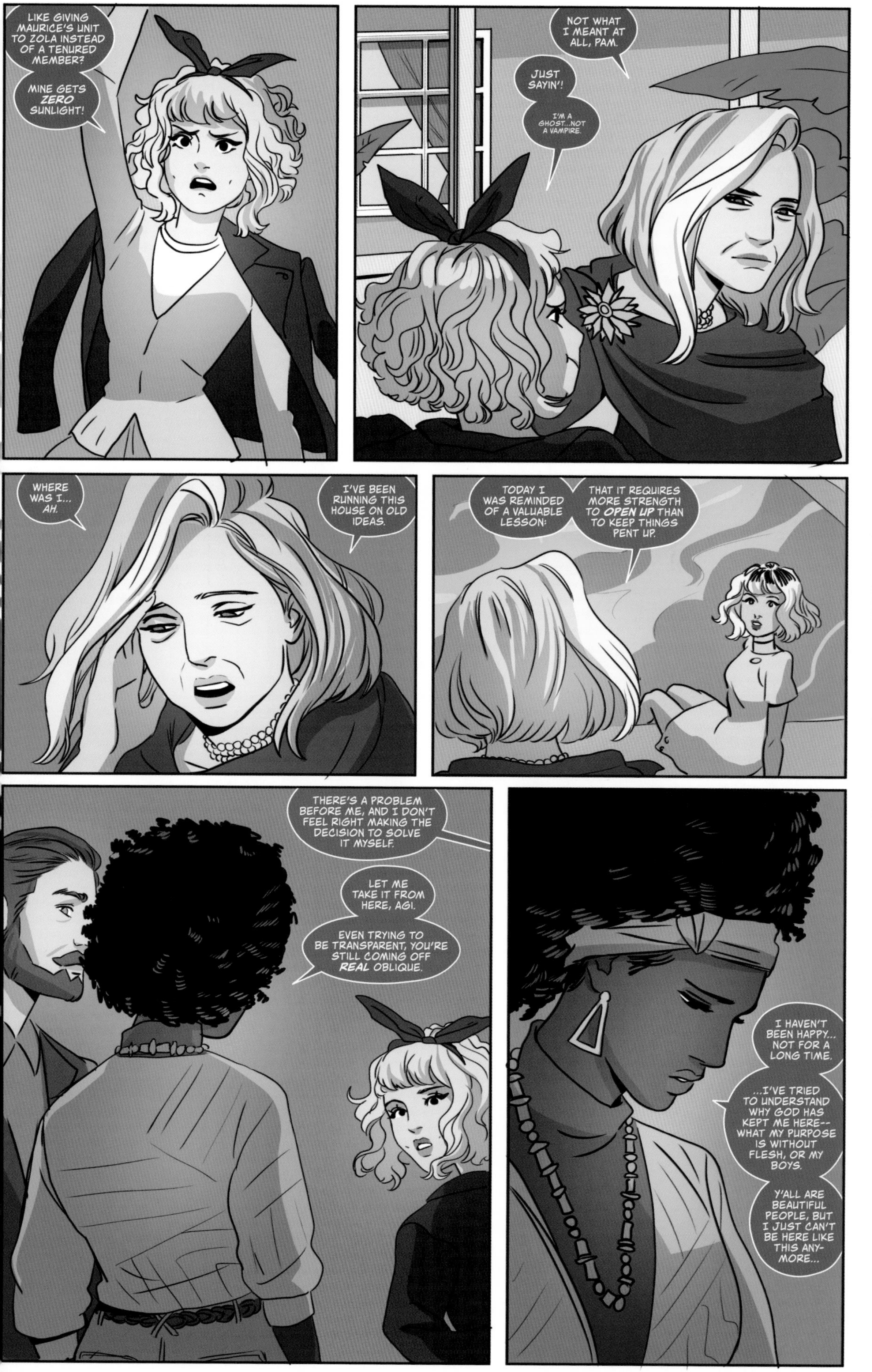
LIKE GIVING MAURICE'S UNIT TO ZOLA INSTEAD OF A TENURED MEMBER?
MINE GETS ZERO SUNLIGHT!
NOT WHAT I MEANT AT ALL, PAM.
JUST SAYIN'!
I'M A GHOST...NOT A VAMPIRE.
WHERE WAS I... AH.
I'VE BEEN RUNNING THIS HOUSE ON OLD IDEAS.
TODAY I WAS REMINDED OF A VALUABLE LESSON:
THAT IT REQUIRES MORE STRENGTH TO OPEN UP THAN TO KEEP THINGS PENT UP.
THERE'S A PROBLEM BEFORE ME, AND I DON'T FEEL RIGHT MAKING THE DECISION TO SOLVE IT MYSELF.
LET ME TAKE IT FROM HERE, AGI.
EVEN TRYING TO BE TRANSPARENT, YOU'RE STILL COMING OFF REAL OBLIQUE.
I HAVEN'T BEEN HAPPY... NOT FOR A LONG TIME.
...I'VE TRIED TO UNDERSTAND WHY GOD HAS KEPT ME HERE--WHAT MY PURPOSE IS WITHOUT FLESH, OR MY BOYS.
Y'ALL ARE BEAUTIFUL PEOPLE, BUT I JUST CAN'T BE HERE LIKE THIS ANY-MORE...

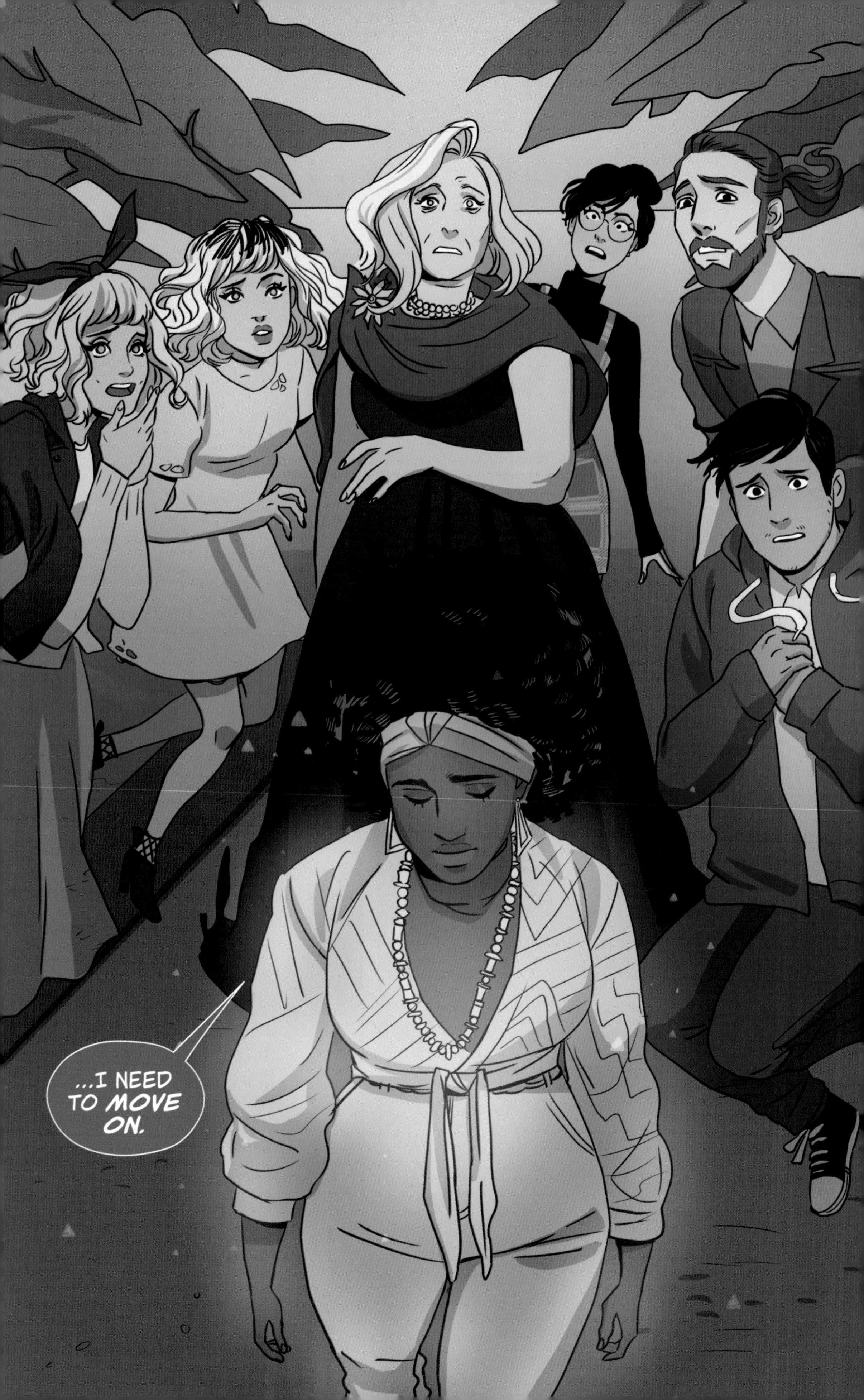
...I NEED TO MOVE ON.

Chapter Eight

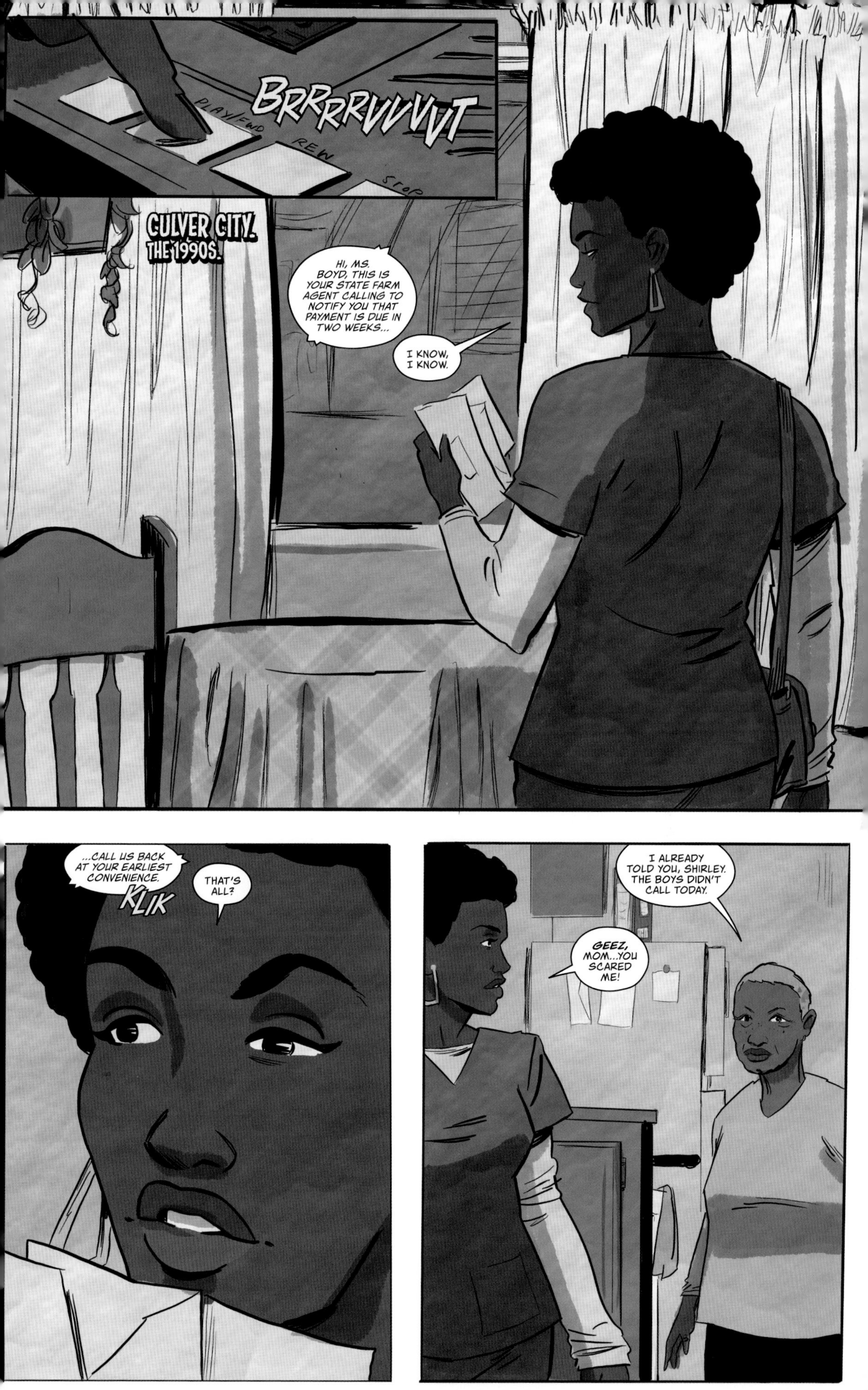
PLAY/FWD
REW
STOP
BRRRRVVVVVT
CULVER CITY. THE 1990S.
HI, MS. BOYD, THIS IS YOUR STATE FARM AGENT CALLING TO NOTIFY YOU THAT PAYMENT IS DUE IN TWO WEEKS...
I KNOW, I KNOW.
...CALL US BACK AT YOUR EARLIEST CONVENIENCE.
KLIK
THAT'S ALL?
I ALREADY TOLD YOU, SHIRLEY. THE BOYS DIDN'T CALL TODAY.
GEEZ, MOM...YOU SCARED ME!

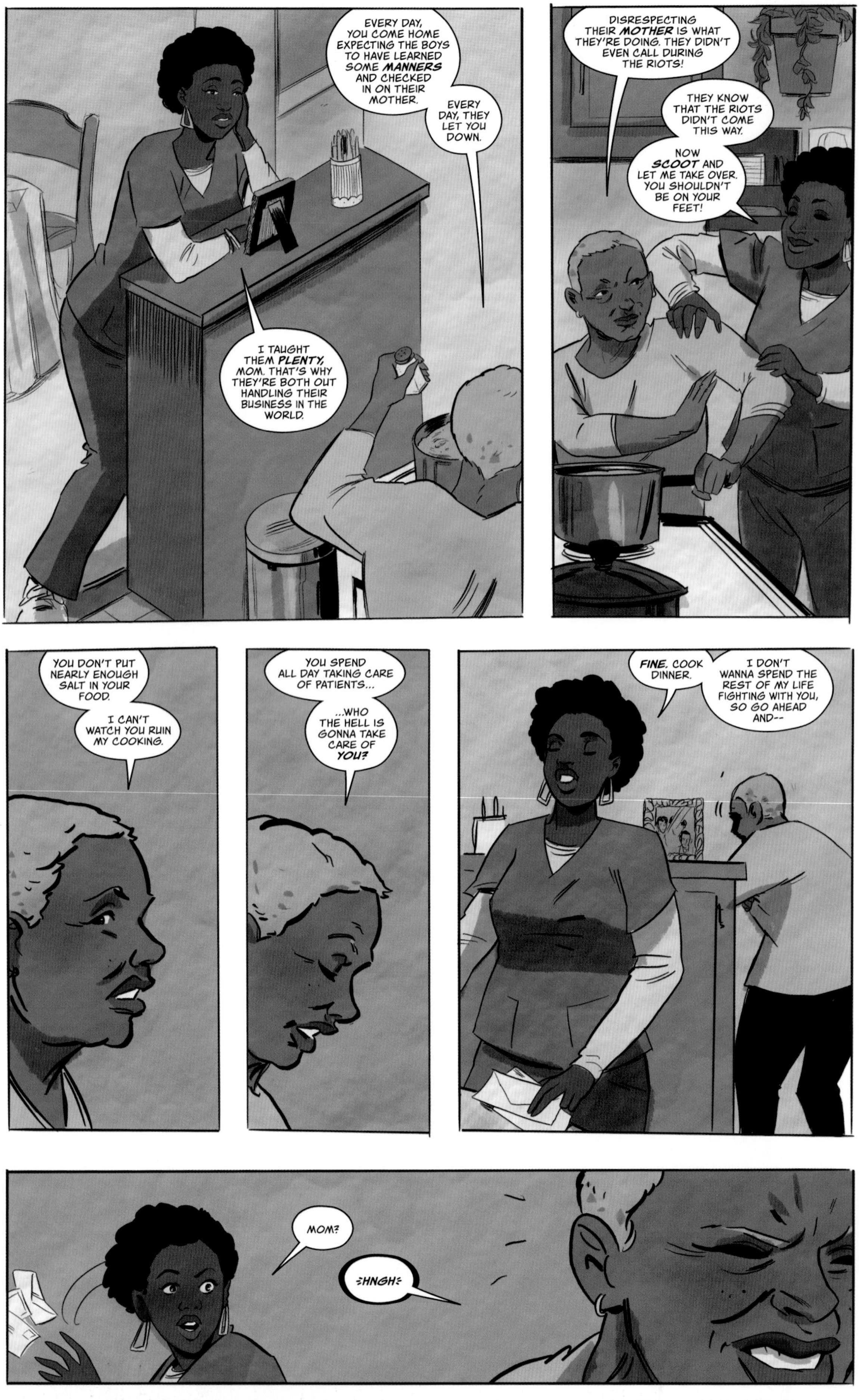
EVERY DAY, YOU COME HOME EXPECTING THE BOYS TO HAVE LEARNED SOME MANNERS AND CHECKED IN ON THEIR MOTHER.
EVERY DAY, THEY LET YOU DOWN.
I TAUGHT THEM PLENTY, MOM. THAT'S WHY THEY'RE BOTH OUT HANDLING THEIR BUSINESS IN THE WORLD.
DISRESPECTING THEIR MOTHER IS WHAT THEY'RE DOING. THEY DIDN'T EVEN CALL DURING THE RIOTS!
THEY KNOW THAT THE RIOTS DIDN'T COME THIS WAY.
NOW SCOOT AND LET ME TAKE OVER. YOU SHOULDN'T BE ON YOUR FEET!
YOU DON'T PUT NEARLY ENOUGH SALT IN YOUR FOOD.
I CAN'T WATCH YOU RUIN MY COOKING.
YOU SPEND ALL DAY TAKING CARE OF PATIENTS...
...WHO THE HELL IS GONNA TAKE CARE OF YOU?
FINE. COOK DINNER.
I DON'T WANNA SPEND THE REST OF MY LIFE FIGHTING WITH YOU, SO GO AHEAD AND--
MOM?
HNGH

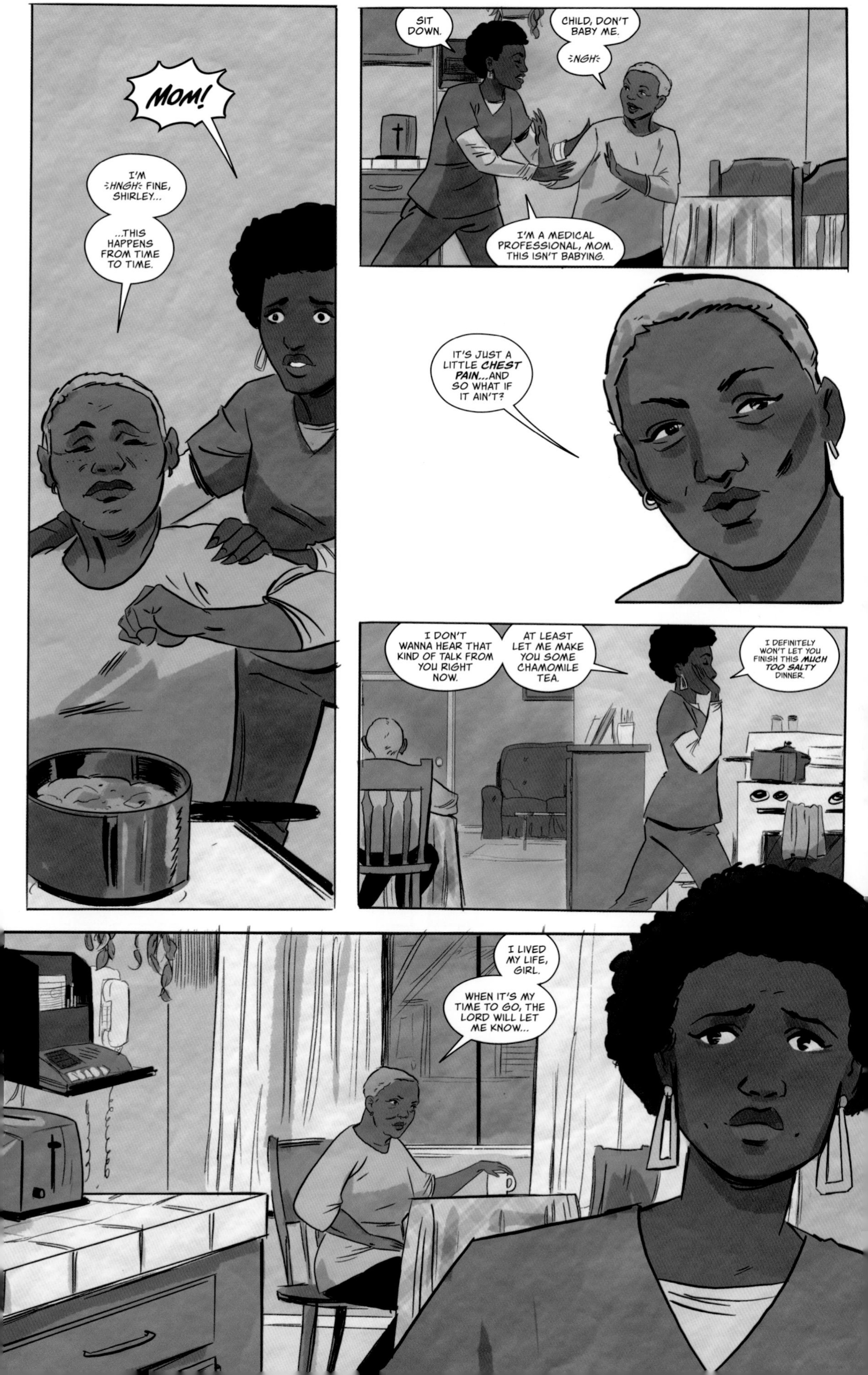
MOM!
I'M ~HNGH~ FINE, SHIRLEY...
...THIS HAPPENS FROM TIME TO TIME.
SIT DOWN.
CHILD, DON'T BABY ME.
~NGH~
I'M A MEDICAL PROFESSIONAL, MOM. THIS ISN'T BABYING.
IT'S JUST A LITTLE CHEST PAIN...AND SO WHAT IF IT AIN'T?
I DON'T WANNA HEAR THAT KIND OF TALK FROM YOU RIGHT NOW.
AT LEAST LET ME MAKE YOU SOME CHAMOMILE TEA.
I DEFINITELY WON'T LET YOU FINISH THIS MUCH TOO SALTY DINNER.
I LIVED MY LIFE, GIRL.
WHEN IT'S MY TIME TO GO, THE LORD WILL LET ME KNOW...

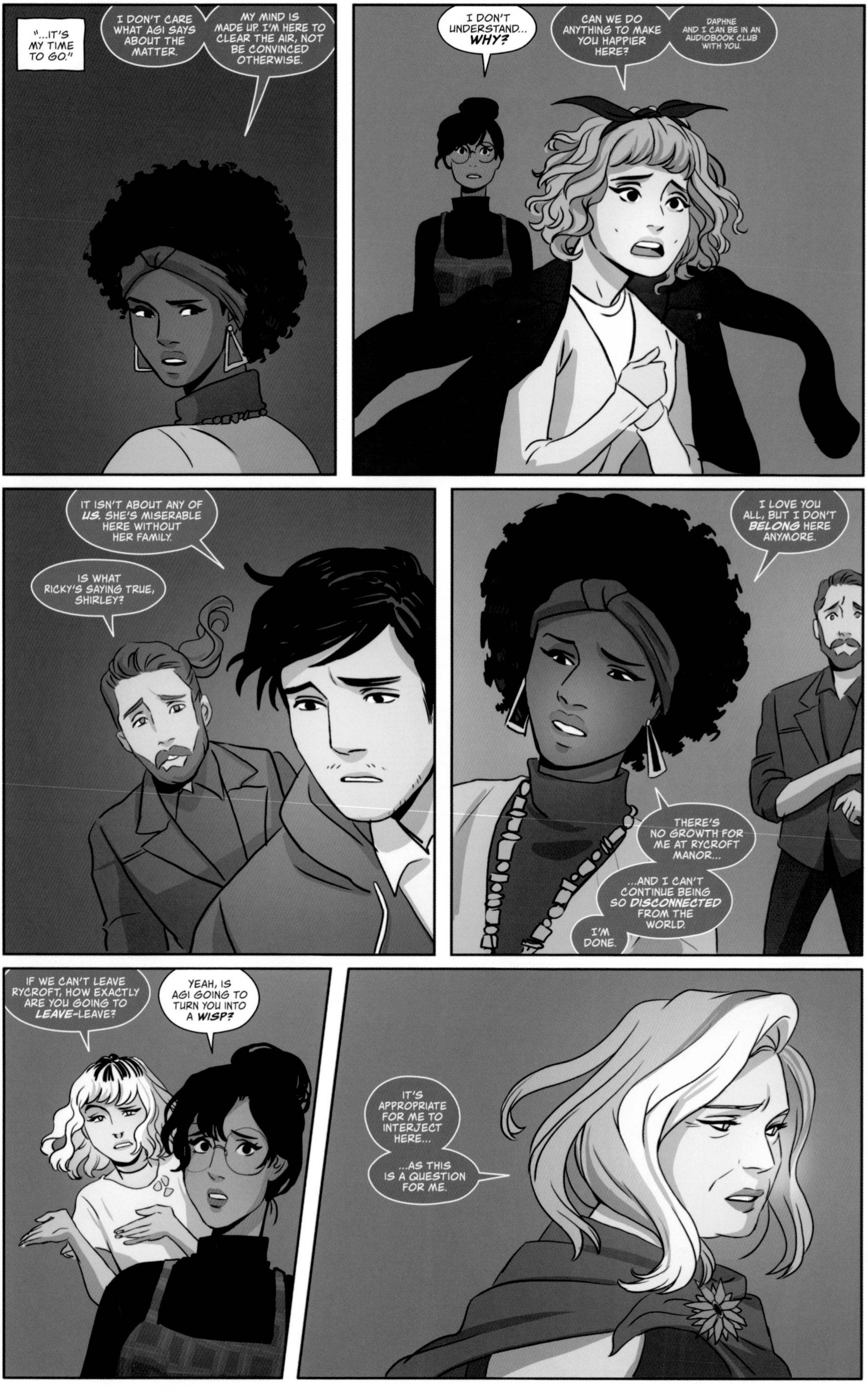
"...IT'S MY TIME TO GO."
I DON'T CARE WHAT AGI SAYS ABOUT THE MATTER.
MY MIND IS MADE UP. I'M HERE TO CLEAR THE AIR, NOT BE CONVINCED OTHERWISE.
I DON'T UNDERSTAND... WHY?
CAN WE DO ANYTHING TO MAKE YOU HAPPIER HERE?
DAPHNE AND I CAN BE IN AN AUDIOBOOK CLUB WITH YOU.
IT ISN'T ABOUT ANY OF US. SHE'S MISERABLE HERE WITHOUT HER FAMILY.
IS WHAT RICKY'S SAYING TRUE, SHIRLEY?
I LOVE YOU ALL, BUT I DON'T BELONG HERE ANYMORE.
THERE'S NO GROWTH FOR ME AT RYCROFT MANOR...
...AND I CAN'T CONTINUE BEING SO DISCONNECTED FROM THE WORLD.
I'M DONE.
IF WE CAN'T LEAVE RYCROFT, HOW EXACTLY ARE YOU GOING TO LEAVE-LEAVE?
YEAH, IS AGI GOING TO TURN YOU INTO A WISP?
IT'S APPROPRIATE FOR ME TO INTERJECT HERE...
...AS THIS IS A QUESTION FOR ME.

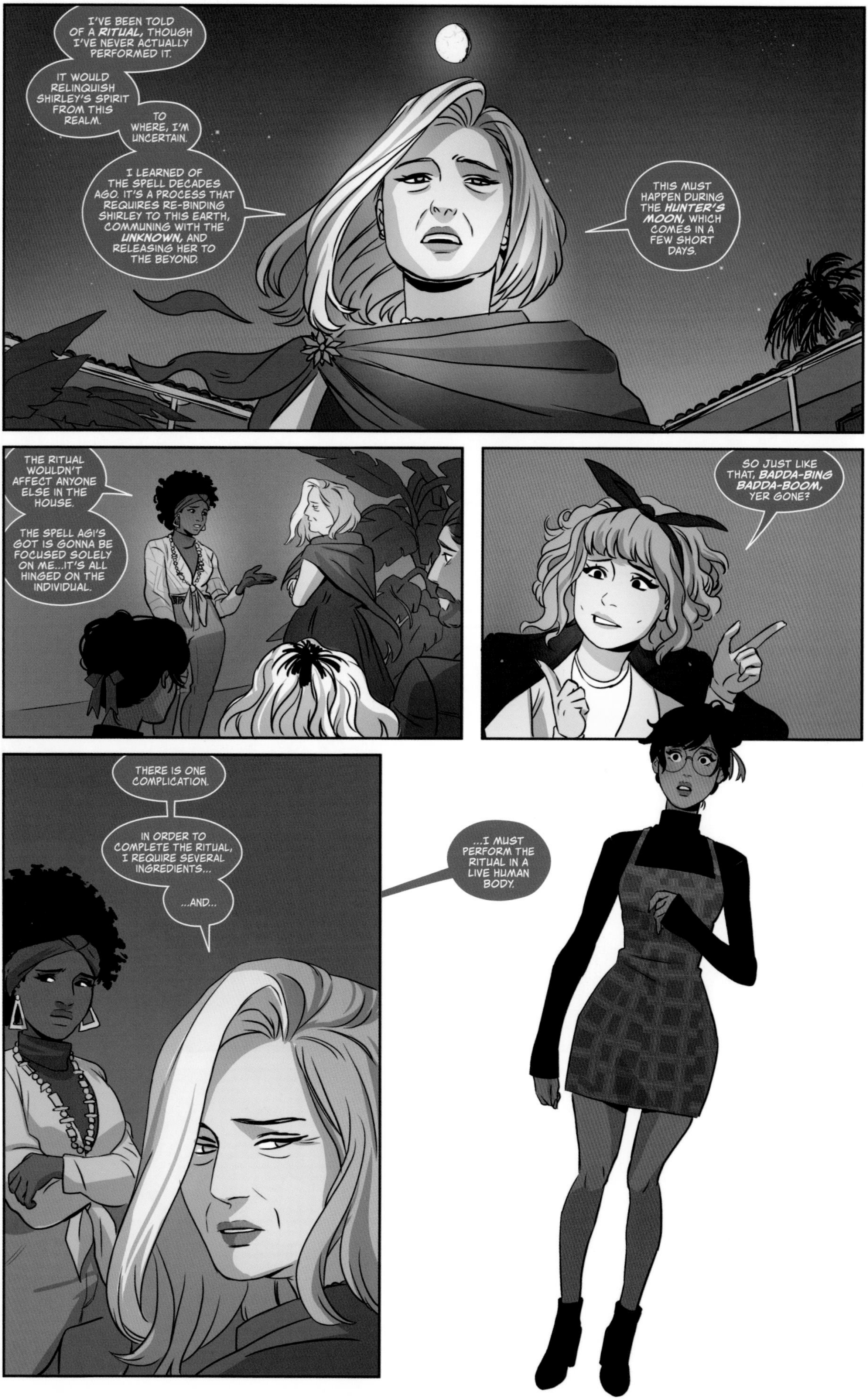
I'VE BEEN TOLD OF A RITUAL, THOUGH I'VE NEVER ACTUALLY PERFORMED IT.
IT WOULD RELINQUISH SHIRLEY'S SPIRIT FROM THIS REALM.
TO WHERE, I'M UNCERTAIN.
I LEARNED OF THE SPELL DECADES AGO. IT'S A PROCESS THAT REQUIRES RE-BINDING SHIRLEY TO THIS EARTH, COMMUNING WITH THE UNKNOWN, AND RELEASING HER TO THE BEYOND.
THIS MUST HAPPEN DURING THE HUNTER'S MOON, WHICH COMES IN A FEW SHORT DAYS.
THE RITUAL WOULDN'T AFFECT ANYONE ELSE IN THE HOUSE.
THE SPELL AGI'S GOT IS GONNA BE FOCUSED SOLELY ON ME...IT'S ALL HINGED ON THE INDIVIDUAL.
SO JUST LIKE THAT, BADDA-BING BADDA-BOOM, YER GONE?
THERE IS ONE COMPLICATION.
IN ORDER TO COMPLETE THE RITUAL, I REQUIRE SEVERAL INGREDIENTS...
...AND...
...I MUST PERFORM THE RITUAL IN A LIVE HUMAN BODY.

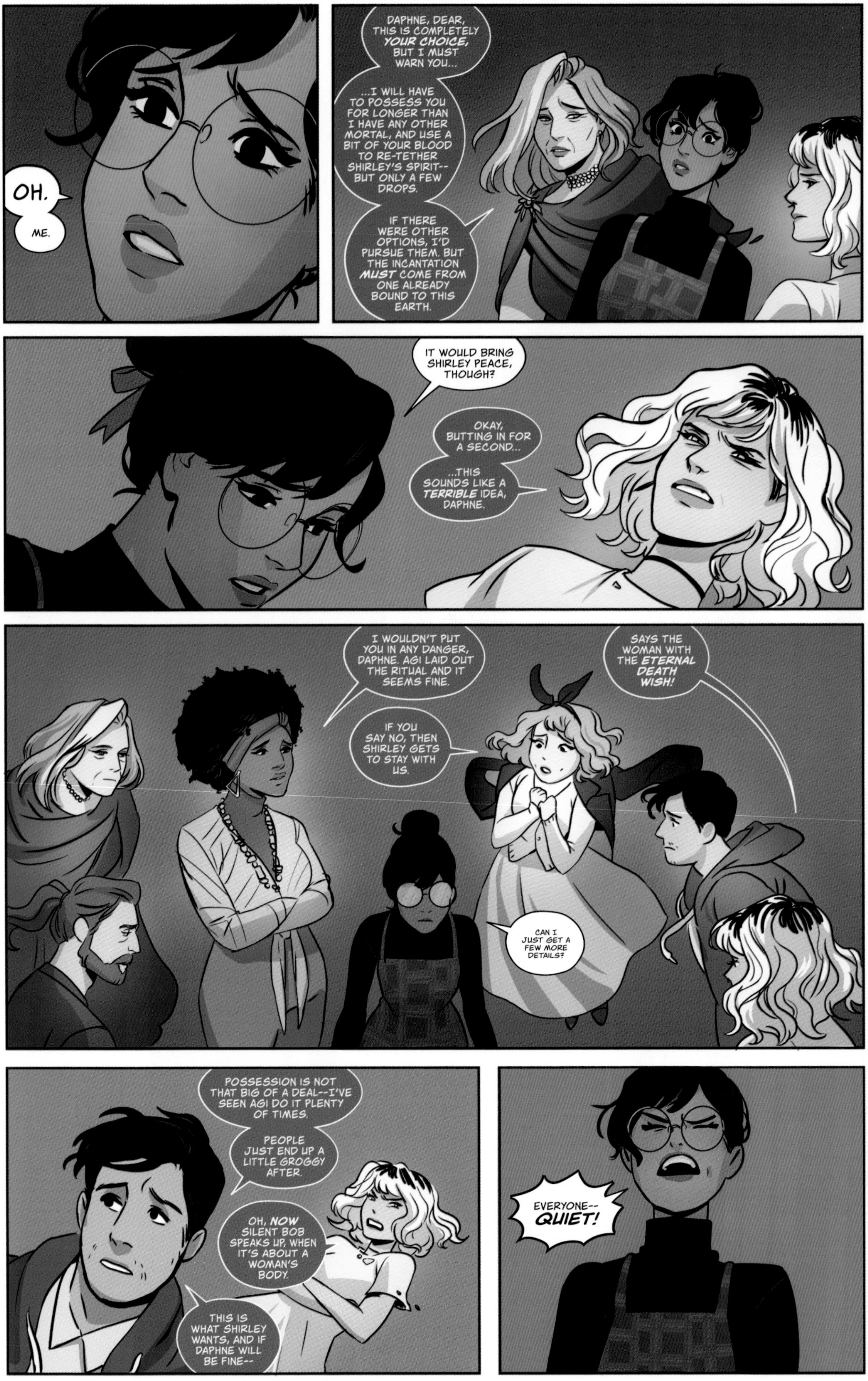
OH.
ME.
DAPHNE, DEAR, THIS IS COMPLETELY YOUR CHOICE, BUT I MUST WARN YOU...
...I WILL HAVE TO POSSESS YOU FOR LONGER THAN I HAVE ANY OTHER MORTAL, AND USE A BIT OF YOUR BLOOD TO RE-TETHER SHIRLEY'S SPIRIT-- BUT ONLY A FEW DROPS.
IF THERE WERE OTHER OPTIONS, I'D PURSUE THEM. BUT THE INCANTATION MUST COME FROM ONE ALREADY BOUND TO THIS EARTH.
IT WOULD BRING SHIRLEY PEACE, THOUGH?
OKAY, BUTTING IN FOR A SECOND...
...THIS SOUNDS LIKE A TERRIBLE IDEA, DAPHNE.
I WOULDN'T PUT YOU IN ANY DANGER, DAPHNE. AGI LAID OUT THE RITUAL AND IT SEEMS FINE.
SAYS THE WOMAN WITH THE ETERNAL DEATH WISH!
IF YOU SAY NO, THEN SHIRLEY GETS TO STAY WITH US.
CAN I JUST GET A FEW MORE DETAILS?
POSSESSION IS NOT THAT BIG OF A DEAL--I'VE SEEN AGI DO IT PLENTY OF TIMES.
PEOPLE JUST END UP A LITTLE GROGGY AFTER.
OH, NOW SILENT BOB SPEAKS UP, WHEN IT'S ABOUT A WOMAN'S BODY.
THIS IS WHAT SHIRLEY WANTS, AND IF DAPHNE WILL BE FINE--
EVERYONE-- QUIET!

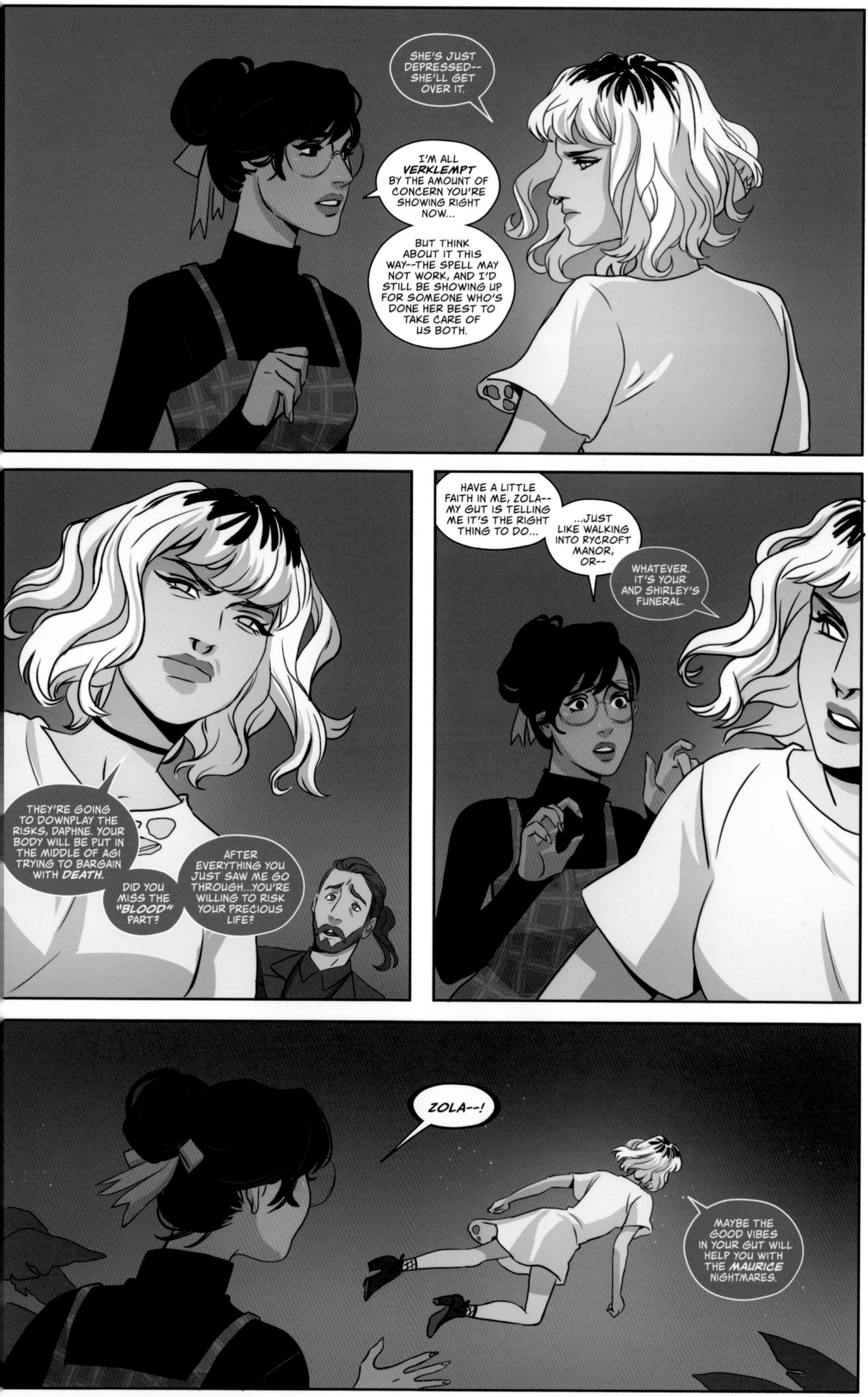
SHE'S JUST DEPRESSED-- SHE'LL GET OVER IT.
I'M ALL *VERKLEMPT* BY THE AMOUNT OF CONCERN YOU'RE SHOWING RIGHT NOW...
BUT THINK ABOUT IT THIS WAY--THE SPELL MAY NOT WORK, AND I'D STILL BE SHOWING UP FOR SOMEONE WHO'S DONE HER BEST TO TAKE CARE OF US BOTH.
THEY'RE GOING TO DOWNPLAY THE RISKS, DAPHNE. YOUR BODY WILL BE PUT IN THE MIDDLE OF AGI TRYING TO BARGAIN WITH *DEATH.*
DID YOU MISS THE *"BLOOD"* PART?
AFTER EVERYTHING YOU JUST SAW ME GO THROUGH...YOU'RE WILLING TO RISK YOUR PRECIOUS LIFE?
HAVE A LITTLE FAITH IN ME, ZOLA-- MY GUT IS TELLING ME IT'S THE RIGHT THING TO DO...
...JUST LIKE WALKING INTO RYCROFT MANOR, OR--
WHATEVER. IT'S YOUR AND SHIRLEY'S FUNERAL.
ZOLA--!
MAYBE THE GOOD VIBES IN YOUR GUT WILL HELP YOU WITH THE *MAURICE* NIGHTMARES.

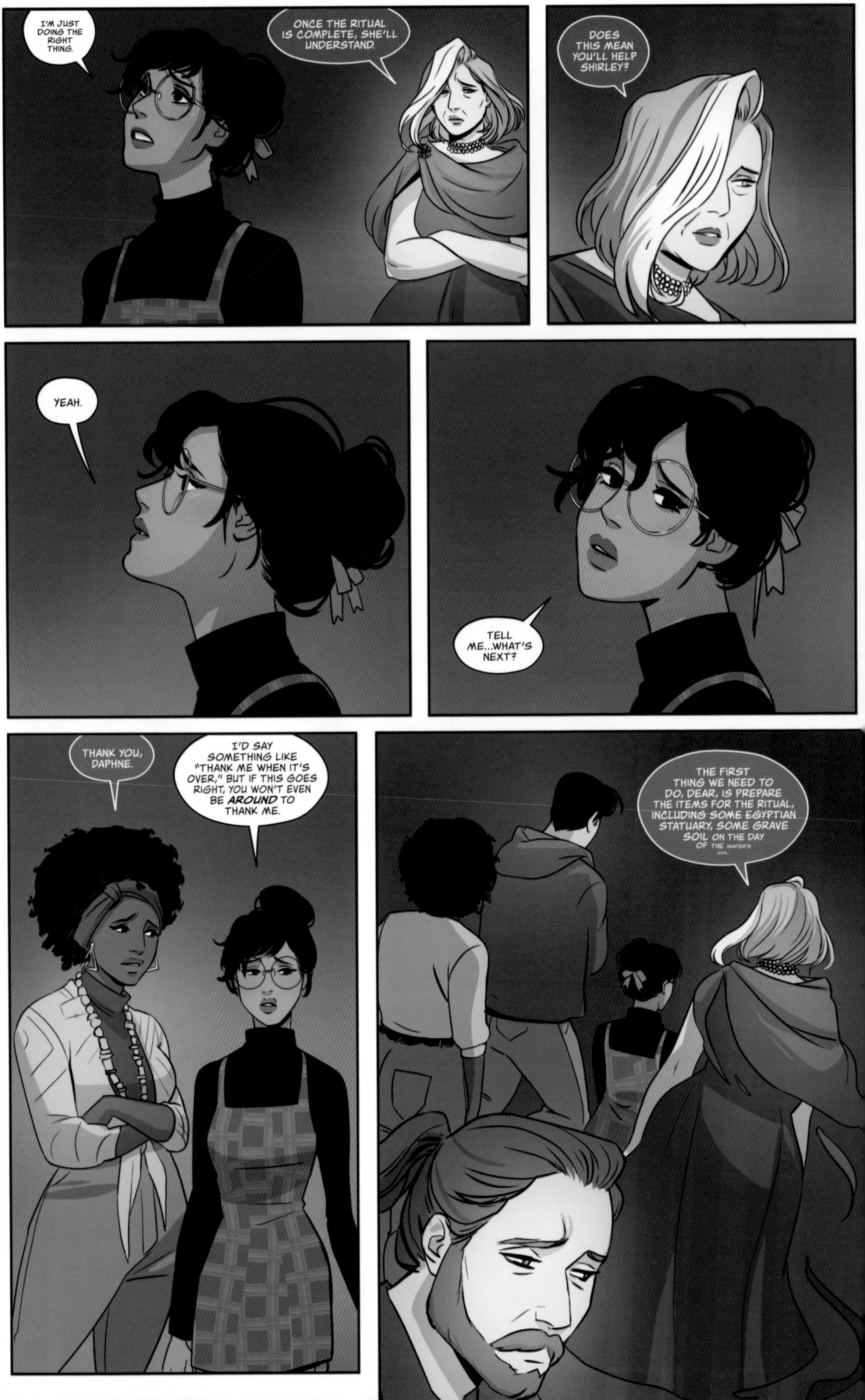
I'M JUST DOING THE RIGHT THING.
ONCE THE RITUAL IS COMPLETE, SHE'LL UNDERSTAND.
DOES THIS MEAN YOU'LL HELP SHIRLEY?
YEAH.
TELL ME...WHAT'S NEXT?
THANK YOU, DAPHNE.
I'D SAY SOMETHING LIKE "THANK ME WHEN IT'S OVER," BUT IF THIS GOES RIGHT, YOU WON'T EVEN BE *AROUND* TO THANK ME.
THE FIRST THING WE NEED TO DO, DEAR, IS PREPARE THE ITEMS FOR THE RITUAL, INCLUDING SOME EGYPTIAN STATUARY, SOME GRAVE SOIL ON THE DAY OF THE HUNTER'S

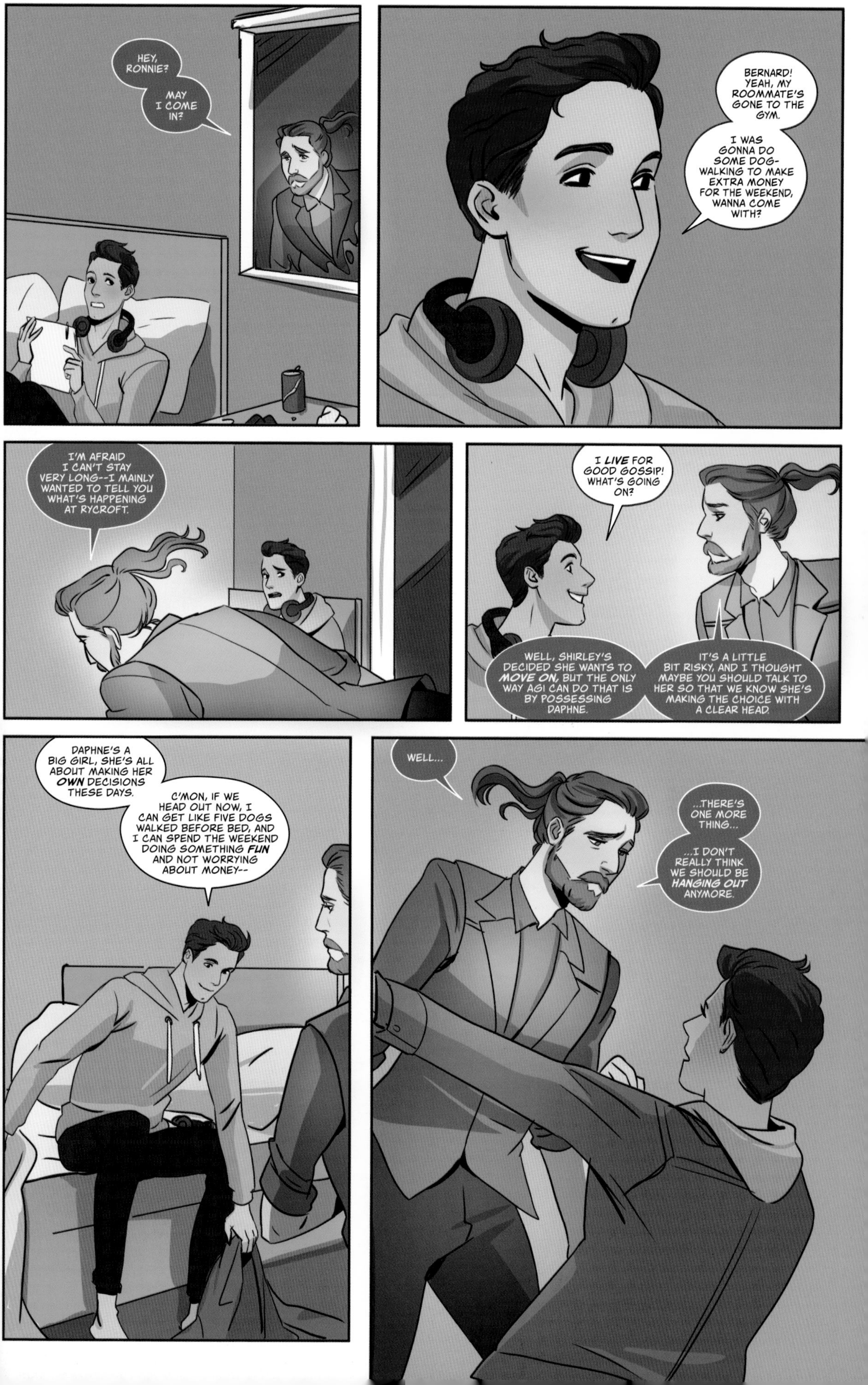
HEY, RONNIE?
MAY I COME IN?
BERNARD! YEAH, MY ROOMMATE'S GONE TO THE GYM.
I WAS GONNA DO SOME DOG-WALKING TO MAKE EXTRA MONEY FOR THE WEEKEND, WANNA COME WITH?
I'M AFRAID I CAN'T STAY VERY LONG--I MAINLY WANTED TO TELL YOU WHAT'S HAPPENING AT RYCROFT.
I LIVE FOR GOOD GOSSIP! WHAT'S GOING ON?
WELL, SHIRLEY'S DECIDED SHE WANTS TO MOVE ON, BUT THE ONLY WAY AGI CAN DO THAT IS BY POSSESSING DAPHNE.
IT'S A LITTLE BIT RISKY, AND I THOUGHT MAYBE YOU SHOULD TALK TO HER SO THAT WE KNOW SHE'S MAKING THE CHOICE WITH A CLEAR HEAD.
DAPHNE'S A BIG GIRL, SHE'S ALL ABOUT MAKING HER OWN DECISIONS THESE DAYS.
C'MON, IF WE HEAD OUT NOW, I CAN GET LIKE FIVE DOGS WALKED BEFORE BED, AND I CAN SPEND THE WEEKEND DOING SOMETHING FUN AND NOT WORRYING ABOUT MONEY--
WELL...
...THERE'S ONE MORE THING...
...I DON'T REALLY THINK WE SHOULD BE HANGING OUT ANYMORE.

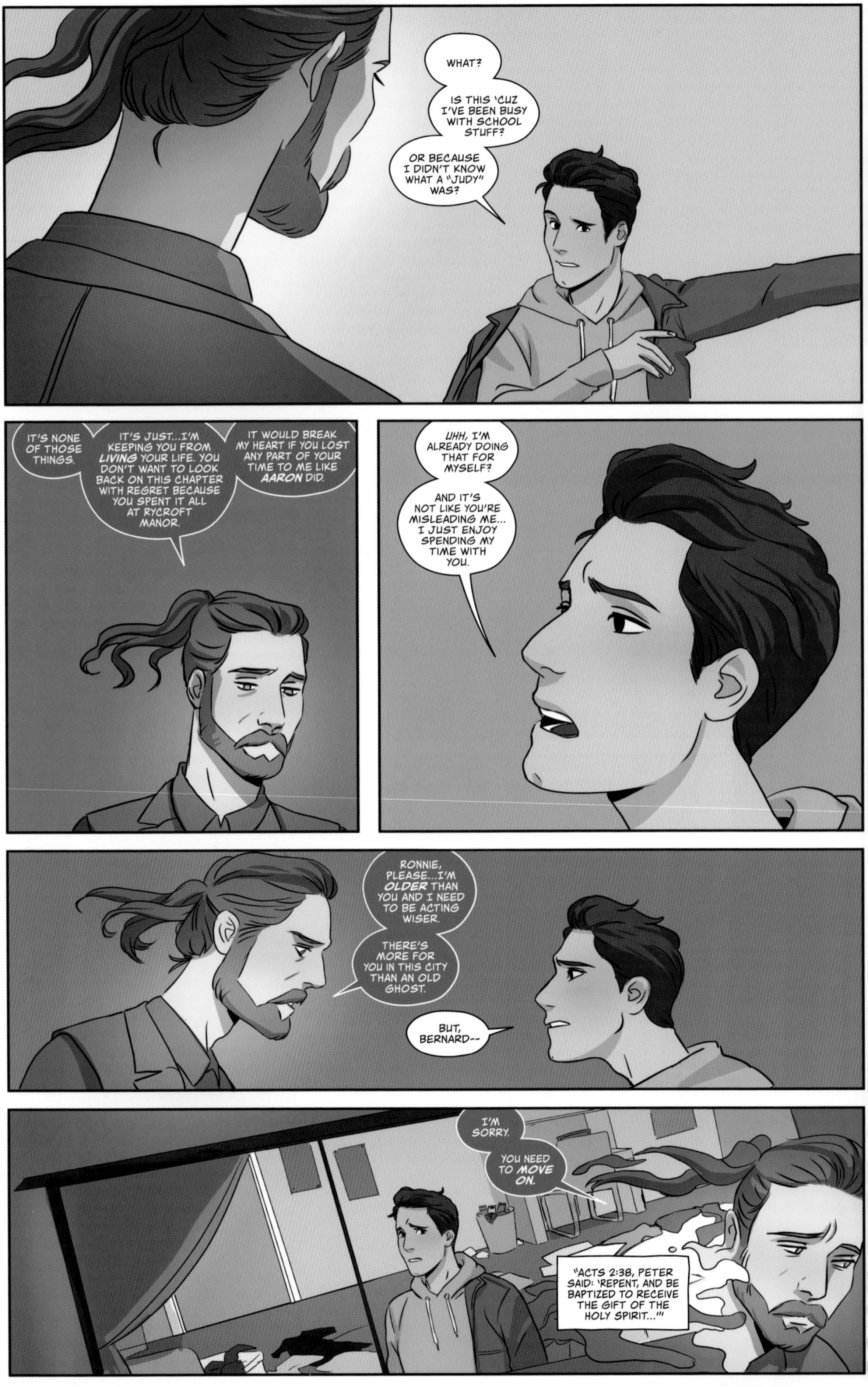
WHAT?
IS THIS 'CUZ I'VE BEEN BUSY WITH SCHOOL STUFF?
OR BECAUSE I DIDN'T KNOW WHAT A "JUDY" WAS?
IT'S NONE OF THOSE THINGS.
IT'S JUST...I'M KEEPING YOU FROM LIVING YOUR LIFE. YOU DON'T WANT TO LOOK BACK ON THIS CHAPTER WITH REGRET BECAUSE YOU SPENT IT ALL AT RYCROFT MANOR.
IT WOULD BREAK MY HEART IF YOU LOST ANY PART OF YOUR TIME TO ME LIKE AARON DID.
UHH, I'M ALREADY DOING THAT FOR MYSELF?
AND IT'S NOT LIKE YOU'RE MISLEADING ME... I JUST ENJOY SPENDING MY TIME WITH YOU.
RONNIE, PLEASE...I'M OLDER THAN YOU AND I NEED TO BE ACTING WISER.
THERE'S MORE FOR YOU IN THIS CITY THAN AN OLD GHOST.
BUT, BERNARD--
I'M SORRY.
YOU NEED TO MOVE ON.
"ACTS 2:38, PETER SAID: 'REPENT, AND BE BAPTIZED TO RECEIVE THE GIFT OF THE HOLY SPIRIT...'"

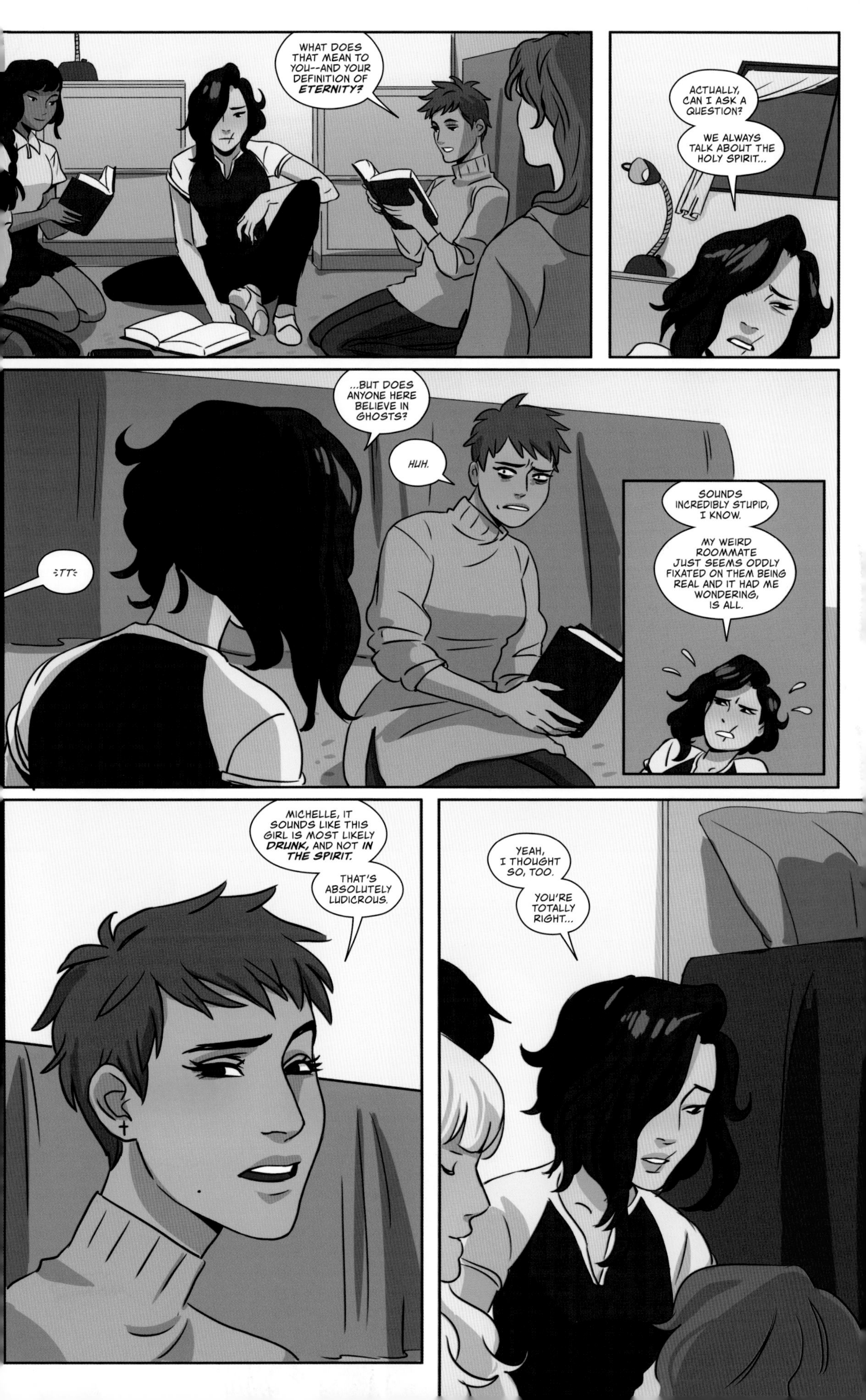
WHAT DOES THAT MEAN TO YOU--AND YOUR DEFINITION OF ETERNITY?
ACTUALLY, CAN I ASK A QUESTION?
WE ALWAYS TALK ABOUT THE HOLY SPIRIT...
...BUT DOES ANYONE HERE BELIEVE IN GHOSTS?
HUH.
TT
SOUNDS INCREDIBLY STUPID, I KNOW.
MY WEIRD ROOMMATE JUST SEEMS ODDLY FIXATED ON THEM BEING REAL AND IT HAD ME WONDERING, IS ALL.
MICHELLE, IT SOUNDS LIKE THIS GIRL IS MOST LIKELY DRUNK, AND NOT IN THE SPIRIT.
THAT'S ABSOLUTELY LUDICROUS.
YEAH, I THOUGHT SO, TOO.
YOU'RE TOTALLY RIGHT...

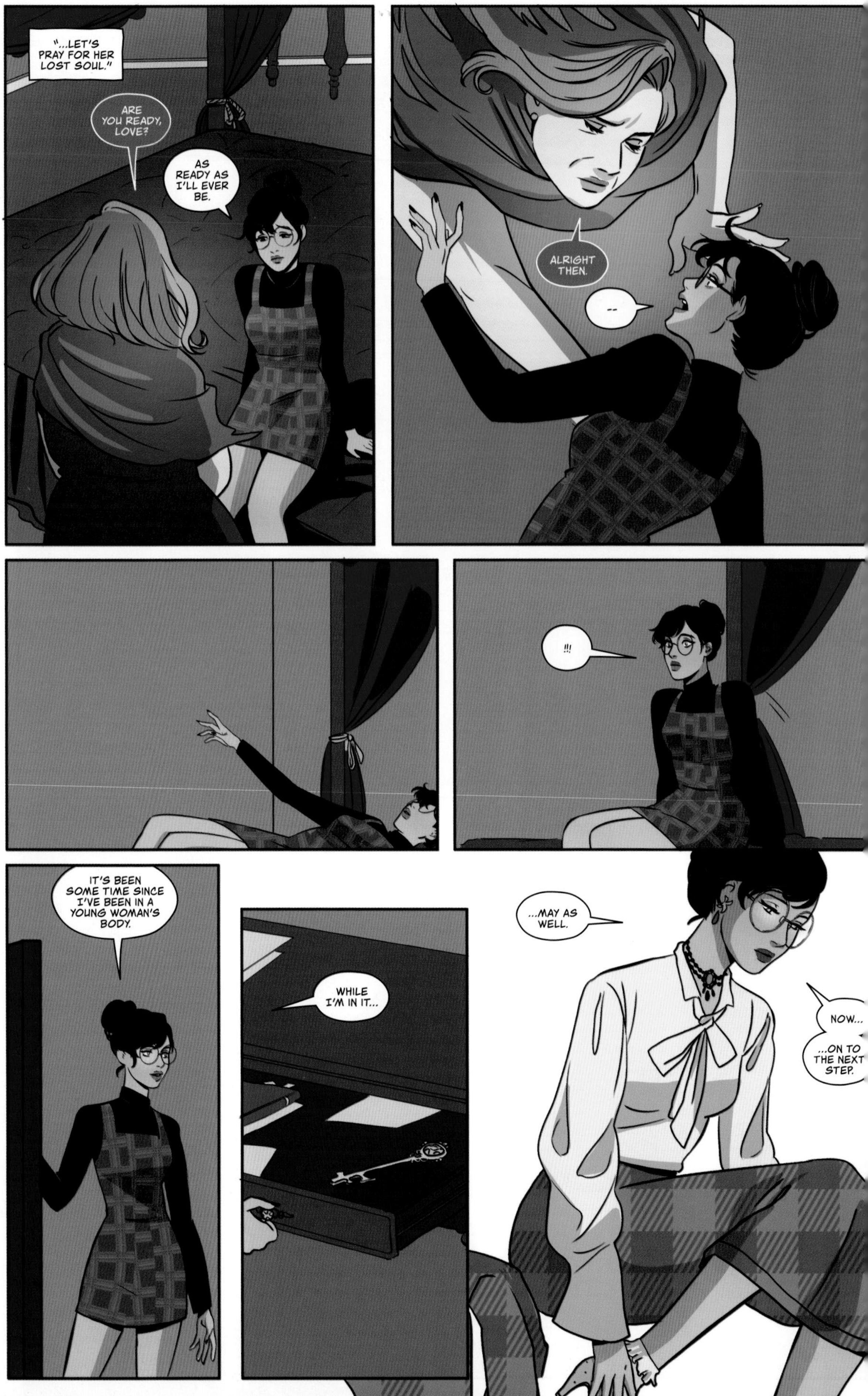
"...LET'S PRAY FOR HER LOST SOUL."
ARE YOU READY, LOVE?
AS READY AS I'LL EVER BE.
ALRIGHT THEN.
--
!!!
IT'S BEEN SOME TIME SINCE I'VE BEEN IN A YOUNG WOMAN'S BODY.
WHILE I'M IN IT...
...MAY AS WELL.
NOW...
...ON TO THE NEXT STEP.

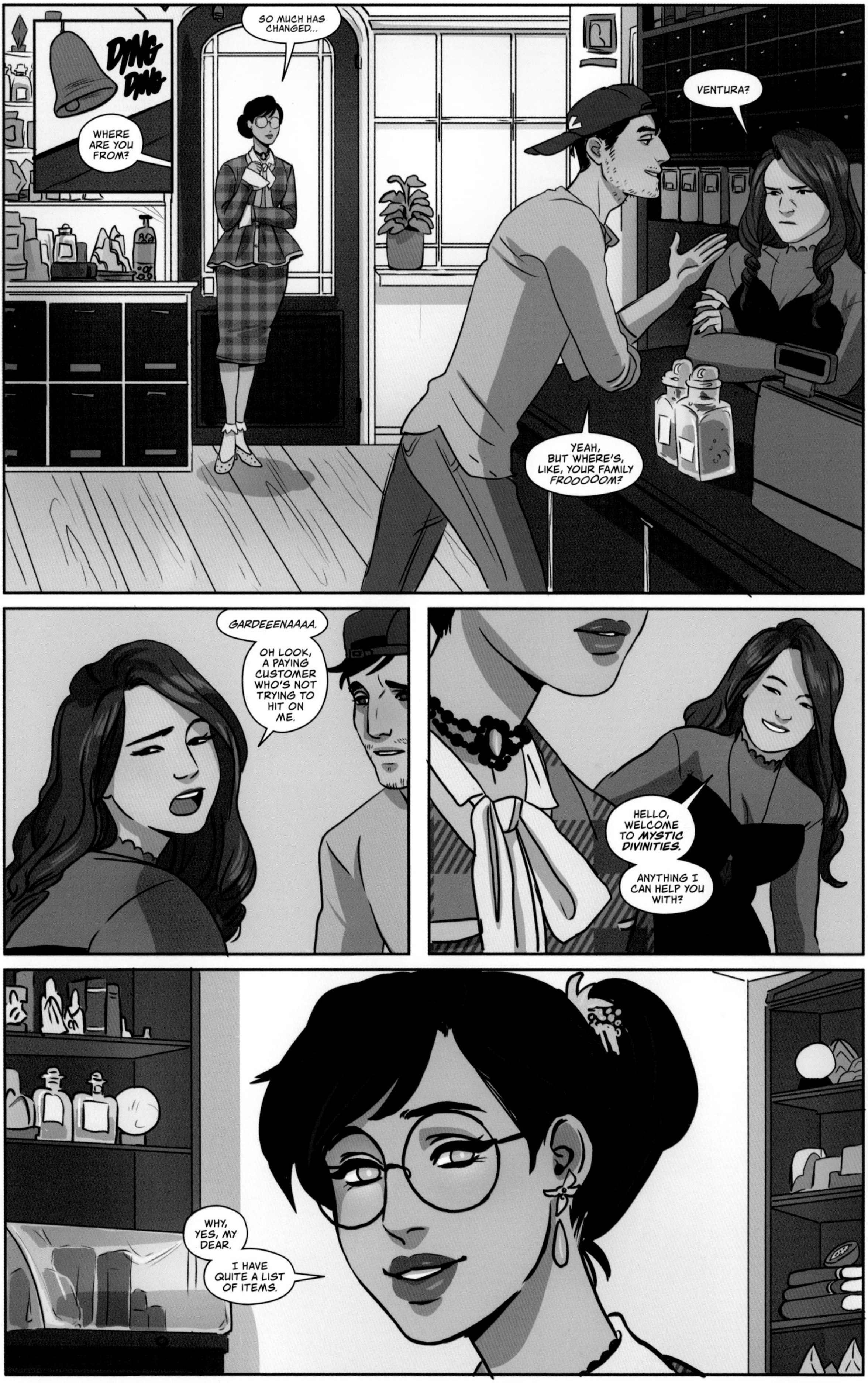
DING DING
WHERE ARE YOU FROM?
SO MUCH HAS CHANGED...
VENTURA?
YEAH, BUT WHERE'S, LIKE, YOUR FAMILY FROOOOOM?
GARDEEENAAAA.
OH LOOK, A PAYING CUSTOMER WHO'S NOT TRYING TO HIT ON ME.
HELLO, WELCOME TO MYSTIC DIVINITIES.
ANYTHING I CAN HELP YOU WITH?
WHY, YES, MY DEAR.
I HAVE QUITE A LIST OF ITEMS.

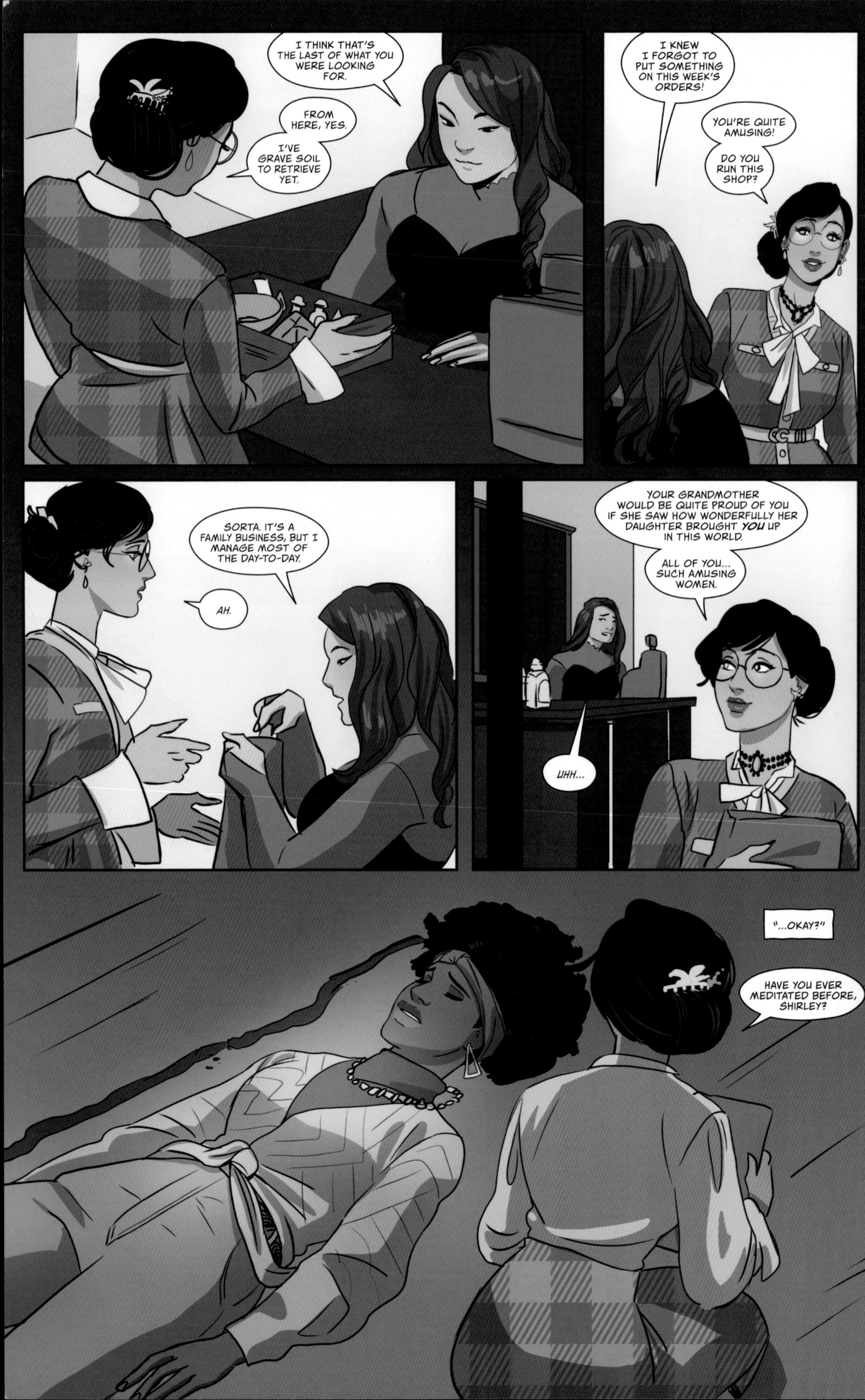
I THINK THAT'S THE LAST OF WHAT YOU WERE LOOKING FOR.
FROM HERE, YES.
I'VE GRAVE SOIL TO RETRIEVE YET.
I KNEW I FORGOT TO PUT SOMETHING ON THIS WEEK'S ORDERS!
YOU'RE QUITE AMUSING!
DO YOU RUN THIS SHOP?
SORTA. IT'S A FAMILY BUSINESS, BUT I MANAGE MOST OF THE DAY-TO-DAY.
AH.
YOUR GRANDMOTHER WOULD BE QUITE PROUD OF YOU IF SHE SAW HOW WONDERFULLY HER DAUGHTER BROUGHT YOU UP IN THIS WORLD.
ALL OF YOU... SUCH AMUSING WOMEN.
UHH...
"...OKAY?"
HAVE YOU EVER MEDITATED BEFORE, SHIRLEY?

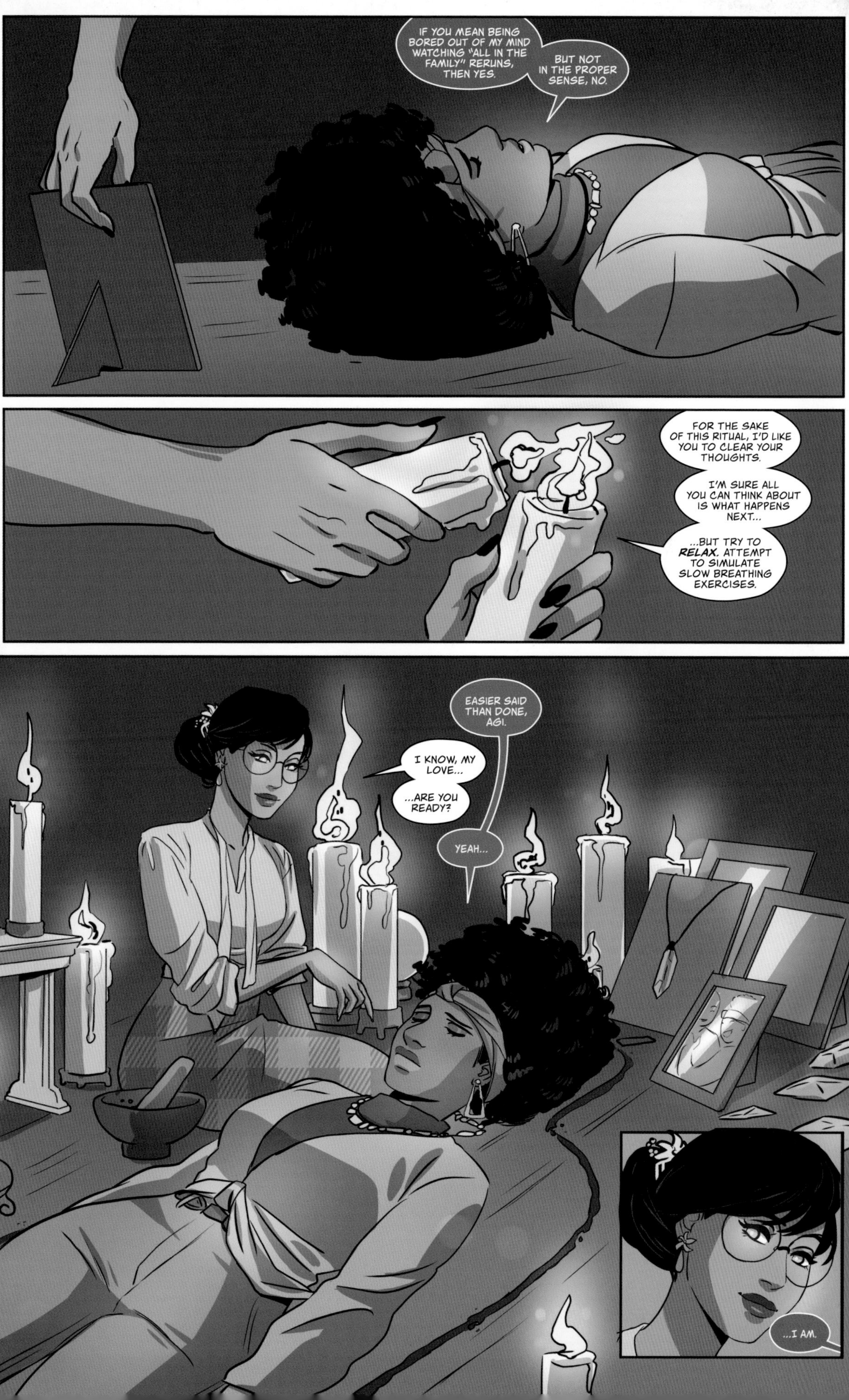
IF YOU MEAN BEING BORED OUT OF MY MIND WATCHING "ALL IN THE FAMILY" RERUNS, THEN YES.
BUT NOT IN THE PROPER SENSE, NO.
FOR THE SAKE OF THIS RITUAL, I'D LIKE YOU TO CLEAR YOUR THOUGHTS.
I'M SURE ALL YOU CAN THINK ABOUT IS WHAT HAPPENS NEXT...
...BUT TRY TO RELAX. ATTEMPT TO SIMULATE SLOW BREATHING EXERCISES.
EASIER SAID THAN DONE, AGI.
I KNOW, MY LOVE...
...ARE YOU READY?
YEAH...
...I AM.

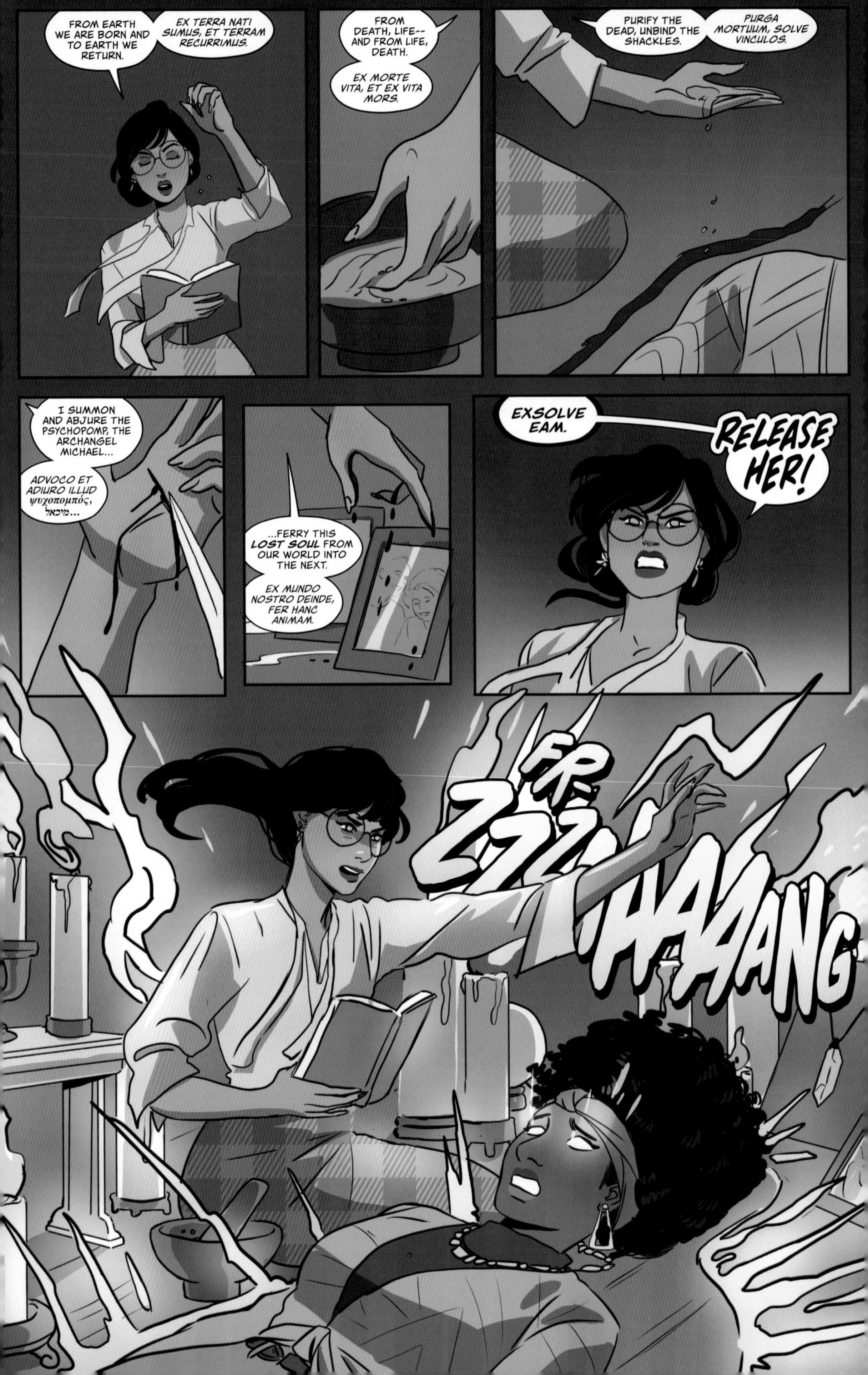

FROM EARTH WE ARE BORN AND TO EARTH WE RETURN.
EX TERRA NATI SUMUS, ET TERRAM RECURRIMUS.
FROM DEATH, LIFE-- AND FROM LIFE, DEATH.
EX MORTE VITA, ET EX VITA MORS.
PURIFY THE DEAD, UNBIND THE SHACKLES.
PURGA MORTUUM, SOLVE VINCULOS.
I SUMMON AND ABJURE THE PSYCHOPOMP, THE ARCHANGEL MICHAEL...
ADVOCO ET ADIURO ILLUD ψυχοπομπός, מיכאל...
...FERRY THIS **LOST SOUL** FROM OUR WORLD INTO THE NEXT.
EX MUNDO NOSTRO DEINDE, FER HANC ANIMAM.
EXSOLVE EAM.
RELEASE HER!
FR-ZZZAAAAANG

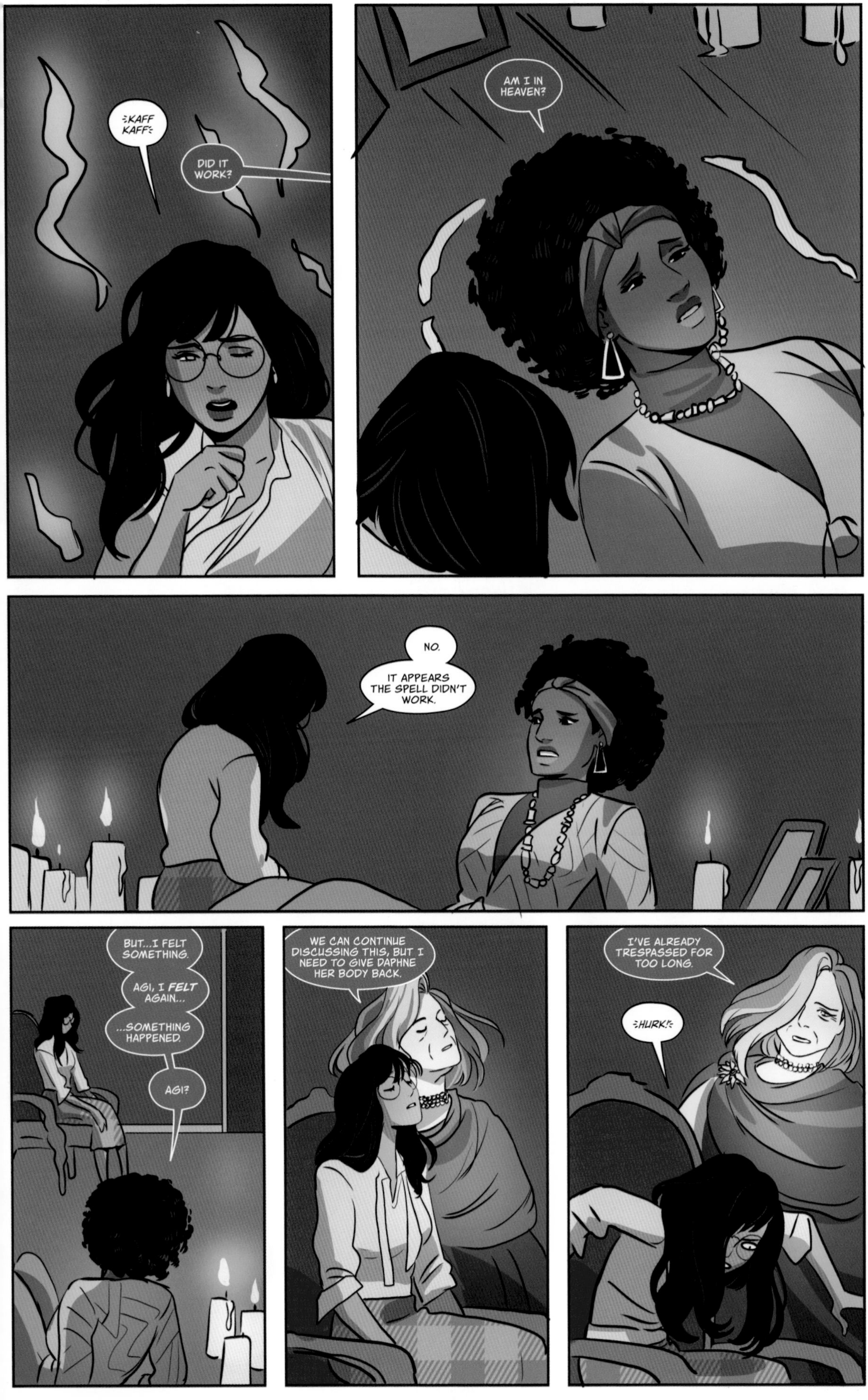
KAFF KAFF
DID IT WORK?
AM I IN HEAVEN?
NO.
IT APPEARS THE SPELL DIDN'T WORK.
BUT...I FELT SOMETHING.
AGI, I FELT AGAIN...
...SOMETHING HAPPENED.
AGI?
WE CAN CONTINUE DISCUSSING THIS, BUT I NEED TO GIVE DAPHNE HER BODY BACK.
I'VE ALREADY TRESPASSED FOR TOO LONG.
HURK!

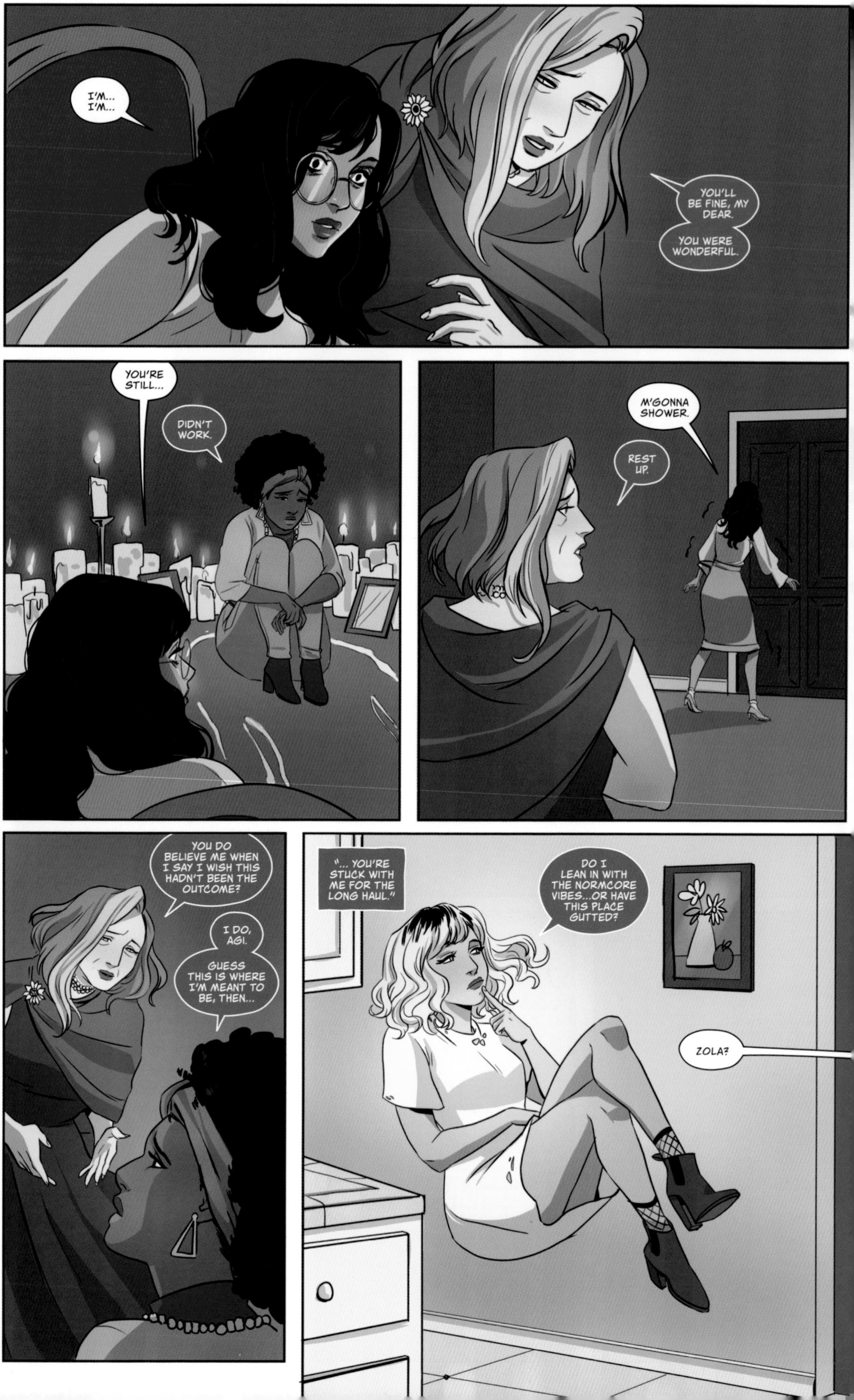

I'M... I'M...
YOU'LL BE FINE, MY DEAR.
YOU WERE WONDERFUL.
YOU'RE STILL...
DIDN'T WORK.
M'GONNA SHOWER.
REST UP.
YOU DO BELIEVE ME WHEN I SAY I WISH THIS HADN'T BEEN THE OUTCOME?
I DO, AGI.
GUESS THIS IS WHERE I'M MEANT TO BE, THEN...
"... YOU'RE STUCK WITH ME FOR THE LONG HAUL."
DO I LEAN IN WITH THE NORMCORE VIBES...OR HAVE THIS PLACE GUTTED?
ZOLA?

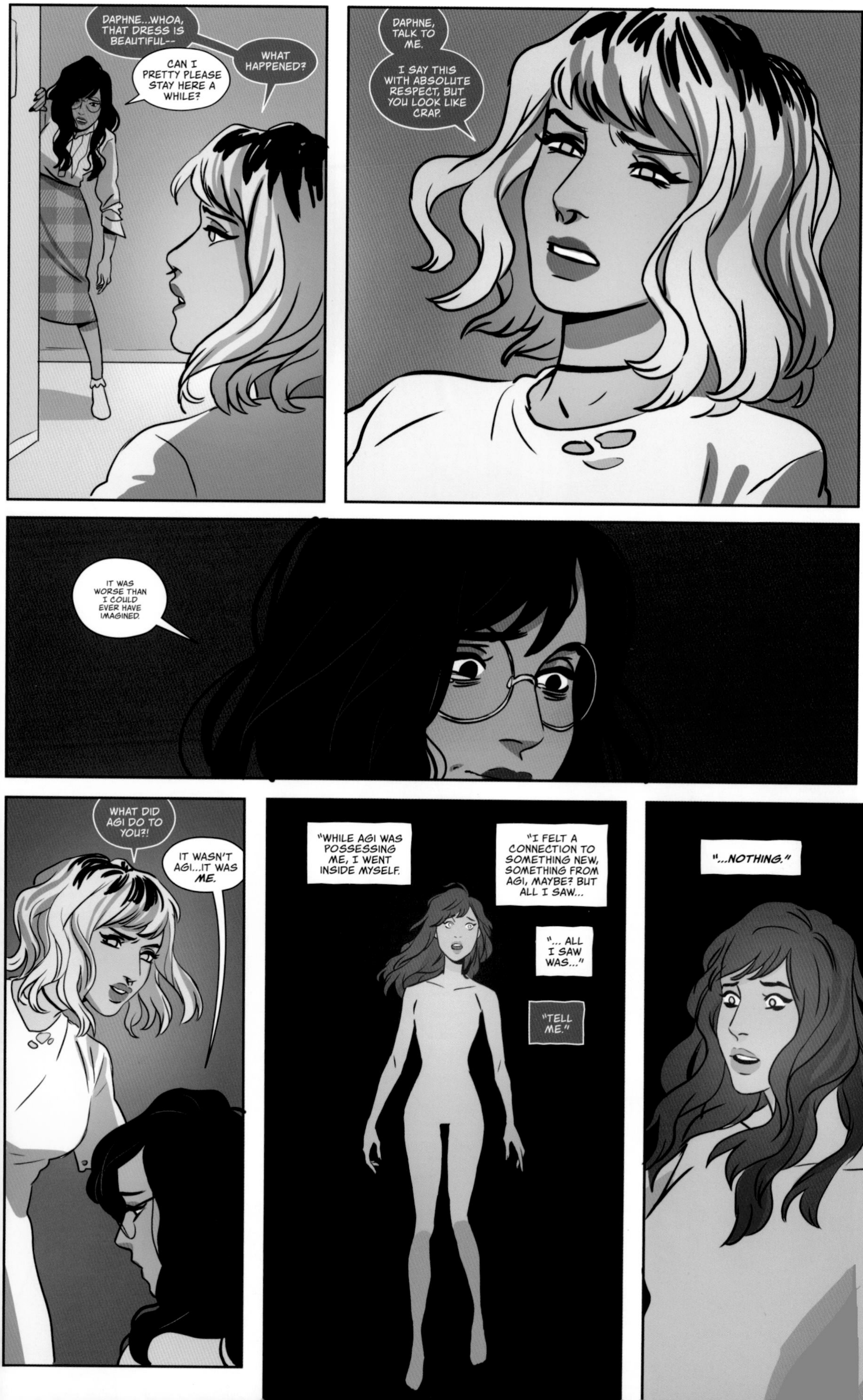
DAPHNE...WHOA, THAT DRESS IS BEAUTIFUL--
CAN I PRETTY PLEASE STAY HERE A WHILE?
WHAT HAPPENED?
DAPHNE, TALK TO ME.
I SAY THIS WITH ABSOLUTE RESPECT, BUT YOU LOOK LIKE CRAP.
IT WAS WORSE THAN I COULD EVER HAVE IMAGINED.
WHAT DID AGI DO TO YOU?!
IT WASN'T AGI...IT WAS ME.
"WHILE AGI WAS POSSESSING ME, I WENT INSIDE MYSELF.
"I FELT A CONNECTION TO SOMETHING NEW, SOMETHING FROM AGI, MAYBE? BUT ALL I SAW...
"... ALL I SAW WAS..."
"TELL ME."
"...NOTHING."

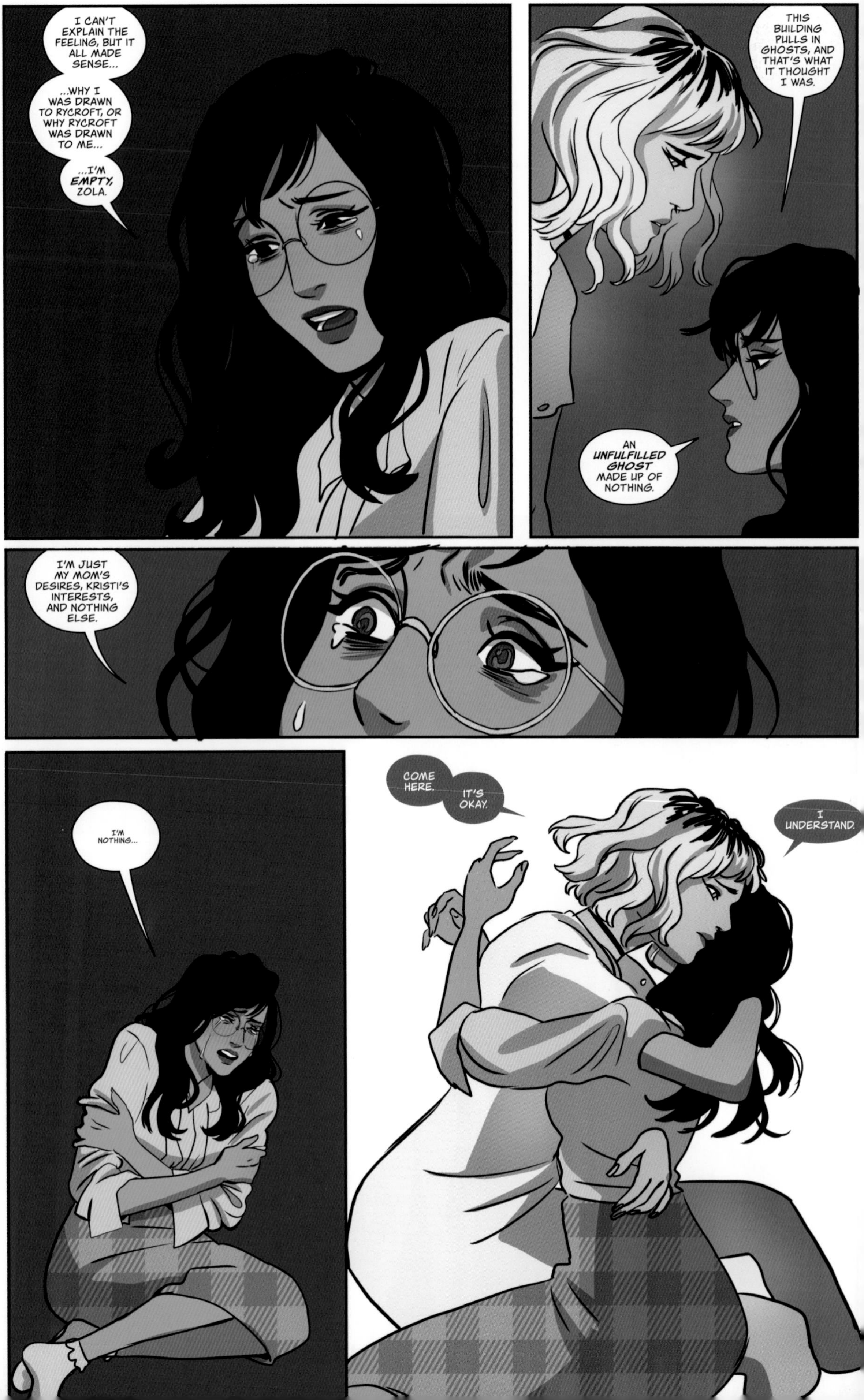
I CAN'T EXPLAIN THE FEELING, BUT IT ALL MADE SENSE...
...WHY I WAS DRAWN TO RYCROFT, OR WHY RYCROFT WAS DRAWN TO ME...
...I'M *EMPTY*, ZOLA.
THIS BUILDING PULLS IN GHOSTS, AND THAT'S WHAT IT THOUGHT I WAS.
AN *UNFULFILLED GHOST* MADE UP OF NOTHING.
I'M JUST MY MOM'S DESIRES, KRISTI'S INTERESTS, AND NOTHING ELSE.
I'M NOTHING...
COME HERE.
IT'S OKAY.
I UNDERSTAND.

HEY.

HI.

HOW ARE YOU FEELING?

CRAGGY.

BUT ALSO A LITTLE MORE CLEAR-HEADED.

SHIRLEY KEEPS TALKING ABOUT THINGS HAPPENING FOR A REASON.

WHAT HAPPENED LAST NIGHT WAS A *WAKE-UP CALL.*

RYCROFT MAYBE BECAME A PLACE FOR ME TO LOSE MYSELF IN, 'CUZ IT WAS EASIER THAN CONFRONTING THE HARD STUFF.

YOU READY TO FIND YOURSELF?

EVEN IF IT FEELS LIKE I'M CREATING A BUILD-A-BEAR FROM SCRATCH...

...YES, I AM.

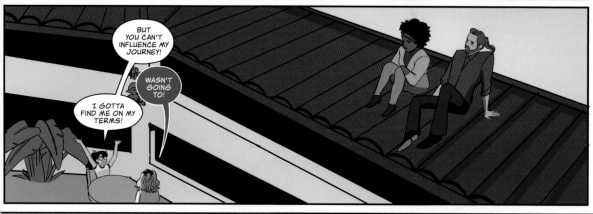

BUT YOU CAN'T INFLUENCE MY JOURNEY!

WASN'T GOING TO!

I GOTTA FIND ME ON MY TERMS!

I SEE WHY THE GIRLS LIKE IT UP HERE.

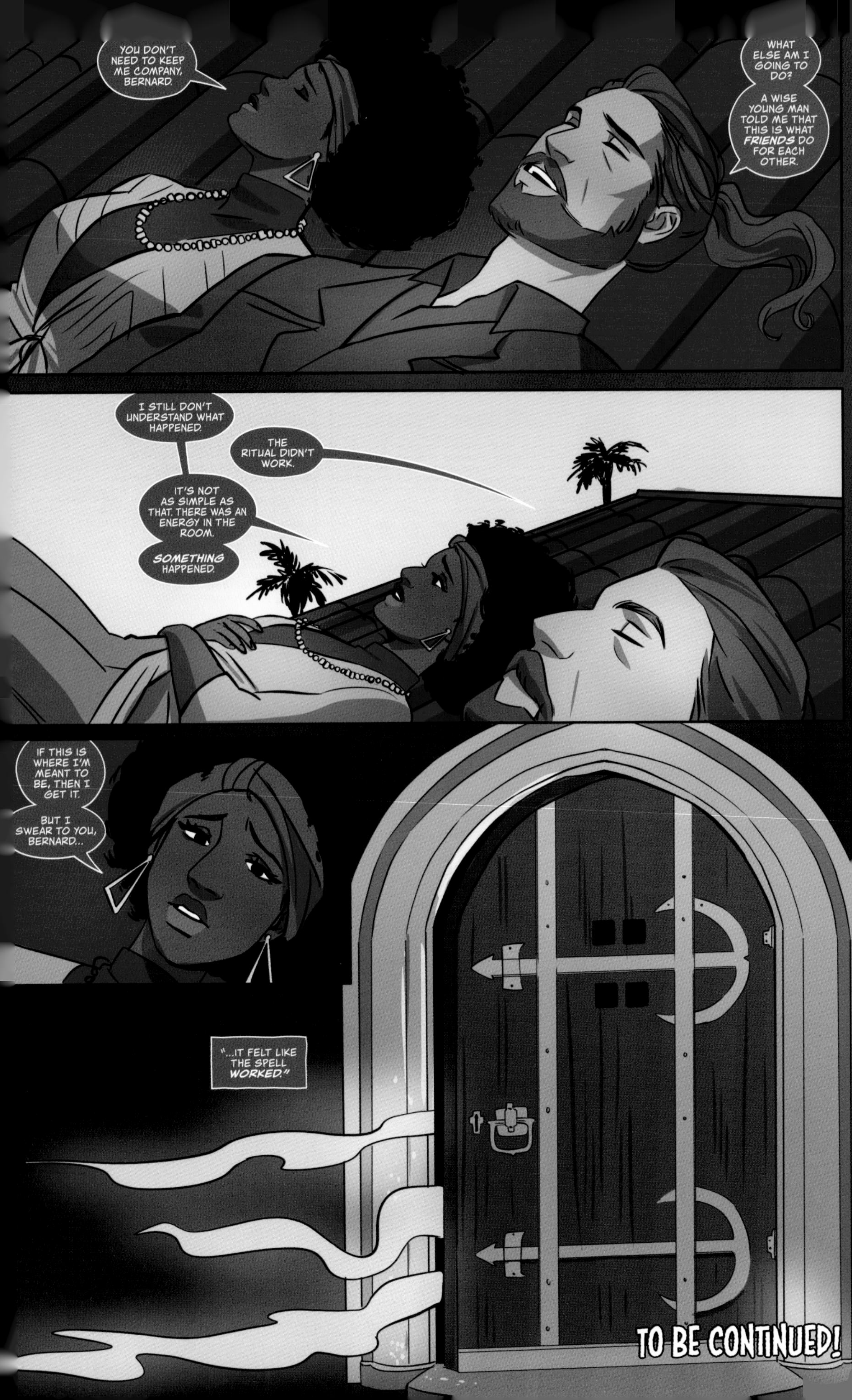
YOU DON'T NEED TO KEEP ME COMPANY, BERNARD.
WHAT ELSE AM I GOING TO DO?
A WISE YOUNG MAN TOLD ME THAT THIS IS WHAT FRIENDS DO FOR EACH OTHER.
I STILL DON'T UNDERSTAND WHAT HAPPENED.
THE RITUAL DIDN'T WORK.
IT'S NOT AS SIMPLE AS THAT. THERE WAS AN ENERGY IN THE ROOM.
SOMETHING HAPPENED.
IF THIS IS WHERE I'M MEANT TO BE, THEN I GET IT.
BUT I SWEAR TO YOU, BERNARD...
"...IT FELT LIKE THE SPELL WORKED."
TO BE CONTINUED!

Cover Gallery

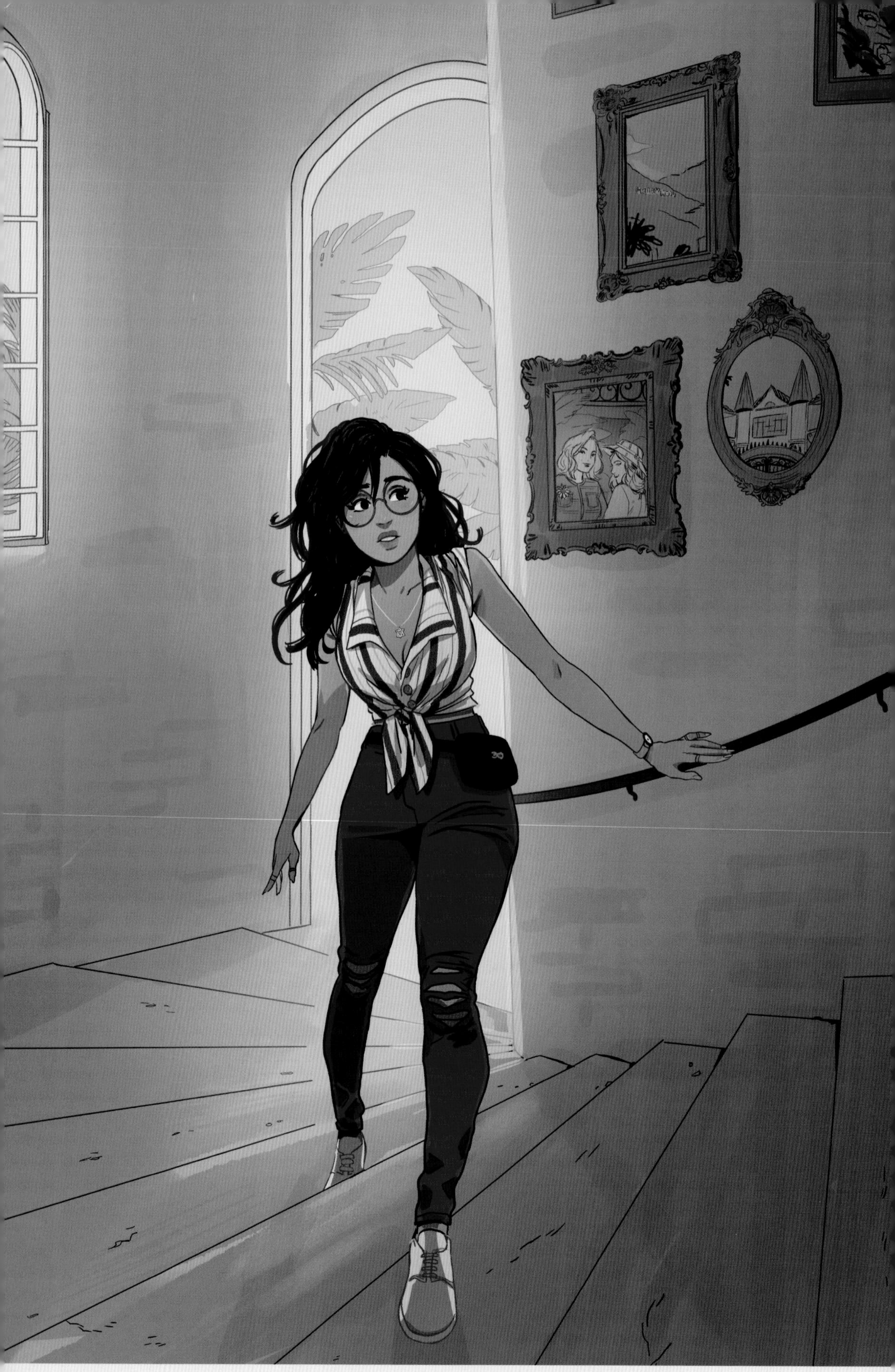

Issue Five Main Cover by **Siobhan Keenan**

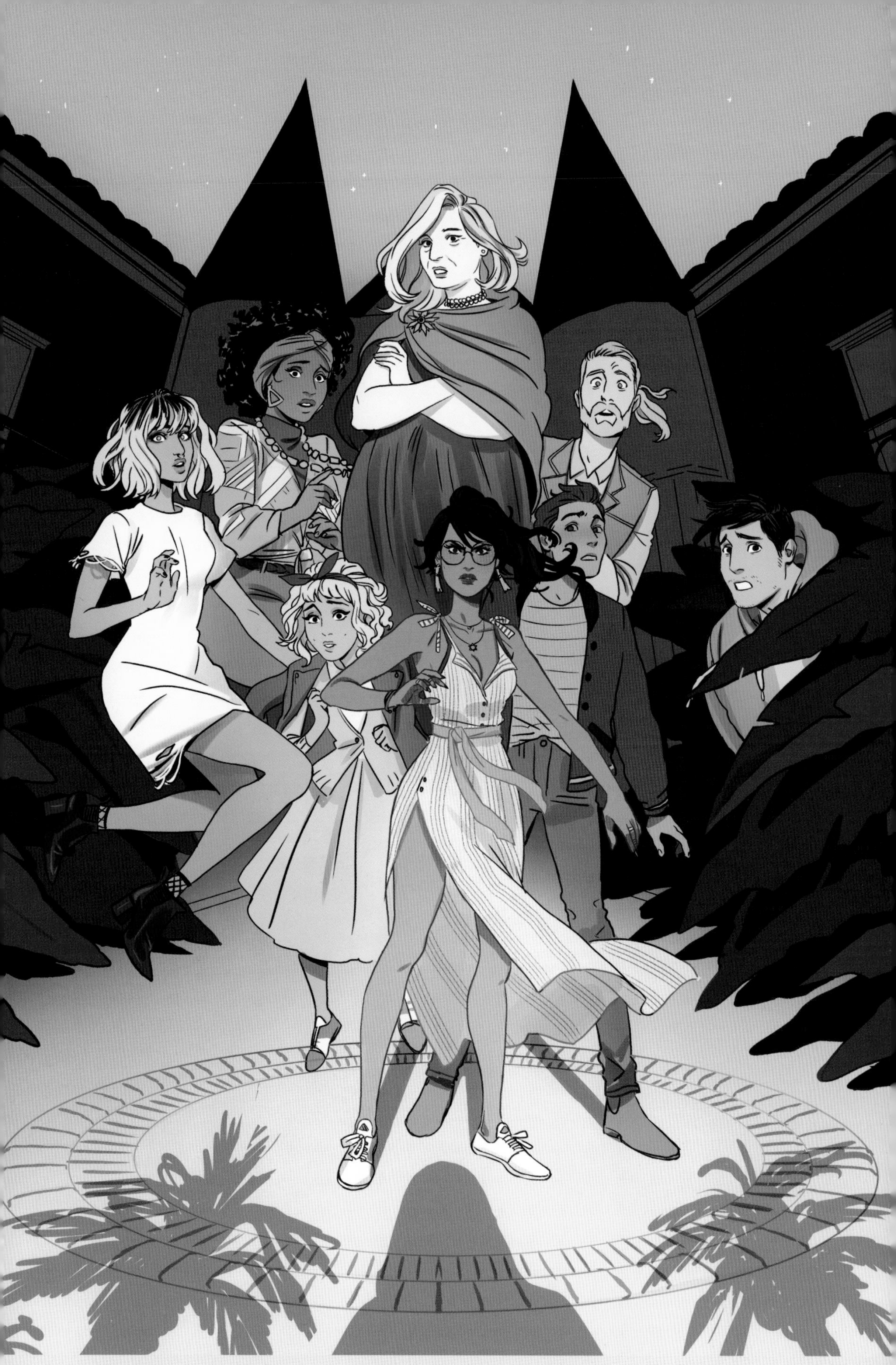

Issue Six Main Cover by **Siobhan Keenan**

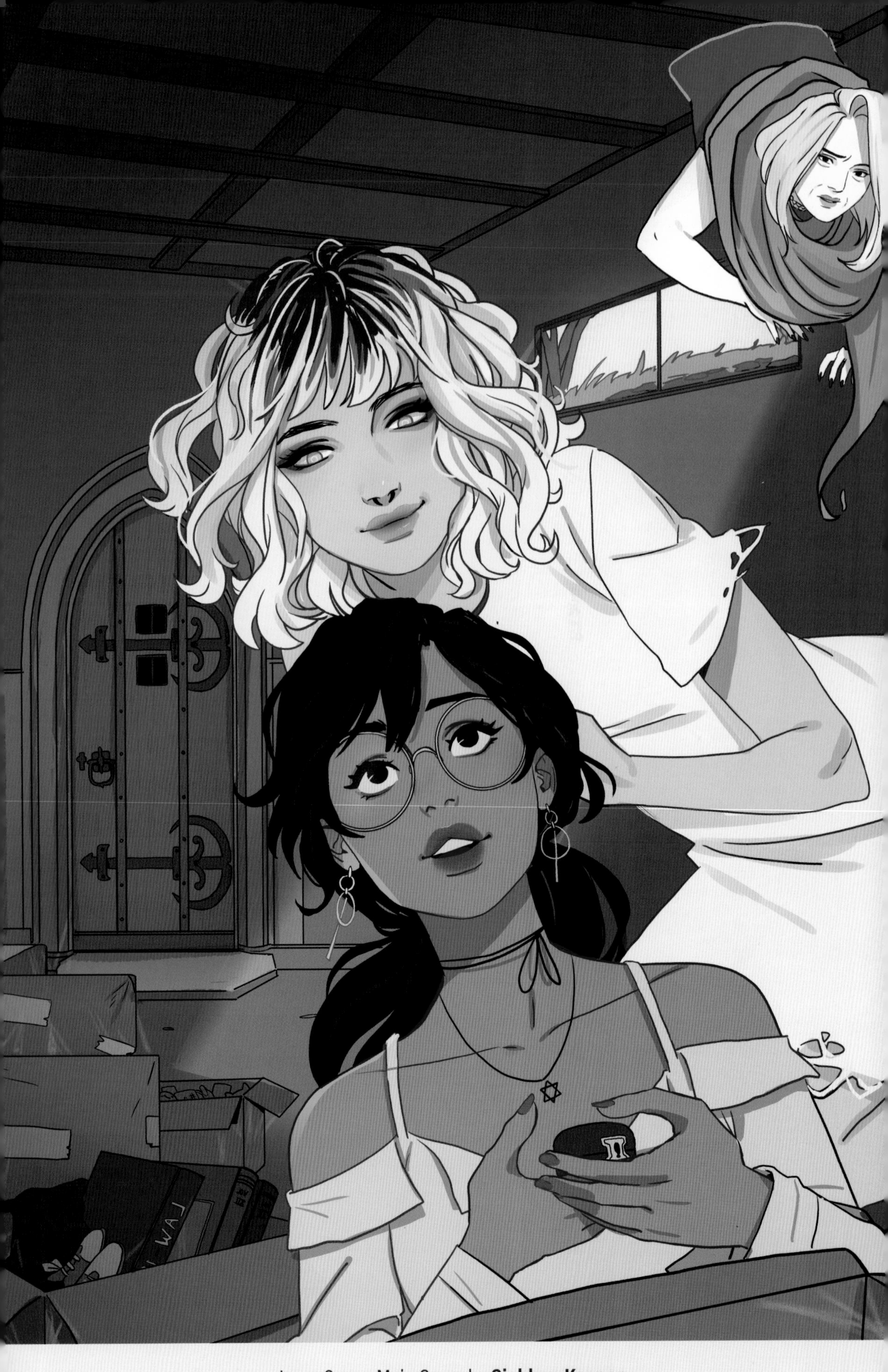

Issue Seven Main Cover by **Siobhan Keenan**

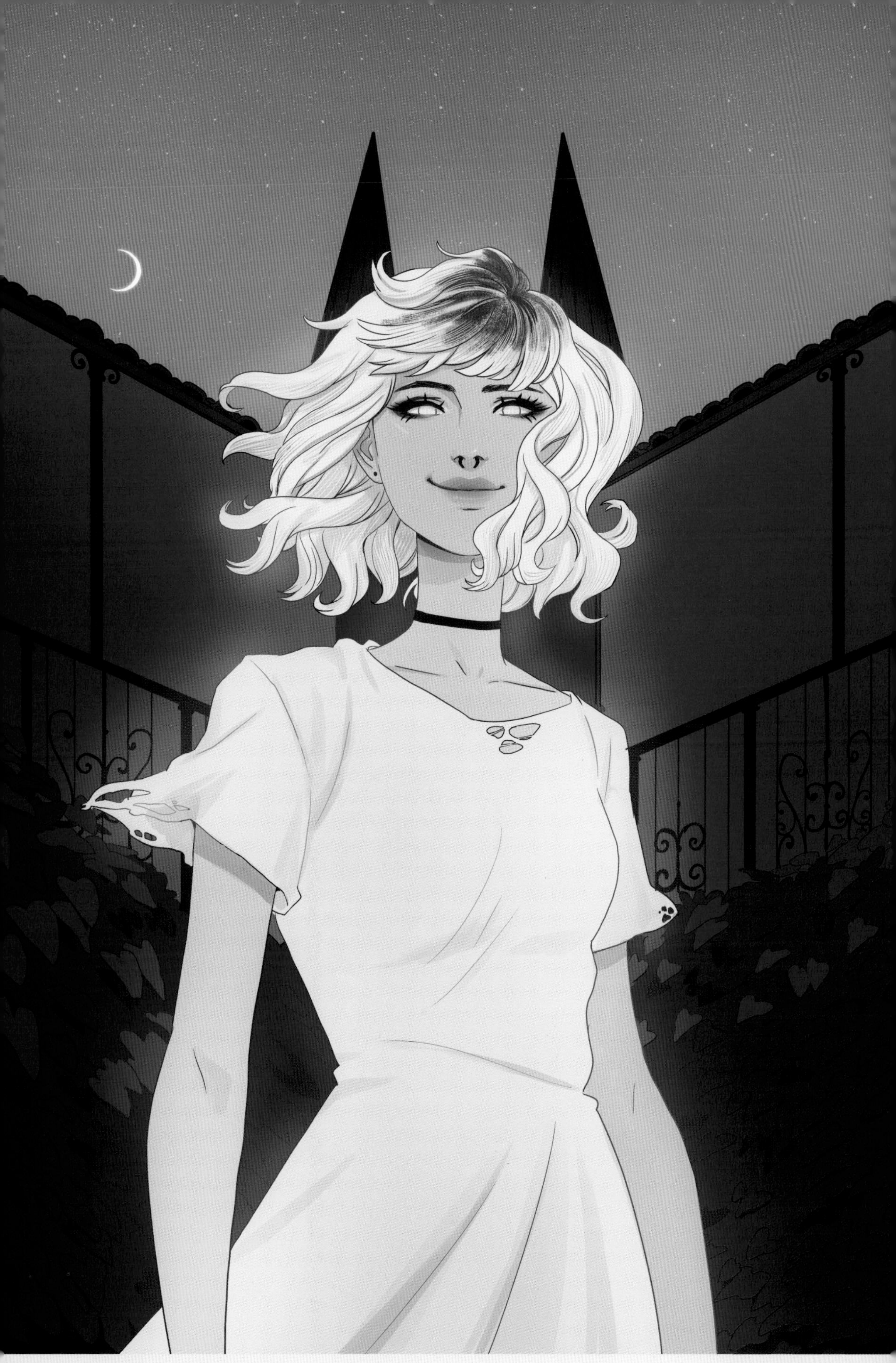

Issue Eight Main Cover by **Siobhan Keenan**

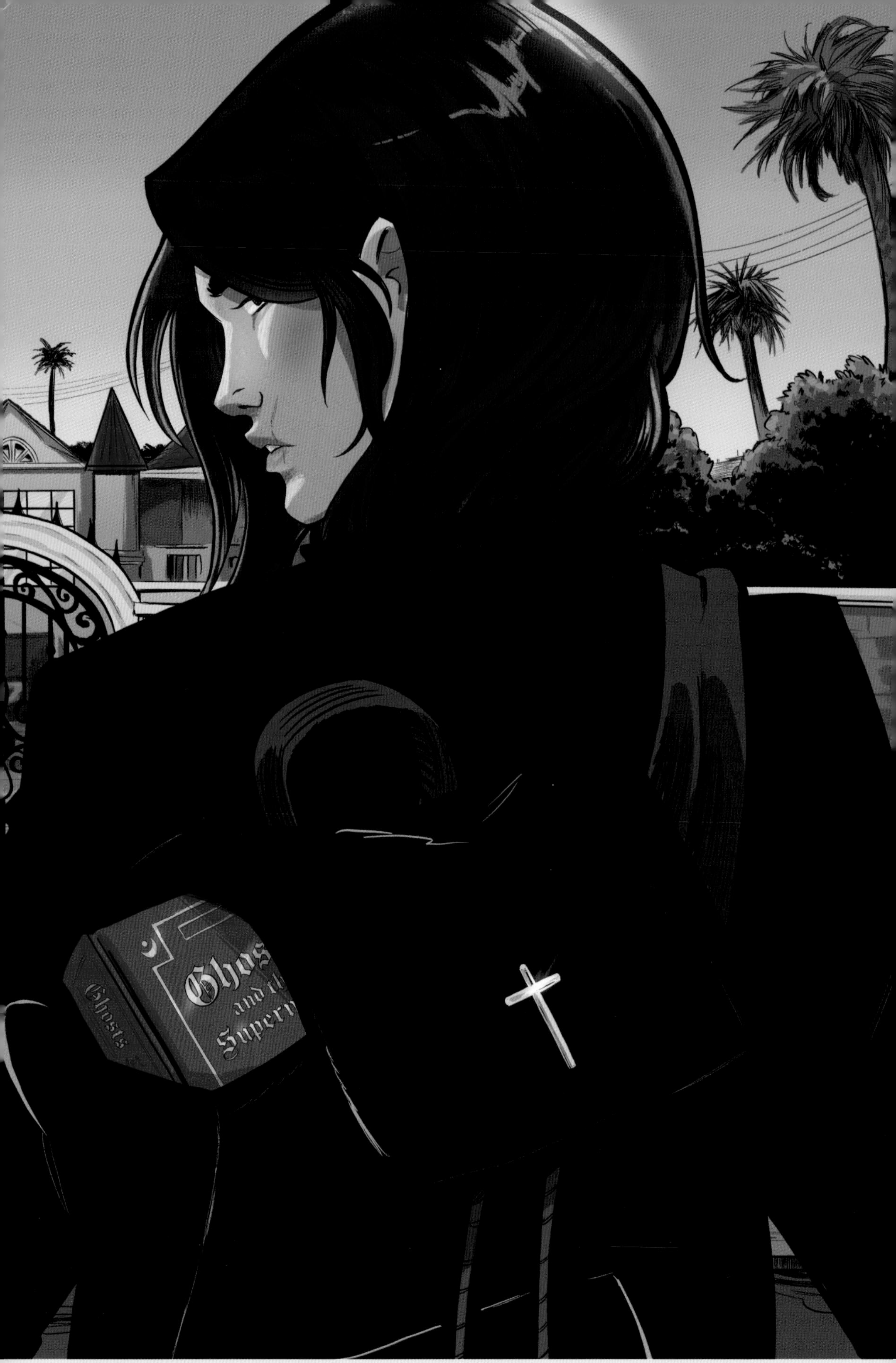
Ghosts

Issue Five Variant Cover by **Sina Grace** with Colors by **Cathy Le**

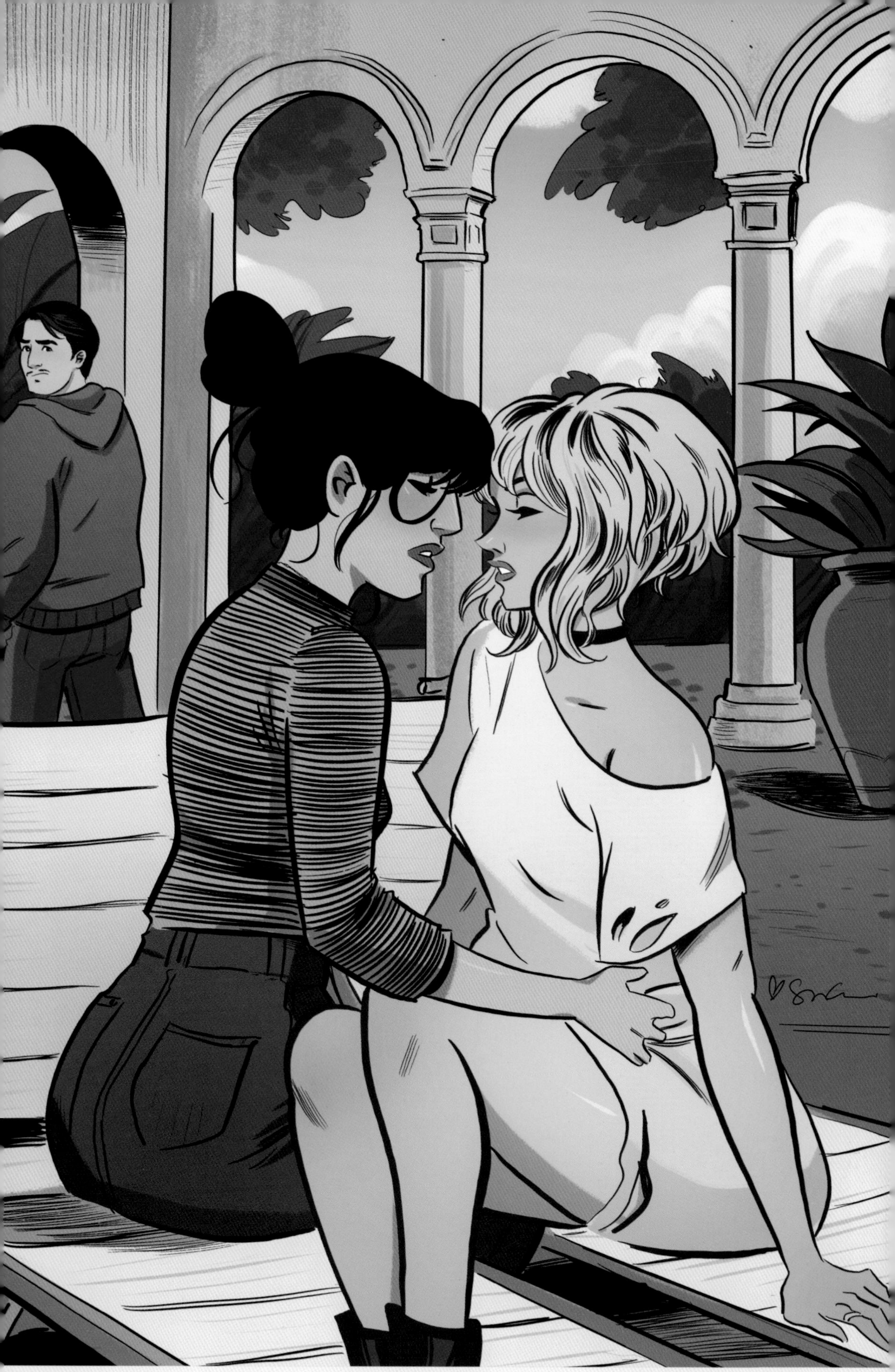

Issue Six Variant Cover by **Sina Grace** with Colors by **Cathy Le**

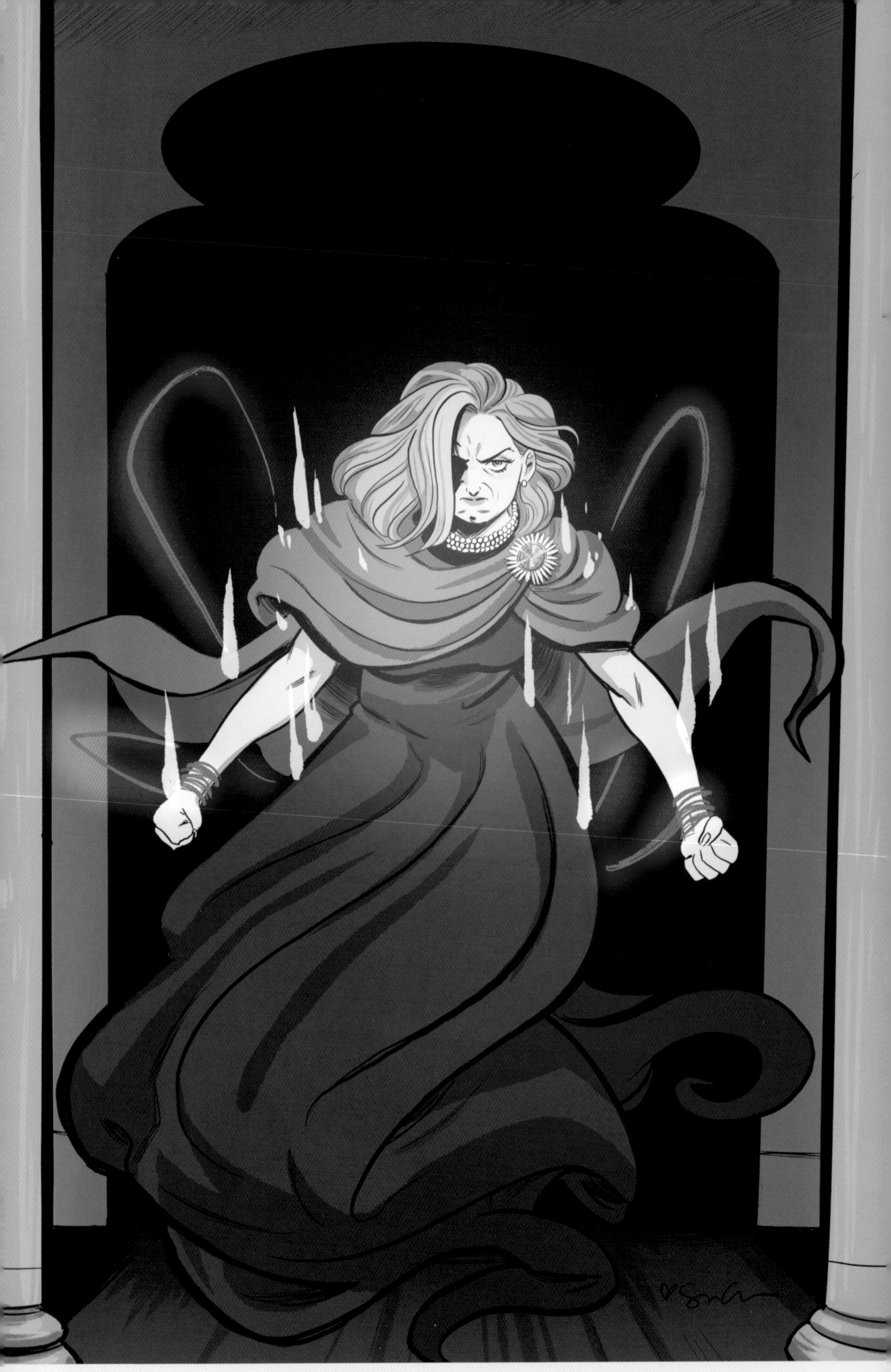

Issue Seven Variant Cover by **Sina Grace** with Colors by **Cathy Le**